MVP

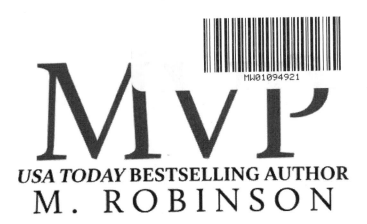

USA TODAY BESTSELLING AUTHOR

M. ROBINSON

This book is a work of fiction. References to real people, events, establishments, organizations, or locations are intended only to provide a sense of authenticity, and are used fictitiously. All other characters, dead or alive are a figment of my imagination and all incidents and dialogue, are drawn from the author's mind's eye and are not to be interpreted as real.

Dedication

TO ALL MY VIPs!!!

THANK YOU, THANK YOU, THANK YOU…I CAN'T SAY IT ENOUGH.

Acknowledgements

Ben: I LOVE you.

Dad: Thank you for always showing me what hard work is and what it can accomplish. For always telling me that I can do anything I put my mind to.

Mom: Thank you for ALWAYS being there for me no matter what. You are my best friend.

Julissa Rios: I love you and I am proud of you. Thank you for being a pain in my ass and for being my sister. I know you are always there for me when I need you.

Ysabelle & Gianna: Love you my babies.

Rebecca Marie: THANK YOU for an AMAZING cover. I wouldn't know what to do without you and your fabulous creativity.

Heather Moss: Thank you for everything that you do!! XO

Michelle Tan: Best beta ever!

Heather Harton: You have been with me since the beginning. Thank you so much for being you. My GILF!

Alexis Moore: I love our crazy banter and your support!

Jen Dirty Girl: I love your voice! And you.

Tammy McGowan: Thank you for all your support and boo boo's you find! You love to give me heart attacks. Just saying.

Alexis Moore: You rock!!

Michele Henderson McMullen: LOVE LOVE LOVE you!!

Theresa Harrell: Thank you for loving Sebastian and Ysa as much as I do.

Barbara Johnson: You ALWAYS make me laugh. Xo

To all the blogs A HUGE THANK YOU for all the love and support you have shown me. I have made some amazing friendships with you that I hold dear to my heart. I know that without you I would be nothing!! I cannot THANK YOU enough!!

To all my new author friends that I have made! That has most definitely been a privilege!

Last, but most definitely not least, to my VIP GROUP. Oh my God ladies…words cannot describe how much I love and appreciate every last one of you. The friendships and relationships that I have made with you are one of the best things that have ever happened to me. I wish I could name each one of you but it would take forever, just please know that you hold a very special place in my heart. You VIPs make my day, every single day. THANK YOU!!!

To all the readers that have shown me an outpouring of love and support. I would be nowhere without you. You are forever my VIPs!!

PROLOGUE

Y

Be careful what you wish for…

Life can change drastically over the course of a few hours; can you imagine how much it can change over the course of a few years? I wanted to find myself, I wanted self-worth, I wanted love; I wanted it all.

Was I expecting too much?

Was it my fault?

Can someone truly have a happy ending?

I didn't know…I didn't know anything anymore.

My life ended and began when I met Sebastian Vanwell, and there I was, three years later; alone, confused, frustrated, and angry.

Trust and resentment, two completely different meanings on such opposite ends of the spectrum. I didn't know which way was up anymore. I had no idea who I was or what I was doing. I was just as lost, as I was the moment I stepped out of The Cathouse.

I love him, but was love enough?

Can love truly conquer all or is that just in fairy tales?

I was so confused.

All I knew was that there I was, leaving Sebastian a Dear John letter on the kitchen table with my suitcase all packed and ready to go. I walked out of our home, the place we built together out of dreams and love with Chance by my side.

I walked out on Sebastian.

I got into the taxi that took me to the tarmac. I took a deep breath and stepped out on the street to make my way toward the steps to board the jet.

Could I do this?

Am I making the right choice?

Is this who I am?

Is this what I want?

They say what goes around comes around…did everything finally catch up with me?

I grabbed my suitcase and boarded the plane.

There I sat with my hands folded in my lap and my dog by my side.

The only thing that I knew to be true was that I was going to Miami.

I was going home.

Back to VIP.

S

I had only ever loved one woman. From the first day that I stared at those mesmerizing and entrancing bright green eyes, I was lured in. It was a magnetic pull that capsized me to live and breathe for her and only her. She was soul mate, the one person in this world that was made for me and only me. I wouldn't let her go without a fight…

I lost her once.

I wouldn't make that mistake again.

I had so many regrets in my life and she will never be one of them. It didn't matter how we met or started out. I knew it the moment her tiny frame fell into my arms. We were meant to meet and be together, it was all for a reason; a greater purpose that I knew from the second she told me her name.

Mine.

The instant connection we shared and the gravitational pull we had toward each other was inevitable. That's what happens when two halves of a heart come together and become one. They're bonded for life. The errors of my ways had finally caught up with me, but how did you prove to the other half of your heart that it beats for only her and her alone?

How did I make her understand that I would die before I ever hurt her again? There was no Sebastian without Ysabelle.

She was my everything…

My girl.

I am not an honorable man and I knew that. I had paid for my mistakes tenfold. I had hurt women that I had held dearly in my heart for as long as I could remember. However, I thought I was doing the right thing. Call me a coward, call me selfish, call me a cheater, call me a bastard; I deserve it. There wasn't anything that you can throw at me that I wasn't already aware of. I've waited thirty-four years for her, this I knew. I did love her, I still love her, I'll always love her.

Though, there I stood, holding a letter from the woman who owned my body, heart, and soul. *Fuck that.* She was much more than that. The human body needed water to survive; it could go three days without it before it started to shut down. Ysabelle was my water.

Sebastian,

I love you. Don't for one second think that I don't…I just don't know if that's enough anymore. As much as I want to, I can't forget the past. My heart says or feels one thing and my mind is spinning telling me another. I've listened to my heart once before and I can't go through that again…I won't.

We want different things.

I'm sorry. Don't hate me.

Yours always,

Ysa.

It was taking everything in me to not fall apart. I couldn't do that. I needed to stay levelheaded and hold my ground to get her back. I needed to stay strong. I was not the same man I was three years ago…

I was over to the front door in six strides and what I found breaks my heart.

Fuck me.

There was a torn picture of Olivia on the floor. I ran my fingers through my hair, wanting to pull it the fuck out. This was so fucked up. How would I fix this? How would I get her to understand that I wanted her?

Just her.

I would fight for her if it were the last thing I would ever do.

And I would like to see someone stand in my way because I'd take them the fuck out.

The Madam didn't know whom she's fucking with.

Mine.

And now I had to prove it to her, once and for all.

CHAPTER I

Y

"God, your pussy feels amazing," he groaned in my ear, before pulling it into his mouth. "I've wanted this for so long. You have no idea how many nights I've spent stroking myself to you, thinking about this and only this."

"Yes…yes…yes," I surrendered.

"How do you feel this good?" he praised.

My body was his, with his breath and sighs all over. With each thrust, I felt him take a little more from me. I wasn't in the right state of mind, though it didn't matter because he felt so good. The pain with the pleasure. The sin of it all. I surrendered every part of my being to him. That's what I needed.

To feel safe.

To feel loved.

To feel wanted.

"I'm sorry it took me so long to get to this point. I've been an idiot," he murmured, angling my leg higher on his hipbone, hitting that perfect spot inside me that had my burning skin crawling from the inside out. He was different, but yet familiar. A quiet to the storm that had become my life; the chaos that surrounded itself around me was calm and cool. And it was because of him. He was my safe spot. He always had been.

I needed this, I repeated silently, over and over.

His breathing became headier and his skin began to perspire, I knew he was close as my core wept from my wetness for him. I had my eyes closed the entire time; somehow, that made it okay, it made it easier, like it wasn't real if my eyes weren't open. When his lips caught mine, I felt his silky and smooth tongue beckoning my mouth to open for him. I gave him what he wanted and moaned in satisfaction when he bit my bottom lip, just before plunging his tongue into my awaiting mouth.

He kissed me all over, from my breasts to my neck and all over my face. I almost sobbed when he kissed my forehead in a loving and tender gesture.

"Kid," he half-whispered into the side of my neck as he laid soft kisses. "Open your eyes, let me see those beautiful bright green eyes I dream about," he seductively encouraged.

I sighed and took a deep breath, and in that moment, it would seem that I was content, blissful, satisfied even. The exhale being from passion and lust…it wasn't. It was from confusion and sadness. I braved myself and willed my eyes to open and they immediately caught his desire and longing for me. His eyes said everything that I didn't think I could hear…

What was I doing?

"Fuck, your pussy is a vise. I'm so close. Tell me what you need."

"I need you," I carelessly responded, not knowing what else to say.

That seemed to appease him. He thrust in and out a few more times while my neck and back began to arch off the mattress to my own release, but he gently grabbed the back of my neck to keep our eyes locked. In the haven of love and complete devotion he thought we were creating. He wanted us to share the moment and I gave it to him. Exactly how I had with so many men before. It felt nothing like I wanted it to.

"Jesus…" he grunted and his release quickly followed, plunging deep within my core and spreading his seed.

His forehead hovered over mine as we caught our breathing, trying to find a unison pattern. The room smelled like sex…our sex, and it made me nauseous.

"I love you, Kid," he expressed with genuine sincerity in his tone.

"I love you, too, Devon."

And then I broke down crying.

CHAPTER 2

S

A year ago…

"Ysa…" I whispered in her ear.

She peeked one eye open and smirked into her pillow when she caught me staring at her from my side of the bed. I was lying sideways with my left arm holding up my head.

"How many times do I have to tell you that it's stalkerish when you're watching me sleep?" she said as she giggled, trying to play it off like she didn't love the fact that I did this every morning.

Ysa hated mornings. I swear the girl could sleep in every day if I let her.

"Hmmm…I don't wanna…ten more minutes," she mumbled.

"Ysa, it's seven thirty; you need to get up. The bar opens in an hour."

"The bar runs itself, I can sleep in for another half an hour. Leave me alone," she grumbled, pulling the sheet over her head.

"All right, you asked for it," I warned.

"Sebastian! Don't you fucking dare," she threatened, like that was going to stop me. My hand was under the blanket and on her thigh before she even saw it coming. I gripped onto it, squeezing the inner part and making her squirm, laugh, and yell at me all at the same time.

"Are you done? You going to get up now?" I teased, trying not to laugh.

"Oh my God! I hate you. I'm up! Stop," she yelled, thrashing her legs around.

I stopped and instantly lay on top of her, holding myself up on my elbows but locking her in with my body.

She grinned. "What did you say? I don't think I caught that part? Did you just say you hated me?" I taunted while she laughed and blushed.

God, I loved that color on her.

"Maybe. What are you going to do about it?" she taunted, wiggling her eyebrows.

"Oh, your smart mouth is going to be the end of you. I think you like mouthing off to me just so I can put you in your place. Don't you, Ysa?"

She laughed. "Nah, I'm just a smart-mouth kinda girl. Maybe you should put something in my mouth to shut me up."

"I have other ideas about where I want to put something inside of you," I responded, trying to control my erection. Too late. *Who am I kidding? I was hard the second my hand was on her thigh.*

"Oh…I see…" She gyrated her pussy on my cock. "We have time for that, but we don't have time for me to sleep in?"

"We always have time for that," I reminded.

She rolled her eyes. "I have to get up, Sebastian."

"It's all right, I'm up for the both of us."

"You're incorrigible. How can you want in again? We did it twice yesterday."

"I always want in. I'm an exclusive member to your pussy and I can get in anytime I want. Try and stop me." I emphasized my words by rubbing my cock against her slick opening. "And I didn't hear you complaining when I had you coming in my mouth and then again on my dick." I leaned in to kiss her neck. "Multiple times."

She slapped my back.

"Ow!" I jerked back and she used the momentum to slide out and away from me.

She put her fingers in the air in a stopping gesture, backing away, knowing that I was going to come after her.

"No! I need to shower, and according to you, I have a bar to run. No sex," she stated and I cocked my head to the side. "Until later," she reasoned, walking away.

I quickly followed her into the shower and we started the day exactly how it was supposed to be. It had been two months since I found my way back to Ysa. We were falling into a comfortable routine of getting to know each other in ways that we hadn't before. See...before, we were playing house; this time, we actually lived in the house and worked together in a partnership, or at least tried to. I had taken a sabbatical from Yachting Enterprises; I didn't need the money, I had plenty of that.

Ysabelle was my number one priority.

Julia still lived in Miami but moved closer to her parents so they could help with Christian when I wasn't around. She knew where I was. I was completely honest on the direction my life was going to go; no more lies. I had learned the hard way that they caused my own demise. She didn't have an opinion when I told her my decision of going to find Ysa; it was like she was already ten steps in front of me and expected it. I think she was surprised that it took me almost two years to figure out she was the missing piece all along.

I did a lot of soul-searching in those two years, and I truly believed that as much as it hurt to be away from each other, we both needed that time to re-group and evaluate what we wanted out of life. What was important to us as individuals.

I had never been alone before. I always had a woman by my side, even in my college years after Olivia; it was purely sexual, but it was companionship nonetheless. Subconsciously, everything I did after the divorce led me right back to those bright green eyes that showed me the world.

Divorcing Julia was the biggest mistake of my life. I should have never married her in the first place. Again, my mistake. I loved her; I still love her. The same goes for Olivia...I was entirely too young to know what it meant to be absolutely and completely devoted and entranced by someone, to be with someone that you can't be without. To physically ache in ways that you literally felt like you were dying when you were apart. I thought I knew pain and loss when I lost Oli–it wasn't even close to what I experienced when Ysabelle walked away from me that night at The Gala. To have looked into the eyes of the person who completes you and see that you have hurt them with all your actions and possibly your words, killed me inside.

I stopped living the second she walked away from me. I moved in an autopilot state of mind, where I thought I needed to make things right with Julia. She was my wife...again–huge mistake. I did everything for everyone else. All my decisions were based upon what would make someone else happy. I didn't say what I wanted, what I desired, what I fucking needed to keep going.

And that made me a coward.

I had almost two decades worth of regrets.

Ysabelle is my reward. She's my happy ending.

Although, we have progressively moved slower than I would have wanted. Yes. I wanted to marry her, I wanted to watch her belly grow with my children and know I put them there. That we created life together out of our love. I wanted the good, the bad, and the ugly…the fights, the makeups, and everything in between. I wanted a life with her and only her, to grow old together and know that I had spent every day of my life with *my* perfect woman by my side.

I wish it were that easy.

The God's honest truth was that she didn't trust me. Ysabelle could hide from everyone; I've seen it and experienced it first hand. However, Ysa couldn't hide from me. Her emotions, thoughts, feelings, were all governed by a façade that she put up, and she didn't even realize she was doing it. It's fully engrained in her; it's all she knew.

I had the privilege to have knocked it all down, with no right, might I add. Only to have personally placed each slab precisely on top of each other and built it right back up. No one did that but me.

I lived with that regret.

It's no longer on my terms…it's on hers…

And that scared me more than anything.

Y

"Do you see what time it is?" I announced, holding my phone up to his face. He grinned a sexy smile that made me want to kiss and slap him at the same time.

He leaned in and wrapped his arms around my waist, pulling me toward him, my front to his front. My breathing hitched as his lips whispered into my ear. "I can't help that my cock has an attachment to your sweet pussy."

My eyes widened and I sucked in my bottom lip.

"You have no idea how amazing it feels to be inside you, Ysa. I just had you and I want you again." He kissed the side of my neck before pulling away, leaving me half stumbling to catch my composure. "Plus, I'm making up for lost time," he said with a wink and walked away.

Jesus…

He had found me two months ago and I felt like I was being introduced to a completely different side of him. Of course, I knew how demanding and controlling he was in bed. We weren't allowed to do it in public before and it had been somewhat of a surprise to how vocal and affectionate he was. I loved it. Having him back in my life was extremely unexpected; we were away from each other for almost two years. I never anticipated that he would make his way back to me. I knew he loved me and I know he still does, it didn't stop.

We hadn't said it to one another, and I wasn't going to be the one to say it first, even though I felt it in my being. He was the one…

Love is a battlefield.

There are two opponents on each side of the scale; one person moved forward, backward, side-to-side and the scale tips. In order to make it work, you have to work together. It takes two mutual parties becoming one. Communication is key. It's the very foundation that will make or break your unity.

But guess what? Love causes war.

I was twenty-six years old and felt like I was fifty. I've experienced so much beyond my years that a normal person couldn't possibly fathom. I had seen things that people have only dreamt about or read about in books. I've sold my soul to the devil and lived to talk about it. There wasn't one place on my body that hadn't been touched by a man or a woman, except my heart. That has only ever been touched and connected to one person.

Sebastian.

From the first time that I literally fell into his arms, it was home. There was this unspoken bond that I felt as soon as I looked into his eyes; they held more emotion and sincerity than I had ever had the privilege of witnessing before, and it was only for me. It was as if he looked through me as opposed to at me. Every time we locked eyes and got lost in the intensity of our stares, we were one. I had no idea if that was even possible or if it even made sense.

I didn't know anything about love.

All I knew was that being without him was like not being able to breathe–you could survive on an oxygen tank that provided you with a comfortable life, but you already knew what it was like to breathe on your own–so you longed for the way it was before. It would be miserable. There was no going back. That being said…I knew how to look out for me. I knew how to survive because I had to. I controlled everything around me…I always had. I had no control around him and that scared the living shit out of me.

I had more money than I could spend in three, maybe four lifetimes.

I had experienced loss, contentment, survival, happiness, and even love.

I didn't have any regrets in my life, and I didn't know if that made me a good or bad person. After some of the things I had done, it could go either way.

To me…

I've lived.

I've survived.

I had come from nothing and became a VIP.

And a huge part of me will always be proud of that.

I know that sounds asinine, but you haven't lived my life. I never felt any self-worth until I became a VIP. The Madam was a mother to me, just like she said she would be. She took me in and made something from nothing. She gave me tools to become one of the elite. For a girl like me, that was immense. You could criticize and judge me all you want; I've always been honest. That's one trait you can't take away from me. You wanted the rest of our story, and if you didn't, you wouldn't be sitting here reading it.

I am who I am, I always have been. An old dog can't be taught new tricks, but they can adapt…and that's what I was trying to do. I embraced whatever the fuck was handed to me.

It's who I am.

I've always felt like I was Sebastian's puppet, and he pulled the strings until I couldn't take it anymore and cut myself loose. When we were asleep and his arms were around me, I felt safe…I felt home. My eyes would begin to shut and then my mind wandered from consciousness to unconsciousness, and it always returned to the same thing.

Was he with me because I look like Olivia?

Was he with me because Julia wanted the divorce?

Was he going to hurt me again?

Could I really trust him again?

I had let all my barriers and guards down with him once and it blew up in my face. Mocking me.

I'm trying...

But lie to me once, shame on you.

Lie to me twice…

Shame on me.

CHAPTER 3

S

Chances really was an amazing bar; Ysabelle had done a great job with making her vision become a reality. It was located in Providenciales, which was the centralized area for nightlife. The bar was opened from 9am-10pm; Sunday through Wed and Thursday through Saturday 10am-4am. She had spent a small fortune having her place above sound proofed. It was beautiful; it overlooked the water with the sand below your feet. Clients loved to feel like they were at a beach party. The bar was the main attraction, positioned right in the middle with area-lighting set up all around and mirrors behind the liquor, to make it look as if it were reflecting the sun. All the high-top tables were scattered around the bar with tiki huts and flat screens placed everywhere to bring in the sports crowds. She'd spent a lot of money on this place and I couldn't have been more proud of her. The staff absolutely adored her; she was a great boss.

"So I've been thinking," I hesitated as I watched her ass sway in her tight bikini bottoms that showed more ass cheeks than it actually covered.

"That's dangerous," she replied, looking up through her eyelashes while she cleaned one of the tables at her bar. She smiled and cocked her head to the side, knowing exactly what I was thinking. "What?" she goaded.

I shook my head. "Nothing."

She laughed. "Oh, come on…I know that look. You know…you never seemed to care before what kind of bikinis I wore. Just saying."

"I don't care now."

"Right…"

"I just think that maybe you should put on a few more clothes. You are the owner; it might help if you looked more professional."

Her eyes widened. *Shit. Wrong thing to say.*

"That's not–"

She put her hand up in the air to stop me. "Nope, too late; you already said it. But let me remind you that I've run this bar for a year and a half and it was voted top three hot spots in all the Caribbean since it opened." She balanced out her hands. "So…"

"Ysa, that's not what I meant and you know it. I'm fully aware that you know what you're doing. In almost everything."

She smiled.

"I'm purely speaking from a possessive and–"

"Jealous?" she interrupted.

"I'd call it protective…standpoint."

"I'd call it bullshit." She shrugged her shoulders and purposely dropped the napkin on the floor in front of her. "Oh look," she mocked. "I better get that." She bent down on her hands and knees, leaving her ample cleavage to fall forward out of her top, and then sat up on her ankles. "It's really hot in here. You know…I think maybe you're right. This is a topless beach, I should probably dress more professional." Her delicate fingers reached up to the strings tied together at the back of her neck.

"Do it and see what happens," I threatened.

She raised an eyebrow and with one hand, started to pull at the tie. I jumped over the bar, catching her by surprise and propelling her backward onto the sand with me on top of her. My hand caught around her tiny fingers and she laughed. Her eyes were dilated, getting the exact response she wanted.

"You're a bad girl," I breathed out between kissing her. "I think you just wanted me on top of you."

"I'll never tell…" she sang out and tried to turn her face, so I laid more of my weight on her to keep her where I wanted her. She sucked in air when she felt my hand on her inner thigh. "You wouldn't?" she warned, not turning to look at me.

"Bad girls deserve to be punished. Should I punish you?"

She finally turned her face and I looked into her big, beautiful green eyes that were now sedated. She stuck out her bottom lip and shook her head no, pouting and surrendering to me.

"What do I get if I let this go as a warning?" I cautioned.

"What do you want?" she teased.

"Oh, we're playing some high stakes here, Ysa…it's going to be a good one. How about you wear some shorts, or even that see through skirt thing that doesn't really cover anything, but it's more than what your bottoms do."

She gasped, dropping her mouth open in shock.

"You give me that and I won't unleash the fury."

She laughed. "Oh my God, Sebastian, that's fucking cheating."

"Call it whatever you want, but I'm not the one in the position to have to compromise here. That's what happens when you fuck with people that are bigger than you and can hold you down until they get what they want. You should have thought about that before you decided to tempt and provoke me. Actions have consequences, Ysa."

She sighed and rolled her eyes. "Fine! I'll wear the *sarong* three times a week."

"Friday, Saturday, Sunday," I added.

"What the fuck? Those are the busiest days of the week, when the bar is packed all day."

I grinned. "I know."

She narrowed her eyes and I gripped her inner thigh firmer.

"I hate you!" she yelled, laughing.

"You what?" I taunted, squeezing harder and making her squirm. "I'm sorry, what was that?" I emphasized, squeezing over and over again. She started laughing uncontrollably and getting sand everywhere, kicking her legs to try to break free. I stopped and let her catch her breath, not moving my hand or my hold on her. "Let's try that again."

"Ugh! Fine. Friday through Sunday, I will wear a sarong," she stated through gritted teeth.

"And…"

"What?"

Y

Damn him! I knew I shouldn't have provoked him, but I couldn't help myself. I'm a little shit like that. Sex sells and it always will. Just because I'm no longer a VIP doesn't mean that's not what still makes the world go round.

"I hate you!" I yelled, half-laughing.

"You what?" he taunted, squeezing my thigh harder and making me squirm. "I'm sorry, what was that?" he emphasized, squeezing over and over again. I couldn't control my movements when he did that to me. I fucking hated it but at the same time, loved the attention. It hurt, and at the same time, it made me laugh, almost violently. The fury and I had a love/hate relationship. I was kicking sand everywhere; we were going to be covered in it when we stood up.

He finally stopped and I sucked in air and tried to catch my breathing, though he didn't move his hand from my inner thigh and his weight still held me where he wanted.

"Let's try that again," he reminded.

"Ugh! Fine. Friday through Sunday, I will wear a sarong," I agreed, through gritted teeth. It really wasn't that big of a deal, but he didn't have to know that.

"And…"

"What?" I asked, confused.

"You said you hated me."

My heart sped up. *Was he trying to get me to tell him I loved him?*

"I know you don't hate me."

Shit! He was.

"Sebastian…I can't breathe; I need up," I coaxed, not knowing what to say.

His face turned from amused to concerned. He immediately removed himself and held out his hand to pull me up.

"Fuck, Ysa. I'm sorry. I forget how tiny you are. Are you all right? Was I crushing you? Let me get you some water." He turned and walked behind the bar.

I sat down to gather my thoughts; my mind was racing. He quickly came back, handing me a glass of water and took the seat beside me. I couldn't look up at him; if I did, he would know.

He grazed my cheek and gently eased my face to look at him. There it was again…

That connection.

"I see you, Ysa. You can't hide from me," he asserted with conviction and I bowed my head. "Look at me," he ordered. I did. He placed his hand around my neck, pulling me closer to him.

I looked into the eyes of the man that held my heart and I knew what he was going to say.

"I have never felt more complete in my entire life than I do when I'm with you. I know we haven't talked about it; it's sort of like we started fresh that first day on the island."

"Seb–"

He put his finger up to my lips silencing me. "I know I fucked up, Ysa. I knew that the second I met you, and when I went home to my wife, it was the biggest mistake of my life. I should have ended it right then and there because from the moment you fell into my arms, I was yours and you were mine."

I bit my lip, wanting to control the tears that were at bay.

"You are my everything. There is no me without you. I started living that second, I was just too fucking stupid to admit it. I always knew it, though…I can't take back my mistakes. As much as I wish that I could, I can't. I hurt the one person in this world…" He paused like he was reliving the entire affair all over again. "I was careless with your heart when I had full responsibility for it. I hurt you. I'm so fucking sorry. Just know…" He leaned in, almost to the point that our lips were touching, and looked deep into my eyes.

"I love you, Ysa. I always have and I always will. That's a fucking promise. I'm never going to hurt you again. I will prove that to you, even if it takes me the rest of our lives."

I couldn't control the internal battle that surfaced in the forefront of my mind. It was a tsunami of emotions. I loved him. I knew I loved him. I always have. He owned every part of me. My heart had been his since the first day that our lives entwined. However, the fear that I felt in my mind took over and I just couldn't get the words to come out of my mouth. My eyes pooled with tears and he reached over to lift my face so I could look into his eyes.

"Look at me," he said.

I looked at him and I no longer had any control over it, the tears broke free and flowed loosely down my face.

"I know you're afraid. I know you don't trust me. And believe me when I say that I wholeheartedly understand why. I'll tell you again, Ysa. You can't hide from me. You don't have to say anything right now."

My heart was racing as I tried to control my emotions. Sebastian took me in his arms, and even though I didn't tell him I loved him, he knew.

He could just feel it.

And that's just how we were.

CHAPTER 4

S

It had been a few weeks since I told Ysabelle that I loved her. I wanted to say it since the first day I saw her beautiful face with her flowing curly hair walk to me in complete and utter shock that I was standing before her. As I walked Chance, I thought about that day.

There was my girl, dressed in a black bikini, with her curly exotic hair blowing in the wind, sitting on a hammock, reading her e-reader in front of her bar. She did it. Ysa does everything and anything she puts her mind to, it's who she is. I stopped dead in my tracks just to take her in. She was a vision. There was no beauty in this world like Ysa. I found myself catching my breath and bracing myself for the possibility of her turning me away. There was a chance that she would completely shut me out and tell me to go fuck myself from all the havoc and damage I had caused, and I wouldn't blame her for one second. She had every right to.

I wouldn't stop fighting for her. I would prove to her that she's the one. I would get on my hands and knees and beg for forgiveness if that's what it took for her to just talk to me.

I expected nothing but hoped for everything.

She's it for me.

Chance heard shuffling in the sand as I started to walk toward her, he barked and ran over to me, immediately recognizing who I was.

At least someone was thrilled to see me, let's hope your mom feels the same way.

He had grown four times in size since the last time I'd seen him; he was no longer a puppy. It warmed my heart a little that she kept him; he was part of me, a part of us. It calmed my apprehension, which I was terribly trying to control.

She quickly got up and chased after him, blocking the sun from her eyes to see whom he was greeting. I caught her stare from my peripheral vision; she stopped dead in her tracks, just like I had done mere minutes before. She was undeniably caught off guard to see me and even blinked a few times in bewilderment. I smiled at her and petted Chance one last time before brushing the sand off my lap and slowly making my way toward her.

I had to overcome every instinct and impulse to not run to her and scoop her up in my arms, to hold her as tight as I possibly could, never wanting to let her go again. But I couldn't scare her. I had to do this on her terms. It wasn't about me anymore.

"What are you doing here?" she blurted out.

Ouch…not exactly the welcoming I was eager for. I chuckled and smiled from nervousness, hopefully breaking some of the tension, and she smiled and laughed back.

Much better…fuck. I missed that smile and laugh. They light up an entire room.

"You look more beautiful than I ever remember. I thought we could start over." I grinned.

Honesty was the only thing I had going for me.

No more lies.

She cocked her head to the side and simultaneously moved her eyes to my ring finger, it had been bare for a little under a year and a half and that realization seemed to please her.

I took the opportunity and extended my right hand. "My name's Sebastian Vanwell." I nodded, smiling.

She grinned. "Ysabelle Telle," she replied, shaking my hand. "My friends call me Ysa," she added.

We stood there for a while; taking each other in, remembering the bond and connection we had since day one. All of the chemistry and passion was very much alive, breathing and pulsating around us and especially between us. I felt it in my bones, and most of all, my heart.

And that's when I knew I still had a chance.

It wasn't the end for us.

It was just the beginning.

I wasn't expecting her to say *I love you* when I said it. She wasn't ready. But that didn't stop the selfish desire to want to hear it. There had never been any promises between us during our yearlong affair. I never told her I was going to leave my wife and she never told me she was going to leave VIP. That didn't stop me from paying Madam for all of her time, though. I think back on it now and it's sickening how much of a mess I created. Everything I put her through…

Her eyes have always been the windows to her soul. They had always spoken for her. Sometimes, when I looked at them, I saw my girl there. I saw Ysa. Most of the time, I didn't, and I had to take a step back and remember that it was my fault. I had no one else to blame but myself. A daily reminder that I had to be patient, but I'm a man. We aren't a patient gender. I didn't want to start over, but I knew we had to. We had built a life together; at least it was to me. I had two lives that I kept separate and deceived everyone involved, most of all, myself. I was a fool to think that it wouldn't blow up in my face. I lived day to day; I didn't think about the future or the consequences. Not once.

I didn't think about her.

I had broken Ysa in so many ways, and I hated myself for that because I prided myself on being the only person to be able to get through those tough-as-shit barriers. She handed me her heart and I greedily took it. Except, I'd slit minor cuts in it every day; the lies, the betrayal, taking my wedding ring off and putting it back on, all the times I took a shower before I left her condo. Making *love* to her. Leaving her…she knew every fucking time that when I left, I was going home to my family and I just expected her to welcome me with open arms the next time I saw her.

She did.

I'm a fucking bastard.

When I was thoroughly done stabbing her, I made sure to throw her heart right back in her face. Except that time, it wasn't whole like it originally was…there were open wounds everywhere. And *now* I felt like I added salt to them.

Could she ever really forgive me?

Would she ever trust me again?

Only time will tell…

I won't give up.

Y

"Hey! What took you so long?" I asked from the kitchen.

"Oh! Chance has a mind of his own. What's for dinner?" he replied nonchalantly.

"I grilled some Mahi and I'm almost done making the salad. Can you help set the table?"

"Of course." He smiled.

It was amusing to watch Sebastian move around my 1,000 square foot home over the bar. For Chance and me, it was perfect. However, he was 6'4 and weighed 210; it didn't stop my enjoyment from watching him struggle in my tiny kitchen.

I giggled.

He turned. "What's so funny?"

I smiled. "Nothing…I think it's adorable how big you are."

"Oh yeah? You're enjoying my awkwardness of trying to move around, Ysa?"

"Sort of."

He shook his head and laughed it off.

We sat at the table eating with Chance begging at my side.

"Chance! Go!" he scolded.

Chance was very much like his owner and looked at him like, "Who the fuck are you?"

"Stop yelling at him,"

"He can't beg at the table. We give him scraps in his bowl when we're done eating. He needs to learn that."

"That's not how we do things. He's not used to that."

"I've been here for eleven weeks and he's going to have to get used to it."

I shrugged my shoulders. "Right…but what are we going to do when you go back home? He's just goi–"

"What?" he interrupted with a serious tone.

"What do you mean *what*?"

"Where did that come from?"

I cocked my head to the side. "Where did what come from? I'm just saying he's going to revert back to begging when you leave because it doesn't bother me that he begs. He's my boy," I sincerely explained, scratching Chance's head. Much to his approval.

I looked back up at Sebastian. *Why was he getting so pissed at me?*

His head jerked back like I had slapped him. "Ysabelle, you think I'm going home?"

"Umm…yeah…I mean…what?" I scratched my head in confusion. "Christian is in Miami, your career is in Miami, your life is in Miami," I clarified.

His eyes narrowed at me. "So what exactly do you think I'm doing right now?" He pointed back and forth between us. "What do you think this is?"

I instinctively raised my hands in the air in a surrendering gesture. I didn't want to fight with him or get him angry. "Listen…I didn't mean to hurt your feelings. I just assumed that you would go back home."

"Oh yeah? And what about you? What do you do?"

"I stay here, Sebastian. This is where I live. This is my home," I reminded him.

"Fuck!" he roared and stomped away from the table.

Shit…

I downed my entire glass of wine in one gulp, took a deep breath, and stood to turn to him. He was pacing the living room back and forth, running his hands through his hair, frustrated.

"Seba–"

"What do you think we're doing?" he argued, looking right at me. He looked crazed. I needed to stay calm to not provoke him.

"I don't…I don't know what we're doing…I just thought…fuck, I don't know…" I reasoned.

"Let me get this straight, just to make sure I have all the facts here. For the last *eleven weeks*," he stated, emphasizing his words, "we've been doing what exactly? Fucking? Is that all this is to you, Ysabelle?"

My eyes widened. "No…" I half-whispered, surprised.

"Then what? Please, enlighten me…because I thought we were trying to make things work as a partnership for the future, which is exactly where I fucking want to be with you. I had no idea that you intended for me to go back to Miami and leave you here. Do you think I would do that to you? That I would lose you again? Is this supposed to be a fucking game?"

I swallowed the saliva that was forming in my mouth. "I honestly don't know."

His mouth dropped open. "Ysa, I told you I loved you."

"I know!" I yelled.

Jesus…how did we go from one thing to another?

"Sebastian, I know you love me, I know you always have…that's not up for debate. I'm just confused, and it's not because I don't want to be with you or have a future with you. I want that more than anything. How could you say that to me?"

"What the fuck do you expect?" he reasoned.

"Some understanding maybe! I mean, is it not natural for me to assume that you would want to be near your son? How about work or money? What do expect me to think?"

"Fine…I'll give you that. But answer this, what about us? What would happen to us if you lived here and I lived there? Huh?"

"I thought we would make it work. I mean, do the long distance thing…I guess. I didn't think we wouldn't be together."

He nodded, then hesitated a few seconds. "I see."

He sat down on the couch and slouched forward with his hands in prayer motion. Neither one of us said anything for what seemed like a long time. I started to clean up the uneaten dinner, tossing it in the garbage and then proceeding to clear the table.

I didn't mean to hurt his feelings and I knew he was royally pissed at me. I had no idea how to make this better. I honestly thought he would go back to Miami and it never crossed my mind that he would want to stay. Here. With me. We loved each other, even though I hadn't said it. It didn't mean it wasn't true, he knew it, too. When we were together, the whole world disappeared; it was just he and I. I didn't think distance would take away the intense love we shared for each other. At least not for me.

I jumped when I heard the front door slam. All my reasoning and thoughts were gone in a blink of an eye, and all that remained were emotions and feelings; fear, loneliness, sadness, loss…

He walked out that door and he took my soul with him. I placed my hand on my chest; I couldn't breathe. My other hand found the counter to support my trembling body.

What the fuck am I doing?

I didn't think; I just reacted.

I ran toward the door and called out his name.

CHAPTER 5

S

"I don't…I don't know what we're doing…I just thought…fuck, I don't know…" she stammered.

She didn't know? What the fuck did she think I had been doing for the last eleven weeks?

I needed to calm down before I really lost my temper and took out all my own demons and frustrations on her.

This isn't her fault…this is yours, Sebastian. You did this.

"Let me get this straight, just to make sure I have all the facts here. For the last *eleven weeks*"—I stated, purposely emphasizing the last two words. I had left everything for her, my career, my son, my parents. She's home to me; that's where I wanted to be—"we've been doing what exactly? Fucking? Is that all this is to you, Ysabelle?"

Her eyes widened in shock, but I needed to know how fucked-up of a situation I was in. *Did this mean anything to her? Did we? Was I reading her all wrong?*

"No…" she half-whispered. Which further pissed me off; Ysa wasn't this timid. She was passionate and fought for what she wanted. *Did she not want me anymore? Had I lost her?*

I had to know. "Then what? Please enlighten me…because I thought we were trying to make things work as a partnership for the future, which is exactly where I fucking want to be with you. I had no idea that you intended for me to go back to Miami and leave you here. Do you think I would do that to you? That I would lose you again? Is this supposed to be a fucking game?"

I could see the apprehension written all over her beautiful face. "I honestly don't know." And there it was. The truth.

I wanted honesty, and that was it. She didn't trust me, not even a little.

Fuck me.

My mouth dropped open. After everything I had told her and everything I had tried to do…she would think I would just leave her again?

Eleven weeks, Sebastian…it's been eleven weeks. You've caused a year's worth of damage. Be patient.

"Ysa, I told you I loved you." It was all I could say.

"I know!" she yelled.

Yes, Ysa! Fight with me…show me something. Please! I'd die without you.

"Sebastian, I know you love me, I know you always have…that's not up for debate. I'm just confused, and it's not because I don't want to be with you or have a future with you. I want that more than anything. How could you say that to me?"

Oh my God, I felt like I was losing my mind. So I just reacted. "What the fuck do you expect?" I attacked.

"Some understanding maybe! I mean, is it not natural for me to assume that you would want to be near your son? How about work or money? What do expect me to think?"

"Fine…I'll give you that. But answer this, what about us? What would happen to us if you lived here and I lived there? Huh?"

"I thought we would make it work. I mean, do the long distance thing…I guess. I didn't think we wouldn't be together."

I nodded and surrendered. "I see."

My legs couldn't hold my weight anymore. I wanted to break down; I had to sit. I slouched forward as soon as my body hit the couch cushion from the overwhelming need to want to fucking scream and rip my hair out.

This is your fault…you ruined everything…

My conscience was fucking with me. *How could I have been so fucking stupid? What do I do? If I run to her, will she run away? Do I give it time? Do I leave?*

I won't. I can't.

Mine.

But what if it's not enough…

I couldn't take it anymore; I needed a drink. She didn't keep hard liquor upstairs; I needed to go down to the bar. The door slammed louder than I would have preferred, but I was pissed. I was fucking livid with myself. *It's not her fault. It's fucking me.*

I poured myself a shot of whiskey and then took down two more when I heard my name.

"Sebastian," she shouted, panicked.

When I didn't answer, the trampling of feet darted down the stairs at an alarming rate. I saw nothing but pure unadulterated fear when she reached the last step. She took one look at me and ran, rounding the corner and jumping straight into my arms.

"I'm sorry, Sebastian, I'm so sorry. Please don't go! Please don't leave me. I'm so fucking sorry. I love you! I swear I do. You have to believe me; you have to believe me," she openly bawled.

I had never seen her break down like that. I didn't recognize the tiny woman in my arms. I held her tighter and grabbed onto her ass–she understood my silent plea and wrapped her legs around my torso, angling herself higher onto my body and steadying her arms around my neck. Her face was still hidden in the nook of my neck, and I wanted more than anything to take away her pain and worry.

I'll carry your entire burden, Ysa; just give it to me. I'm strong enough for the both of us.

She was hyperventilating between breaths, and I kissed all over the top of her head.

"Ysa…"

She whimpered and clung on to me harder.

"Ysa…my girl…I need you to look at me. I want to see those beautiful bright green eyes that show me the world."

She sniffled and tried to control her breathing before taking a deep breath and finally looking at me.

There she is…there's my girl.

"What's going on in that gorgeous head of yours?" I whispered while laying soft kisses on her forehead.

"I…I…I don't want you to leave."

"What?"

"I'm sorry I made you mad. I'm sorry I hurt your feelings. I don't know what I was thinking; I don't want you to leave."

I unintentionally laughed. "Ysa, I was never going to leave you, even if you kicked me out, I wouldn't leave you. I belong to you. You belong to me."

She sniffled again. *God, she was fucking adorable.* Her eyes were bright green and glowing and her mascara had started to run. She had this whole sexy, seductress, exotic thing going on.

"But…you left. You slammed the door."

"What the fuck? Did you think I was leaving?"

Her forehead wrinkled and she nodded.

"Ysa, I came down here to get a drink. I know you don't keep hard liquor upstairs."

"Oh…" She blushed.

"I won't ever leave you again, I promise."

She bit her bottom lip.

"I love you. We will make this work. But you're home to me. This is my home now. I'm not leaving you."

She smiled and it lit up her entire face. "I love you, too, Sebastian. I always have."

To hear those words come out of the woman that has consumed my everyday existence for the last two years was like winning the lottery. I knew she would hide from me again, I knew we still had countless obstacles to overcome, but in that moment, she was mine again.

All her walls and guards were down.

My girl…

There was no need for more talking, those three words were enough for me and I knew it took everything for her to say them. She was emotionally spent, as was I. The sudden urge to make her mine was overpowering. The immense emotions that we just shared and displayed took over and I wanted to carve my name into her skin. I wanted to brand her for the whole world to see that she belonged to me.

I rounded the bar and sat her on the first table. Her body was perfectly proportionate with mine as I stood in between her legs. She looked up at me with abandonment and yearning; the heady expression was enough for me to lose control. I kicked all the chairs aside and brushed off the entire table's contents to the ground. I roughly grabbed the back of her neck and plunged my tongue into her eager and awaiting mouth. Our tongues did a sinful dance of want and need. It went back and forth between us, each giving the other what they craved. She clutched on to my hair and I pulled on hers, beckoning her head to fall back and give me the liberty to assault her neck.

I inhaled the sweet and tantalizing smell of Ysa, and ran my nose up and down from her chin to her collarbone, leaving a wake of desire behind.

She was my kryptonite.

I slowly removed her camisole and swiftly made my way down to her luscious breasts. Her nipples were hard, waiting for me to take them into my mouth. I sucked and gently bit one while my hand caressed and fondled the other. Her breathing escalated and both of her soft, delicate hands gripped my hair as her hips gyrated forward and toward the edge of the table.

Her legs spread wider and I got down on my knees.

I kissed my way to her lower abdomen and looked up with just my eyes. She was looking down at me, observing everything that I was doing, with a dark, dilated, intensified gaze. I grinned. My teeth latched onto the front of her panties, while my hands went to the sides.

She grinned back.

I growled and deliberately slid them down, throwing them to the side. I grabbed her right foot and perched it on the side of the table as I licked my way to her core, and then proceeded to do the exact same thing with the other. When I was a few inches away from her wetness, I backed away and sat on my ankles. There she was, completely spread eagle for me.

She leaned back on her hands, cocked her head to the side, and raised an eyebrow. She lingered for a few seconds to let me admire the view, and then seductively licked her lips as she started to rotate her hips front and back like she was fucking the table.

I could have come right then and there.

She pulled in her bottom lip and moaned, never stopping the momentum of her movements. “You didn’t eat dinner,” she taunted. “Aren’t you hungry?”

Fuck me...

Y

There I sat, completely open for him. Showing him every last part of me. It didn't matter how many men I performed for, or how many men I'd been with, it was always different with Sebastian. I knew our making love was going to be primal and it was going to look like we were fucking, technically, we were. Though, our feelings and emotions were all love–every last one of them. That's all that mattered; it spoke enough for our actions.

I always loved a man's eyes on me. They all said the same thing.

Want.

Craving.

Lust.

Sebastian's said all that and more.

Love.

Home.

Mine.

You might ask yourself if I missed the power and control of being a VIP. Take a look at me…

Does it look like it's fucking gone?

I leaned back on my hands, cocked my head to the side, and raised an eyebrow. I paused for a few seconds to let him admire the view. When I knew his cock was ready to explode, I took it a step further. I seductively licked my lips and started to rotate my hips front and back, just like I would on his dick.

I sucked in my bottom lip and moaned, never stopping the riding motion of my hips. And just because I could…I fucked with him.

"You didn't eat dinner," I insinuated. "Aren't you hungry?"

He lunged forward, almost knocking me off the table and devoured my pussy. He licked and sucked on my clit as if it centered him, giving him peace and tranquility. I moved my hands to the back of his head and continued the movements of my hips.

"Fuck…" I breathed out, and our stares locked. "I love you, Sebastian. I love you, I love you, I love you," I repeated as I climaxed on his face.

His tongue immediately moved to my opening and he growled the second his tongue dipped inside, licking and eating me clean.

"Goddamn it, you taste good."

I latched on to the sides of his face and shoved my tongue into his mouth, tasting my arousal for him and only him. I heard the rustling of his pants as he just let them fall down his thighs, not bothering to remove any of his clothing. His hands went around to my ass and he effortlessly picked me up off the table and slammed me right down onto his cock. In one thrust, he was deep inside me.

We moaned in unison and took a moment to appreciate the feeling of being connected. Two people in love becoming one, nothing is more powerful or fulfilling.

I was tightly wrapped around his body and his arms leveled me up and down, thrusting me onto his shaft. We had never done that before, and I could maybe count a handful of times that I had done it that way with another man. It took a lot of strength to hold someone up in that position.

Sebastian was marking me. We engulfed each other in the sensations of this perfect and precise angle to both our desired spots.

"Ysa…" he panted. "Let go a little, look at me, I got you, you're not going anywhere."

I loosened my hold and hitched in a breath when I looked into his eyes.

Devotion.

Loyalty.

Yours.

Always yours.

I braced my forehead on his and we never once took our eyes off each other. It took all my willpower to not let my eyes roll to the back of my head. Within seconds, we were both gasping and breathless for air. Our moans were getting louder and heavier, and we were both dripping sweat. I could feel my come dripping down my ass. Within minutes, neither one of us could take it anymore.

We both came together. Hard.

It was all that and more.

CHAPTER 6

S

"What are we doing for the holidays?" I asked as she made her morning protein shake.

It had been almost four months since I had been on the island with her. She ran her hand through her hair, ruffling it all over. It was getting long, almost down to her ass; the longer it got, the less it curled. Now it appeared like she had soft waves. I could smell the lingering vanilla scented shampoo and sunscreen she put on every morning.

Deadly combination for my cock.

"I don't know. That's my busiest time of the season."

I nodded. "I imagine, but how about you let me take you away for a few days. You've said so yourself the bar runs itself and your crew and management can hold down the place for a bit."

"True. You do know we live on an island, though? Where are you taking me that's better than paradise?" she said with a giggle.

"I was thinking we would go to Colorado. Maybe go snowboarding for a few days, rent a cabin in Breckenridge. The city is amazing during Christmas time, all the houses are lit up."

She smiled and sat up on the counter. "You can snowboard?" she asked, taking a sip of her shake.

"Of course, I can snowboard; I've been going since I was a kid. I'm actually pretty good. I'd have to go to my parents' and get my board, though."

"Oh…" The sadness in her tone was evident.

She bowed her head and I stepped in between her legs. "I was thinking another idea, too."

She looked up at me. "You're just full of them today, huh?" She narrowed her eyes as I placed my hand on her inner thigh. "Be nice," she cautioned.

"I'm always nice, especially when I'm in between in your legs," I teased. "What I was thinking, was that you would come back to Miami with me. I haven't been back in almost three four, Ysa. I miss Christian like crazy, and Skype just isn't cutting it anymore."

She nodded. "No, I understand."

"I also want to talk to Julia. She's been extremely understanding of me being here, and I'd like to let her know what's going to happen from here on out. I need to take a meeting with Yachting Enterprise's as well."

Her eyes followed my every word. "Yeah…definitely…that makes sense." She played it off well, but I could see her confusion and intrigue to what I was going to say next.

"I'd love for you to meet my parents."

"Whoa…"

I chuckled at her response. "Not only that, But I'd love for you to officially meet Christian and Julia, Ysa. I want my two worlds to unite so we can all come up with some sort of game plan for everyone involved."

She sucked in air. "Sebastian, that has nothing to do with me."

"It has everything to do with you. My mom would love to meet you. I talk about you all the time; they know where I am. They know everything."

"Everything?" she asked with apprehension.

"They know the important parts. Not so much the specifics. Julia knows I'm here with you. I want to go back together and then come home together."

"Okay…" she replied with obvious confusion.

"Okay?"

Her head was spinning with questions.

Her eyes darted all around the room, trying to process everything I was saying at a rapid speed. I could see the overwhelming perplexity of what I was requesting on her face. She wasn't doing a good job at hiding it. Her emotions were running wild, trying to catch up with her ability to understand how serious I was about us.

"I don't need to come home with you," she blurted. "I live here. I don't want to decide for you what is going to happen. I don't want to be involved in deciding what happens with everyone else. But this is where I am, so if you want to be here, just go, figure out your shit and then come back," she argued.

"I'm not asking you to. I've already made my decision. I'm moving here. I want to sell off my equity and partnership of Yachting Enterprises; I've already spoken to them. They have my final offer and we need to sit down and work out all the paperwork. I don't need to worry about money, ever. I've done very well for myself; Christian will have everything he needs. We will have everything we need. I want to invest in a charter business, here, with you." I paused to let her take in my words. "I want to trade in my yacht that's at the marina in Miami for a fishing boat and sail it back, here, with you. I'd like to talk to Julia and my parents about all of this in person, with you by my side. It's no longer just me, Ysa; it's us, and I want a life with you. Not just today, but tomorrow and every day after that. We're a team now, a partnership, and I want you to be a part of the decision-making process, for me, for us, and everyone else included. It will affect you, me, *us*, as much as them."

I stood there waiting for her to say something, but she didn't make a sound. She stared at me like I had grown three heads or something in the last few minutes. I waited for a response, anything to let me know that we were on the same page. Still nothing. I laid my heart out to her, and she hadn't said one thing. But if the expression on her face and the silence she's displaying were supposed to mean something, then I was royally fucked.

Just when I think we take two steps forward, we take three back.

The silence was terrifying and it was eating away at all my insecurities.

Be patient...

I was about to say something, anything, when her phone rang, taking her out of her coma-induced daze. "I'm going to get that," she announced, shaking her head.

"Are you serious?"

"Yeah...it could be important."

"More important than this?" I demanded, wanting an answer.

She put her hands up in the air in a frustrated gesture. "Just...chill...give me a second." She pushed me backward, away from her, and jumped off the counter, quickly grabbing her cell phone off the dining table and sprinting out the front door.

What the fuck just happened?

Y

I walked outside and closed the door behind me, and just started walking with nowhere in particular to go.

Please don't follow me…I need a minute, or thirty…maybe a lifetime…

My phone kept ringing and I placed it to my ear, not caring to check who was calling. "Hello," I answered.

"Hey, Kid, how's my favorite troublemaker?"

I couldn't get my mouth to move. I could barely form thoughts and sentences, which seemed to be a problem, too.

"You there? Ysabelle?" he added.

I shook my head. "Yeah…hey, Devon, what's up?" I responded, shaken.

"You all right?"

"I don't fucking know…" I honestly replied.

"Okay…do you want to talk about it?"

I shrugged as if he could see me. "I don't even know what just happened…how can I talk about it if I don't understand it," I countered.

"How about you start from the beginning."

I nodded. "Umm…one minute we're talking about going away, and then Colorado, which led to snowboarding…and then he's telling me he's going back to Miami to get his snowboard that is at his parents' house…" I rambled, throwing my hands in the air and walking around in circles. "So then he's asking me to go meet his parents…I don't know his parents…I don't know anyone's parents…I don't even know my own parents. I mean, I know my mom…but she's a cunt…I never met my dad…" I continued, mindlessly babbling. "Yeah…" I nodded repeatedly.

"Then…he's telling that he wants me by his side to talk to Julia and his parents…who I'm just going to meet for the first time…how the fuck does that even make sense. But get this, Devon…they know everything…so, let me tell you how that introduction is going to go, ‘Oh, hi, I’m Ysabelle, yes that Ysabelle, the one that broke up your son’s marriage…yeah…we had an affair for a year until Julia found out and then everything went to shit. But it’s okay because I’m no longer a VIP, I’m only your son’s whore now,’” I reasoned. “Doesn’t that sound awesome? To top it all off, he’s moving here and he wants to open a charter business with his fishing boat that he wants us to bring back together.” I nodded again. “So…that sums it up in a nutshell. How are you?”

“I’m great. You sound…” He hesitated. “…good…”

“Great, actually.” I hadn’t stopped nodding.

“Excellent. So…are you going to pick me up from the airport?”

I stopped nodding and frowned. “Huh?”

“I’m at the airport. I was coming to visit today, you remember? My divorce was finalized last month, you told me to come visit.”

“Holy shit, Devon! I completely forgot. Fuck…I-I-I—”

“Kid, take a deep breath, relax, I’ll take a cab. I’ll see you soon. We’ll continue this conversation, okay?” I nodded like he could see me. “Okay.”

I aimlessly walked into the bar and Sebastian was talking to Jamie, one of my employees.

“There she is,” she announced, making him turn and take in my disheveled appearance. I didn’t give him a chance to comment.

“Devon’s on his way here. Did you remember he was coming today?”

He cocked his head to the side in concern and confusion. “It slipped my mind.”

“Mine, too. I think I’m going to take a shower.”

“Ysa…”

I put my hands up in front of me to stop him. “Sebastian, please, I can’t do this right now.”

Before I could see how my response hurt him, I turned and walked upstairs.

CHAPTER 7

Y

I showered, dressed, and put myself together as best as I could. By the time I was done, I walked out into the living room; Devon was sitting on the couch with his son, Ethan, in his lap. Sebastian was nowhere to be found.

"Hi," I sighed.

He laughed. "You look like you got ran over by a bus."

"I feel like I did. How was your flight?"

"It was good. Ethan flirted with the girl next to me so it made it that much better."

"That sounds about right." I went into the kitchen. "Do you want anything to drink or eat?" I hollered.

"Yeah, I'll take a water. We ate on the plane."

"Who the fuck eats on a plane? Did you ride first class?"

"No, Princess Kid, we did not. I bought something at the airport and ate it on the plane. Ethan has his snacks. He'll be good for a bit."

I grabbed two bottles of water from the fridge and handed him one, then sat on the opposite couch, facing him.

"He's gotten big," I acknowledged, nodding at his two-year-old son.

"That usually happens when you feed them."

"He looks more like you than that Miami whore." He was about to scold me for calling her that, but then nodded in agreement. "Can I say I told you so, now?" I smiled.

He chuckled. "I'm surprised it took you this long."

"So how much did she take you for?"

"You know, I do know a thing about business, and marriage is very much a business deal. Two parties coming together and uniting, assets are very important to take into consideration when making such a huge commitment."

I laughed. "Why, thank you, Mr. Hill, for clarifying in such great detail how that works."

He smirked. "We had a prenup."

I gasped. "You did know she was a whore!" I yelled.

He rolled his eyes. "No…but it's life and I have to take care of myself. She got more than enough in the settlement and with child support, she won't ever have to work again."

"Ugh, you're such a nice guy. I would have left her with nothing. She fucking cheated on you…with a bar-back, at your bar! Might I add. She's a piece of work."

"I'm aware."

"I mean, damn…if you're going to cheat, don't downgrade; she was already fucking the boss. Now that's disgusting."

He shook is head.

"What? I mean, and the obvious, too; she hurt you and shit."

"Oh lord…have I told you how much I've missed you?"

I looked up in thought. "Not today."

We sat there for an hour just shooting the shit. I was grateful that he was there; I needed to take my mind off Sebastian. Devon was always there for me, he was my go-to person and it meant everything to me that he still was. When I first opened up my bar, he came and stayed with me for a month to get things settled and showed me how to run the place. I didn't even have to ask him, he offered. During that time, I opened up to him and finally told him everything; my mom, running away, VIP, The Madam, Sebastian, all of it.

Granted, we were drunk when having this serious conversation…there was no way I would have been able to do it without liquid courage. He just sat there and listened, never judged, never asked any questions, nothing. He'd always been my shoulder to lean on, it didn't matter what happened or would happen in my life, I knew I always had him. He's known me since I was sixteen years old, and literally picked me off the street when I had no one, taking a chance on me when I never had that before. He was my best friend, a brother, and my only family outside of VIP. The first person I'd ever said "I love you" to and meant it.

And *that* meant everything to me.

S

Ysabelle is going to be the death of me.

I couldn't believe she just walked out on me like that. With no explanation, no excuse, no warning, just up and left after I poured my heart out to her. I'm trying to be honest and upfront with what I want…after all this time and everything we've gone through.

I want her.

For the first time in my life, I was thinking about what I wanted. Me. I'm fighting a battle that I didn't know if I would ever win. I couldn't lose her again; I wouldn't survive it. It's frustrating to no end to not have a clue as to where the fuck I stood, where the fuck we stood. One minute I felt like we were making progress, going in the right direction, and then the next, I didn't recognize the woman standing before me.

She lets me in and then shuts me out.

She swallows me whole and then spits me right back out.

Am I wanting too much too fast?

We went almost two years without seeing or speaking to each other, isn't that enough time for her to decide what she wanted? Did she not think about me at all during our time away from each other? How could she not?

I thought about her every fucking day. I never stopped thinking about her.

"Ethan!" I turned when I heard a yell from behind me. "You can't run away from me like that, buddy." Devon picked up his kid, dropping the duffle bag onto the sand.

He nodded at me. "Hey, man," he greeted, walking up to me.

"Hey."

I had met Devon twice before, the first was at his bar with Ysabelle, on one of our first encounters, and the following time, I went to his bar to ask about her. If it weren't for him, I probably would've never found her. I knew their history; Ysabelle had told me all about him. He took care of her when she had no one and for that, I'm eternally grateful to him.

"How you been?" he asked.

I sighed and he laughed.

"Don't you just love her?" he sarcastically questioned.

"Mmm hmm…"

"Where's our trouble maker, anyway?"

I nodded toward the stairs. "She's upstairs."

"You guys okay?"

"I hope so."

He placed his hand on my shoulder. "Hang in there, man. She's worth it."

"Trust me, I know. She's waiting for you," I acknowledged.

He geared his head toward the stairs. "You coming?"

"Nah, you guys catch up."

Watching him with his son made me think about Christian. I missed him. He was growing up so fast and I didn't want to be an absentee father, he was seven and before I knew it, he'd have his first girlfriend and be applying to colleges. I had to go back to Miami.

I just hoped that Ysabelle would come with me.

Y

"So…spill it, what's going on with you and Romeo downstairs? He looks like a
kicked puppy. What did you do?"

My mouth dropped open. "What makes you assume it's me?"

He raised an eyebrow and kissed Ethan's head, leaving him to play with his Legos on the dining table. I scooted over when I realized he was coming to sit by me. We both tucked one leg under the other to face each other.

"That man is devoted to you, Kid. You'd be a fool not to notice."

"I know."

"So…then what's the problem?"

I shrugged. I didn't want to talk about it.

"Okay, let me guess and stop me if I'm wrong."

I nodded, slightly amused.

"From what I gathered over the rampage you had on the phone earlier, I'm assuming he wants a life with you. There's nothing wrong with what he's requesting, and to be completely honest, most women would be on their knees wagging their tails from the commitment."

I rolled my eyes.

"Yes…I'm fully aware that you aren't most women."

I smirked.

"What are you so scared of? The Ysabelle I know looks at fear and laughs in its face, and then she goes back and gives it blue balls."

That won him a laugh. "Ugh! I'm not scared…I mean…I don't know. I–" I stuttered. "I guess I didn't expect this. I mean, I am devoted to him; I love him with everything I am. But sometimes, I feel like it's overwhelming how much emotion is behind our relationship. Does that make any sense?"

"Of course."

"We have this history that isn't good, there's so much hurt and pain from both ends. Mostly his, though…he's the first person that ever hurt me, and I can't help but feel responsible for that."

"What? Now you lost me."

"You know who I am, Devon, I've known you…what? Ten years now? It took me almost nine of them to finally let you in. I'm not made like that. But I let him in, wholeheartedly and pretty much immediately, and I got fucked in that; emotionally, mentally, physically, I was put through the ringer. And I just kept going right back for more…I was needy and pathetic. That's not who I am and I pride myself on being strong and independent. I mean…look at everything I have. I. Did. That. With no help from anyone else." I paused to gather my thoughts and take a deep breath for what I was about to say. "I'm terrified that if I become that person again, I won't be able to find my way back to where I am right now. I've grown so much since I left VIP and I don't want to ruin or jade that."

His eye widened and he nodded. "That's some deep shit, Kid."

"Tell me about it."

"However, what if it doesn't?" he countered.

"What do you mean?"

"What if you do get the happily ever after? Men fuck up…we don't understand women at all and pretend like we do. I can sympathize with him, and not that I'm trying to excuse what he did because it was wrong, but people make mistakes, it's human nature.

Men are selfish; we want what we want when we want it, plain and simple, black or white, all or nothing. There's no grey area for us. You just have to decide what it is that you want."

"I want him," I instinctually declared.

He smiled. "Then that's your answer."

CHAPTER 8

S

I could hear them laughing from the stairs before I even made it to the third step. It was 11pm and I had been at the bar all day, thinking. I hadn't seen or spoken to her since this morning. I can't say that I wasn't hurt by the fact that she hadn't even texted me. I gave her space that I assumed she wanted and let her spend the day with him. It didn't stop me from feeling…fuck…I don't even know. Frustrated, maybe?

I opened the door and what I saw nearly knocked me on my ass. Ysabelle was laying on the love seat with her head on Devon's lap as he caressed her hair.

What the fuck?

They were laughing and didn't even realize that I had walked into the room. There were two empty bottles of wine on the coffee table, and both of their glasses were nearly empty. I couldn't help but take in the familiarity of the way they looked at each other. When she stumbled on her words and his fingers grazed the side of her cheek, I nearly lost my shit.

I slammed the door shut.

They both jumped, looking over at me. "Heeeyyy," she addressed with glossy eyes and flushed cheeks.

She was drunk.

"Hi?" I questioned.

"Where have you been all day?"

"Running your bar."

She lazily smiled, not picking up on my irritated tone.

"Kid," he chimed in, leaning her forward and putting her arm around his neck to help her up. "I think you need to go to bed."

I was over to them in three strides and shoved him in the chest. "I got her," I warned and he nodded, releasing his hold on her.

She leaned upward, placing her hand on his chest for balance and gazed at him. "I'm so happy you're here. I missed you so much." Her arms went around his neck, putting all her weight on him and his arms instinctively went around her. "I love you, Devon."

His eyes locked with my manic glare.

"What would I do without you?" she whispered, loud enough for us both to hear and then kissed the side of his neck.

Never tearing his neutral gaze from mine, he kissed the top of her head. "I love you, too," he repeated.

I roughly grabbed on to her arm and jerked her to me, cradling her like a baby and carrying her into *our* bedroom, kicking the door closed behind me.

She inhaled my scent and half moaned "Sebastian" as I gently laid her on the bed and she spread out like a cat. I walked into the bathroom and grabbed three Ibuprofen from the cabinet.

I reached for her and sat her up. "Ysa, you have to take this."

She half-opened her beautiful eyes and smiled at me. I never wanted to yell at her more than I wanted to in that moment. It wasn't the time; I would have to wait. I placed the pills in her mouth and helped her take a sip from the bottled water that was on the nightstand. She was already half asleep when I started taking off her clothes. I left her in her panties and scooted her on her side of the bed, laying her on her pillow and covering her with the sheet. She groaned, displeased, and rolled over to my side, grabbing my pillow and sighing in contentment.

I sat back on the armchair and rubbed my temples, in an effort to calm the migraine that was forming, to no avail. I watched her sleep for a few minutes before a sound from the living room reminded me of the reason she was in this state in the first place. I took one more look at her, kissed her on the forehead, and walked out into the living room. He was cleaning up their mess of alcohol and food and paused when he heard me close the bedroom door.

"What the fuck are you still doing here?" I demanded, trying to keep my composure. I wanted nothing more than to beat the fuck out of him.

Mine.

He wiped his hands on the dishrag, threw it on the counter, and walked in my direction, stopping a few feet in front of me.

"Ysabelle invited me. That's why I'm here, and I'm not leaving until she tells me to go." He shook his head. "I'm not leaving."

"Who the fuck do you think you are? You think I'm fucking stupid? You don't think I see the way you look at her, how given the chance, you find a way to touch her?" I snickered and stepped in front of him until we were mere inches apart. "But guess what, motherfucker, she's mine. And I will destroy anyone who tries to take her away from me. Do you understand? I get this nice guy act you have going on and I'm sure it gets you lots of pussy. I don't give a flying fuck whom you are to her, you come in between us and I will take you the fuck out." I roughly pushed him, but he didn't lose his footing, he was expecting it.

"Now, I'm going to ask you this one fucking time, and trust me, I'll know if you're lying."

He held his head higher, not cowering. I balled my fists.

"Have you ever fucked her?"

"No," he responded with no hesitation.

"Do you want to?"

He paused. "No."

"Liar," I stated through gritted teeth. "You're in love with her, aren't you?"

"It doesn't matter…she loves you," he informed, not missing a beat. "She spent the entire day talking about you. I'm here as her friend. I've been in her life longer than anyone, especially you. I've seen her at her worst and I've seen her at her best. But unlike you, I've never fucked her over. I know who you are, Sebastian. Don't try to play the nobleman act with me. Now…let me remind you that just because I haven't been inside her, doesn't mean I don't know her in more ways than you do."

My fist connected with his jaw before he even got the last word out. He stammered a little, but caught himself on the coffee table.

I cocked my head to the side. "You want to try that again?" I threatened.

He raised an eyebrow and rubbed at his jawline, backing away from me. I cracked my neck as soon as he left my sight, but he quickly reemerged with his duffle bag and his sleeping son in his arms.

Fuck.

I immediately felt like a bastard, I completely forgot about the kid.

"Let Ysabelle know that something came up and I had to go back to Miami. I'll call her tomorrow afternoon," he informed and left.

And that was that…

There was nothing left to say.

Y

My head was pounding.

I covered my eyes from the sunlight. It was too fucking bright.

"How you feeling?"

Of course, he was watching me sleep.

"I'm hurting."

"I bet. Sit up," he ordered.

I slowly peeled my eyes open, one at a time. Sebastian was holding a glass of ice water and buttered toast. I sluggishly sat up, pulling the sheet with me and leaned against my headboard, grabbing the water and gulping it.

"Here," he said, handing me Ibuprofen.

"Oh, I love you; you're so good to me," I responded, smiling.

He half-smiled at me, as I took a bite of toast.

"Where's Devon?"

"He said something came up in Miami and he had to leave."

"What? Is everything okay?"

He shrugged. "I guess, I didn't really talk to him. How much do you remember from yesterday?"

"Oh…" I hesitated. "Ummm…things start getting a little hazy after we opened the second bottle of wine. Was I a shit show?"

He chuckled. "I've seen worse. You definitely couldn't fend for yourself. I put you to bed, though."

"When did Devon leave?"

"After you passed out."

"Oh. I hope he's okay. You guys didn't get a chance to hang?"

He shook his head no. "I barely talked to him. He just said he had to leave and that he'd call you later."

"Okay. I think we should do a cuddle day. Watch movies in bed and eat junk food. I don't feel good."

"Ysa…" he said in a serious tone.

Damn it. "I know, Sebastian. I'm sorry about yesterday."

"We need to talk about it."

I nodded. I didn't really want to have a serious conversation while feeling like shit, but I knew better than to say that out loud. He deserved an explanation.

"You can't keep running away from me like that."

"I know."

"You know where I stand and sometimes I think I know where you do, but then something like yesterday happens and I'm back to square one again. I love you. I know what I want and it's you."

"I love you, too."

He smiled. "You have to talk to me, Ysa. You have to tell me what you're feeling because I can't help you if I don't know. I'm not a mind reader."

"It's hard for me."

"I know, but what do you want?"

"You," I simply stated. "I talked to Devon and it really helped."

He sighed. "I need and want you to talk to me."

"I know. I promise, I'll try. It's just that Devon has always be–"

"I don't want to talk about Devon, Ysabelle," he abruptly interrupted. "I want to talk about us, me and you. That's all that matters, no one else," he added.

"I understand."

He leaned forward and kissed my forehead and then the tip of my nose, before resting his forehead on mine. "Will you come back to Miami with me? It would mean everything to me to have you by my side. I need you."

I would do this for him.

For us.

I took a deep breath.

"Yes."

CHAPTER 9

S

A few days later, I bought the plane tickets, first class. Ysabelle was insistent on that, she said something about hating to fly, and sitting too close to a person she didn't know gave her anxiety. I didn't care if I had to rent a fucking private plane if that's what it took to get her to go with me. Three weeks later and we left the next morning. I rented us a suite on South Beach for a week; it would give us time to get everything in order without having to rush. Luke, Ysabelle's GM, was going to be watching the bar and Chance while we were gone. It was the first time she would be leaving the bar for that extended amount of time, but I knew that wasn't what was bothering her.

I could tell she had reservations, but didn't express them to me. I didn't push her for any information; she was coming back with me and I knew that was huge for her. Not to take into account everything else that went along with it, I couldn't fault her for being overwhelmed; it was a lot. And as much as I wanted her to open up to me and tell me everything she was feeling, and that *we* would work it out together, I knew that would only add fuel to her already lit fire. She was coming back with me and that was good enough for me.

For now.

"You almost done packing?" I asked, walking into the bedroom.

Her luggage was on the floor and she had piles of clothes scattered on the bed; she had been packing all morning. Let me rephrase that…she would pack, and then unpack, and then start all over again. The nervousness she displayed was adorable.

"I'm getting there," she sighed. "I left all my stuff at my condo when I left Miami and the stuff I own now is not...Miami..." she reasoned.

I held back the laughter that was at bay and sat on the armchair. "Ysa, you look fucking amazing in anything. Although I prefer you in nothing." I smirked, getting her to glance up and smile.

There's my girl.

"Do you want me to help?" I suggested.

"No, I'm almost done. I think..."

"No...I think I can help."

I gripped her wrist, bringing her over to me and she giggled. She straddled my lap with her ass on my cock, facing away from me.

"I actually love what you're wearing right now," I huskily praised while my hands moved from her hips to the sides of her body, up to her breasts. I slowly touched them and she curved her back.

Vixen.

"You know what the color white does to me. Do you do it on purpose?"

She sucked in air when one of my hands moved to the back of her neck and I nudged her backward, making her hips sway on my cock.

"Why do you provoke me?"

She deviously gazed into my eyes. "Because I can," she snickered and I immediately jerked her head back by her hair.

"You know I like it rough, Mr. Vanwell," she added, baiting me.

"Oh...it's Mr. Vanwell is it?" I murmured, inclining her head back further. Her body was stretched out for me; she felt tinier in that angle. I could do anything I wanted to her and she would let me, begging me to keep going. That's just the kind of woman she was.

Mine.

My hold on her hair grew harder and she whimpered, not in pain. In submission. I slowly inched her head back further until her breasts were upright and her eyes beheld the ceiling. I could see every rib protruding as her back was perfectly extended in the shape of a U.

"I'll ask you again...why do you provoke me, Ysa?"

She didn't hesitate. "Because I'm yours."

"Prove it."

She didn't move or make a sound while I used my other hand to untie the strings of her bathing suit top and bottom; they fell to the side. My nails dug into her soft, delicate skin from her neck all the way down her incredible body. They left a trail of red, almost like a rake had been taken to her skin. Nothing. No sound. No movement.

Her pussy was bare for me and I could see her throbbing clit.

I placed my lips right by her ear. "I'm not going to touch you," I whispered. "I know you want me to. I can see your greedy cunt just begging to be played with."

Her breathing hitched.

"Tell me what you want," I added, tugging her hair back slightly to get her to speak.

"I want to come," she panted.

"Show me."

She hesitated.

"Now," I urged.

Her fingers found her pussy and she started touching herself. I licked my lips and sucked on her earlobe.

"Harder," I demanded.

She stimulated herself at a quicker pace, monopolizing the little bundle of nerves until her body started to tremble. I bent her back further and my other hand reached for the front her neck. She withered and moaned.

I caressed her neck and then lightly squeezed; her breathing slowed, but her body was quivering. She was close. I gripped a little more until I could feel her pulsating vein beating rapidly, her body burned and her face reddened.

"That's it…fuck that tight, wet, perfect pussy that I can't get enough of. Do it. Let me see you come apart like you know I love." I clutched until I knew she couldn't take one more breath and then held her there for a few seconds. When her eyes watered, I immediately let go of her neck and simultaneously tugged her hair further back. She gasped for air and came apart on my legs with such force that her entire body shook and she screamed out my name.

My girl.

Y

I tried not to panic as we boarded the plane, I hated flying. We were going back to Miami, together. I hadn't been back in over two years. I was going to meet his parents, his son, and his ex-wife, officially. I barely comprehended the severity that this would implement on our relationship, but I was going with it. That's what I do.

To make matters worse, I had no fucking clue what to do about Madam.

Yes…I just said Madam.

Brooke knew we were coming. I called her a few days ago to tell her and she screamed in my ear for a good five seconds before I got another word in. She was thrilled that she would be seeing me and finally meeting Sebastian. That wasn't what was plaguing me. It was Madam; I knew Brooke would tell her that I was in town. I had skipped out on the last two VIP reunions. However, we talked maybe once a month, but they were always brief and Sebastian had absolutely no idea. I never told him. I figured we had enough obstacles to overcome and get through, the last thing I wanted to do was add the burden of The Madam.

I wasn't fucking stupid enough to think that he would be okay with it. I knew he would flip the hell out. It would cause another major rift. We were already in limbo and I didn't need to add Satan, so to speak. But in all honesty, I wanted to see her. I missed her. I didn't miss VIP, not really. I mean, I think it was the familiarity of what was comfortable for me. VIP was home for such a huge part of my life. I found myself there, and when I left, I took a huge part of that with me. I still use my sexuality and wear it on my sleeve; I still craved attention, except now it was from one man versus all men.

My independence was such a strong factor and it's hard for me to give and take that. I knew Sebastian wanted all of me, and sometimes I worried if I was capable of truly handing that over to him. I didn't know if that was in the cards for us. Could he ever truly love me if I could only offer him fifty-percent? Would that be enough for him? For us?

I was emotionally torn and it ate away at me the closer we got. All I could do was keep trying, and that's why I was sitting there beside him, going back to a past I didn't know if I was ready to face. Again, I did the only thing that came natural to me; I pretended to have my shit together.

"You okay?" he questioned.

"Yeah, I just really hate flying," I lied.

"I find that really hard to believe, Miss World Traveler."

I laughed. "That was so different. I flew on private planes that were bigger than what we're flying in now. You felt like you were on land. Plus, I was usually fucked up on drugs or at least alcohol," I carelessly replied.

Shit.

"I mean–"

"So I talked to my mom and she was thinking about having a dinner for all of us at the house I grew up in," he interrupted.

I nodded. I would have agreed to anything at that point. I was too much of a coward to look at him, terrified of what I'd see.

"Great. I'll let her know as soon as we land. I think she was trying to aim for tomorrow since it's Sunday."

"Right…Sunday fun-day," I nervously chuckled.

We rode in silence the rest of the ride.

Lost in our own thoughts.

S

We landed around 6pm, and by the time we made it back to the suite, it was almost 8. Ysabelle took a shower and I ordered room service. When I was done, I called my mom.

"Hello," she answered.

"Hey," I replied.

"Honey, how was the flight?"

"It was good, no turbulence. How are you guys doing?"

"Your dad's on call and I'm just cleaning up."

"Great. I talked to Ysabelle and tomorrow sounds like a plan."

"Oh, fabulous. I already went grocery shopping; I was thinking we would just grill out. I've invited some of the neighbors who would love to see you. Julia said she would be a little late and arrive around 2pm with Christian and a friend."

"A friend?" I asked, caught off guard. "One of Christian's friends?"

She paused. "Ummm…I'm not quite sure, honey. I guess we will find out tomorrow. Anyway, I'm so happy to get to see my boy. I've missed you so much."

"I've missed you, too. Ysabelle is excited to meet you, both of you guys."

"As are we. If you guys would like to head over around noon, that would be perfect, it would give us some alone time before everyone arrives around 1."

"That sounds great, I'll see you tomorrow."

"Perfect, I love you."

"Love you, too," I repeated, hanging up.

I saw Ysabelle in my peripheral vision, standing in the doorway from the bedroom to the living room. Her expression was unreadable.

"That was my mom. I told her we're on for tomorrow."

She nodded. "Yeah, I heard. Your son's bringing a friend?"

I guess she could hear the other line.

"I don't know, I guess Julia said she was bringing a friend."

She cocked her head to the side. "Oh…maybe she's bringing a guy? Is she dating someone?"

I shrugged. "I don't know and I honestly really don't care. Good for her if she is."

Her eyes narrowed like she was trying to see if I was lying. I wasn't. I didn't care if Julia had a boyfriend; it just caught me by surprise.

"Right," she half-whispered and turned into the bedroom.

I couldn't tell if she believed me or not, and a part of me knew…

She didn't.

CHAPTER 10

S

Ysabelle tossed and turned and I feigned sleep.

"I know you're not sleeping," she announced into the dark room. "And you know I'm not sleeping, so since neither of us is sleeping, maybe we should talk."

She'd always been able to open up to me when we were shielded by darkness, I made sure to make a mental note of that.

"I'd love to talk," I encouraged.

"Sebastian, what if they don't like me?"

"They're going to love you as much as I do," I simply stated.

My parents were the most supportive people ever. I knew that they would have reservations about her, but once they got to know her like I did, they would love her. It was hard not to. I wished she could see that.

"How do you know that? I mean, really…I've never met anyone's parents. I don't know how to act in front of them and I want them to like me so bad. I want to make a great impression and not just be the woman who broke up your marriage."

I wanted so badly to turn on the light and look into her eyes, to take away every reservation, but I knew better. This is how she preferred intimate conversations and I could give her that. The darkness made it easier for her to tell her secrets that she held so dear to her heart. Although, I reached for her and she let me, laying her head on my stomach. I placed one arm behind my head while the other played with her hair; I knew when she was under distress, this soothed her. I loved feeling the soft and silkiness between my fingers.

She sighed contentedly. "Is Julia going to be a bitch to me? I mean…I don't blame her if she is; I'd just like to be prepared on what to expect."

"Julia is fine. You don't need to worry about her or anyone else."

"Does she hate me?"

"We've never talked about it. I know that you feel responsible for the demise of my marriage, Ysa, but you couldn't be more wrong."

"What do you mean, Sebastian? We had an affair, an emotional affair the worst kind. I was the other woman, I knew you were married and still got involved with you. She has every right to blame me."

"Julia and I made sense on paper. Our marriage was great; I'm not going to lie about that. I thought I was happy, but the minute I met you, I knew I wasn't. I never was."

She breathed out, wanting to say something.

"Tell me, please, tell me what you're feeling. I need to know," I urged. I waited for what felt like an eternity. Her body tensed; the internal battle she was fighting was radiating and I knew it was wrecking havoc on her fear. I grabbed the side of her face, making her look at me. The trepidation on her face was evident, even in the dim lighting. "It doesn't matter what you say to me, Ysa, I'm not going anywhere. Please don't be afraid of me."

She bit her bottom lip.

"If you tell me, I promise to try to make it better. I will ease every one of your concerns."

She glanced down and nervously drew what felt like a heart on mine. "If I didn't look like Olivia…"

Shit.

"I mean…if we still met on the yacht that night and I looked like someone else, would you have still wanted me?"

I took a deep breath, contemplating how to express what I felt in my being. "Initially, your appearance was a major draw to me. I can't lie about that. But the second you opened your smart mouth…" I chuckled. "…I was yours. You may look like her, Ysa, but you're nothing alike. It's like night and day and I noticed that immediately. I was drawn to you as a person, but your appearance was the first thing I noticed. I'm grateful to Olivia for that. I truly believe she came into my life so that I could meet you. You're my soul mate."

She smiled and laid her head to the side, finally looking up at me. "I love you, Sebastian."

"I know."

And I did.

Y

The next morning came at rapid speed. I slept in Sebastian's arms all night and it was the first time my mind didn't wander. We woke up fairly early and ate breakfast on the terrace that overlooked the water. Miami was beautiful, but it was nothing like my paradise at home. We had casual conversation and I tried to control the turmoil that plagued me in the back of my mind, completely ignoring it and hoping it would go away.

It didn't.

I dressed in a sherbet colored maxi dress and Sebastian said I looked like ice cream. Then he proceeded to eat me, literally. It helped. He rented an Audi A8 for the week and I couldn't help but remember that this was the same car Madam had given me after we broke up. It was the same color, white with tan leather interior.

We drove in silence, holding hands and listening to XM radio, BPM station. Sebastian was dressed in dark blue cargo shorts, a white button-down shirt that made his bright blue eyes pop, and flip-flops.

We drove through a gated Mediterranean community. "This is a beautiful neighborhood."

"It is. Welcome to where I grew up, Ysa." He kissed my palm and lingered there for a few seconds. "You okay?"

"I think so," was all I could reply with.

We pulled up to a large roundabout driveway with a sprawling staircase that led up to the front door. The house was dark green with tan trim and white accents. It was immaculate.

"What do your parents do again?" I questioned, exiting the car.

"Mom's a housewife and Dad's a cardiologist."

"Oh yeah, I remember."

The front door opened as he rounded the car.

"My baby!" his mom shouted. She swiftly made her way down the stairs and pulled him into her arms.

"Hey, Mom," he greeted, squeezing her and hauling her up in the air.

She looked so tiny in his arms. It was endearing to see the love that displayed in front of me. I had never been around a family before. I could see the love that they shared for one another and it made me happy that he grew up around that. He placed her back onto the ground and grabbed her hand to bring her toward me.

"Mom, this is my girl, Ysabelle," he introduced.

I extended my hand and she curved her head to the side and laughed.

"Honey, we do not shake hands in this house."

She immediately pulled me into her arms for a hug. My eyes widened as I stared up at Sebastian, who had the most gratified smile on his face.

"Oh...okay," I breathed out, wrapping my arms around her.

She hugged me like she had known me for years.

She hugged me like she loved me.

She hugged me like a mom hugs their daughter.

And in that moment, I knew I'd never known the touch of a mother. I bit the inside of my mouth to hold the tears that were at bay. My eyes were getting watery and when I glanced back up at Sebastian, he knew exactly what I was feeling and said, "I love you," with just his lips.

She pulled back and held my hands out in front of me, taking in my appearance.

"Wow, you're gorgeous. Sebastian didn't do you justice, honey."

I smiled. "Thank you. I can see where Sebastian gets his kindness."

She beamed and grabbed Sebastian, putting her arm around each of our waists as we walked inside. The inside of the house was just as breathtaking as the outside. Although it looked luxurious, it had a home feel to it. I instantly fell in love.

"Son," his dad called out from the living room.

They both moved simultaneously, embracing each other much like he had with his mother.

"Dad, this is Ysabelle," he announced, bringing him over to me.

I took in his appearance, and although Sebastian had his mother's eyes, he was the spitting image of his father. The man was handsome, devastatingly handsome. They made a gorgeous couple. He hugged me just like his wife had and I took in the comfortable and welcoming embrace.

We made our way into the backyard where there was a huge Olympic size pool. The pavers matched the modern décor, and the outdoor grill had a granite countertop. We sat on the patio furniture as his mom gathered some drinks. I had a glass of wine and Sebastian had a beer.

"So, Ysabelle, Sebastian tells us that you own a bar and it does very well," she questioned, taking a sip of her wine.

I smiled. "Yeah, it does extremely well actually. I'm really lucky, I love it."

"That's amazing. What made you want to get into that?"

"Oh, I love being near the water, there's something about it that calls to me. I decided that I might as well do something that makes me happy."

She nodded. "I agree. Are you from Miami?"

Oh man…

"No, not originally. I had lived here for about eight years before I moved to the island."

"Oh lovely! Where are you from?"

Sebastian and I locked eyes. "Tampa," I nervously responded.

"Great! I love Tampa; we go there often for medical conferences. Sebastian used to love going to The Florida Aquarium when he was younger."

I chuckled.

"So, Dad, how's work?" he asked, taking the focus off of me.

I've never loved him more.

We spent the next hour talking about Sebastian growing up and I loved hearing the stories about his childhood. It made me feel closer to him to hear about his life. When his mom got up to get baby albums, he put his foot down and said that it wasn't necessary; she didn't listen.

"Isn't he precious? I swear he was born gorgeous. All the nurses at the hospital couldn't believe he was a newborn because of how strong his facial features were. He was always such a great baby, sleeping through the night almost immediately. I mean, look at that face."

I giggled. "Oh my God!" I yelled, looking at a picture of him in the bath. He was only a few months old and his chubby little body was squirming around.

"Mom, I think that's enough," he said, grabbing the photo album and she slapped his hand, making me laugh.

"Nonsense," she reprimanded.

As we looked through all the pictures, it was then that I realized how much Julia really was a part of his life. I played it off nicely, smiling and pretending that it wasn't hard for me to see.

It was.

When we got to the older years and Olivia showed up–it was uncanny. This girl really did resemble me. I couldn't believe it; it was almost like looking into a mirror. I had to excuse myself to use the restroom; it was too much to take.

It was like a reality check.

Mocking me.

CHAPTER 11

S

I fucking knew it.

That was exactly why the second my mom brought out the photo albums, I knew it was going to be a bad idea. It was like witnessing a train wreck. It was written all over her beautiful face the second Julia's pictures started showing up. She tried to play it off, but she couldn't hide from me; I wanted so badly to jump over the table and stop it before it happened. I witnessed it in slow motion as Olivia came into the pictures; she looked like she had seen a ghost. I wanted nothing more than to jump over the table and rescue my damsel in distress; instead, I watched her eyes water and then she abruptly excused herself from the table.

I couldn't blame my mom, it wasn't her fault–she was just trying to include Ysabelle in my life. It didn't come from a bad place. She was proud of me, she always had been. She wanted to show off her only child, like any mother would want to do.

"Honey, I'm so sorry; I completely forgot," she sympathized.

"It's all right. I know that."

"I feel awful. What should I do?"

I placed my hand on her shoulder. "I got it, Mom. I'll be right back."

I knocked on the bathroom door.

"Just a minute," she announced.

"Ysa, it's me."

"Okay…just give me a minute; there's something in my eye."

Bullshit.

"Let me see, I can help."

"No, I'm fine. I'll be out in a few," she choked out like she was crying.

"Please let me in."

I silently prayed she would and I waited for what felt like an eternity for the door to be unlocked and opened. She leaned on the doorframe with her head tilted on it. Her face was flushed and her eyes glossy.

She looked shattered and my heart broke a little more.

"Hi," she murmured.

I sighed. "Tell me. Talk to me."

She shrugged.

She was closed off again; the walls were back up. I wouldn't get anything out of her. She wouldn't allow it.

I leaned in, kissed her forehead, and said the only thing I knew to be true. "I love you."

"I love you, too," she whispered.

We walked out onto the porch hand-in-hand. She downed her entire glass of wine in one gulp and poured herself another. I proceeded to talk to my parents about our plans for the future and she never let go of my hand. However, she wasn't there anymore; she had checked out on me. My parents were extremely supportive, just as I knew they would be. They made me promise that I would visit often and I informed them that they were welcomed anytime. We didn't discuss any of the details other than it's where I belonged.

Ysabelle nodded and smiled when it was appropriate. From an outsider looking in, she would have appeared happy and content; it couldn't have been further from the truth.

The neighbors began to arrive. I recognized most of them. I introduced Ysabelle to everyone and everybody doted over her. She played her part perfectly. It was then I finally understood how she could have been a VIP. She did what was expected of her; it was like she turned on an internal switch that made her seamlessly flawless. I was captivated by how effortlessly easy it was for her to hide everything she was feeling. She was stronger than anyone I had ever known, including me.

This woman was an enigma, a paradox of everything that I loved and hated all at the same time.

"Dad!" Christian shouted, taking me out of my daze.

"Buddy!" I replied, catching him in my arms.

"I've missed you so much, Dad."

"Me too, bud, me too." I held him tighter, breathing in the son that I adored.

"Hey, bud, I want to introduce you to someone," I stated, standing up and grabbing Ysabelle around the waist.

She smiled.

"Christian, this is Ysabe–"

"I know who she is, Dad; Mom told me she's your girlfriend," he declared, taking both of us by surprise.

I looked over at Ysabelle whose eyes had widened and then back at Christian.

"That's right." She kneeled down to his level. "Hi, Christian, I've actually met you before. You've gotten so big I hardly recognized you."

He smiled. "I know, my baseball coach says I'm going to be just as big as my dad," he boasted.

She laughed. "I bet just as handsome, too. Got any girlfriends?"

He shrugged. "I got a few."

We all laughed at that. That went smoother than I would have anticipated.

I caught Julia from the corner of my eye. She was dressed in a long skirt with a tank top; her hair was pulled up in a tight bun. She looked exactly as I remembered her, always impeccably put together. There was a man standing next to her that had his hand around her waist. He looked about my age, but my complete opposite with tan skin, dark hair and eyes. She quickly caught my gaze and smiled, making her way over to me while holding his hand.

"Sebby," she greeted. "It's so good to see you." She pulled me into a tight hug and I returned it.

She pulled away and looked right over to Ysabelle. I could feel her apprehension and Ysabelle's nervousness.

"Ysabelle, it's nice to see you again," she said, extending her right hand.

Ysabelle nodded. "It's nice to see you, too," she addressed, shaking her hand.

There was an awkward pause as Julia took Ysabelle in and as soon as it appeared, it was gone.

Julia, always the lawyer.

"I'd like you both to meet, Anthony, Anthony this is Christian's father, Sebastian, and that's his girlfriend, Ysabelle."

Y

Holy shit balls...

I recognized him immediately.

What do I do? What do I do? What do I do? I panicked.

"Sebastian, Ysabelle, nice to finally meet you," he greeted.

I smiled. "Nice to meet you, too." I turned to Sebastian. "I'm going to get something to drink do you want something?"

He shook his head no in confusion.

I nodded, smiled at everyone and excused myself as inconspicuous as possible. I franticly walked into the kitchen, looking in every direction. "Where do they keep the hard liquor?" I asked, aloud to myself.

"There's a bar in the den, you're in the wrong room."

I gasped and turned, coming face-to-face with Sebastian.

"What the hell was that?"

"What do you mean?"

"Ysa..." he warned.

"I need a drink and then I'll tell you."

He nodded. "Follow me."

He poured two shots of whiskey and we took them down simultaneously. I tapped on the counter for another and took that one down. "One more," I said, holding up a finger. "Anthony was a client of VIP," I blurted during mid-shot. I recognized his angry face immediately. "Oh no! He has a thing for blondes, obviously, I was never with him."

"Fuck," he sneered.

"Yeah...he doesn't recognize me and the only reason I remember him is because Brooke...well, let's just say he has some interesting fetishes. But hey"—I held my hands in the air—"good for Julia," I half-laughed, trying to make light of the small world we lived in.

Sebastian looked livid. *Was he jealous?*

"I mean…it's not a bad thing that he was a client. You would be surprised how many men were clients that you would never think would be. VIP is a very successful business. I'm sure he's not still a client, Sebastian, if that's what you're worried about. But I mean…you were a client…so…just trying to paint you a picture here," I reminded.

"That's not what I'm worried about."

"Then what is it?"

"I would hate for Julia's life to be torn twice because of VIP."

"Yeah…me, too," I murmured.

He took a deep breath and then smiled lovingly at me. "Come on."

The next hour was interesting to say the least, Sebastian was at my side the entire time but I could tell that he wanted to talk to Julia. The information that I shared was hovering over him and I'm not quite sure what he intended on doing with it, but something told me that it wouldn't be pretty. We socialized with everyone until Sebastian started talking to Matt, a fellow baseball player from high school. Matt informed me that his wife was at the table with the rest of the women that had babies. I was avoiding that table like the plague but found myself standing there nonetheless. Lesley had their six-month-old baby girl in her arms.

"So you can only imagine the transition from being just the two of us, to the three of us now. But we absolutely adore her, I mean she is such a great baby and she sleeps through the night. We are actually talking about having another one because she is that amazing," she giggled.

This was exactly why women with babies made me nervous, it's like they completely forget how to talk about anything else.

"Yeah…that make sense," I casually replied.

"Oh, Ysabelle, can you do me a favor? Can you hold her while I go get her bag from inside, she needs to be fed soon."

It sounded like a request, however it wasn't, she handed her right over to me and didn't even take into consideration the look of distress that I knew was evident all over my face. She placed her in my arms and just turned around. I had never held a baby before. I held her under her armpits, which was the way she handed her over to me and she wiggled and squirmed. I looked all around me to see if anyone was witnessing the shit show that was happening right before them.

When she started whimpering from being uncomfortable, I started moving her up and down, literally, hoping it would calm her.

Jesus…I am not maternal.

Shouldn't a woman just know how to handle this? Isn't it like inbred in us or something?

"It's okay, little person, stop moving, where the hell is your mom?" I said to myself.

"Why are you holding her like that?" Sebastian questioned, catching me off guard and coming up beside me.

"How else am I supposed to hold her?"

"Definitely not like a football," he laughed, enjoying my misery.

When she started wailing, he grabbed her from me and cradled her in his arms–she was immediately content, looking at ease and safe in his arms. Nothing of what she displayed when I held her.

I placed my hair behind my ear, trying to act nonchalant. "I've never held a baby before. Sorry…"

He cocked his head to the side. "Really?"

I nodded. I hated feeling embarrassed and weak.

"It's all right, Ysa. See how I'm holding her, they like to be coddled and close to your body, the heat is comforting to them."

"Right…I'll make sure to remember that."

"Here, try again," he ordered, handing her back over to me.

I held her the exact way he had just done and she wasn't having it. She screamed bloody murder, making everyone turn to look at us. I nervously smiled as Sebastian once again grabbed her from me.

Fuck…this day just keeps getting better and better.

"It's okay," he soothed her, rocking her back and forth until she lamented.

"I guess I'm not good with babies," I half-laughed, trying to make light of the situation.

He grinned. "You're nervous, they can sense that."

"Or…I'm just not made to do that."

"What do you mean?" he coaxed.

"Oh! Sebastian, you are amazing with her," Lesley boasted, bringing our attention to her. "Look at how happy she is. Ysabelle, he's going to be a great father–he's not nervous at all. Matt still gets a little scared when I leave her with him. You're so lucky."

Oh yes…so lucky.

Sebastian drew me into the side of his body and I instantly felt at ease. I guess I could relate as to why the baby relaxed in his arms, it worked for me, too. He calmed me as much as he calmed her and I loved him for that. He kissed the top of my head, as if he knew what I was thinking. We were that in sync with one another, always had been.

I found myself in the bathroom, staring at my own reflection in the mirror. I couldn't help but be bothered by the fact that I felt nothing when I held that baby girl. It was more like a burden than a blessing.

Was that how my mother felt when she had me?

Was it hereditary that I wouldn't be a good mother? Was that God's way of showing me that it wasn't in the cards for me? I would never bring a child into this world, knowing that I didn't have that maternal gene. It wouldn't be fair to him or her; I wouldn't wish my mother on my own worst enemy.

Maybe some women were not made to procreate, and I was one them…

Could Sebastian be satisfied with it just being him and me forever?

I knew in the back of my mind that he wouldn't.

And for the first time since he came back into my life…

I contemplated it not working out between us.

CHAPTER 12

S

I could sense that Ysabelle needed some alone time, so I let her be, against my better judgment. I needed to remember that she processed things in her own way and if I pushed her, she would push back.

I took the time to find Julia.

"Hey, can you excuse us for a minute?" I announced to Anthony, who nodded before she followed me inside.

"What's up?" she asked, sipping her wine.

"Not much, I just wanted to take a few minutes and see how you were doing."

"I'm great, thanks for asking. How are you?"

"Really good."

"I can see that. I'm happy for you, Sebby."

I smiled. I knew she meant it.

"I could say the same for you. You seem smitten."

She blushed. "I am, he's a nice guy. We've been officially monogamous for maybe the last few weeks. He's a lawyer, too. We met when my client decided to run his off the road. It's random, I know."

"How much do you know about him?"

"Enough…why?"

"Maybe we should sit down," I suggested, pulling out the dining room chair.

"Okay."

I set my elbows on my thighs. “I don’t want to be the one to have to tell you this but I also don’t want to see you get hurt. I never wanted to see you get hurt.”

She nodded. “You’re scaring me.”

“Ysabelle recognizes him.” I raised an eyebrow, waiting for her reaction.

She cocked her head to the side. “Oh, I see…did you think I didn’t already know that?”

I jerked back.

“Anthony has been very honest since day one, as have I. I’m done with the lies as much as you are, Sebby. I have no problem with his past, hell, I have one, too. We all do. I don’t have a problem with it. And you seemed not to either, seeing as you’re with her,” she prompted with attitude.

“Julia, you’re twisting my words. My concern isn’t coming from a place of jealousy,” I reminded. “I care about you and I always will. You’re the mother of my son and always will be. I don’t want to see you get hurt, again. So all I’m trying to say is be careful; that’s all.”

“I appreciate that and I could say the same to you.”

“Excuse me?”

“She loves you, Sebby, don’t twist my words,” she repeated right back to me. “But…sometimes that’s not enough. Trust me, I know.”

“Juli—”

“Christian is very excited to see you and I know he’s missed you terribly, as I’m sure you have, too.”

“Of course. We have a lot to discuss, Julia. I’m actually here because I wanted to let you know about my plans. We need to work out something with Christian for the future.”

She nodded. “I figured as much. I take it you’re planning on taking residence.”

“Yes,” I simply stated.

“All right. How long are you in town for?”

“All week.”

“Sounds good, give me a call tomorrow and I’ll check my schedule. We can meet up for lunch?”

I nodded.

“You look good, Sebby.”

“You do, too.”

She walked back to Anthony and I caught Ysabelle's stare from the corner of my eye; she shyly smiled at me and turned to continue the conversation with my mom.

It was late evening when we drove back to the suite.

"That wasn't too bad. Huh?" I squeezed her hand.

"Compared to what?" She grinned.

I made some phone calls and scheduled out my week when we got back. I didn't realize how much I needed to take care of before I headed back to the island. It would be taking up most of my time while we were there. I found Ysa in bed with her e-reader. I laid my head on her stomach and looked up at her.

"What porn are you reading tonight?" I teased.

She rolled her eyes. "How many times do I have to tell you, it's not porn! It's romance. There's a storyline."

"Oh yeah? Romance...read me the last sex scene in your book."

"What?"

"You heard me, find the last sex scene in your book and read it to me. Then you can tell me if it's smut or not."

She narrowed her eyes at me.

"Do it," I dared.

Never one to turn down a challenge, she lay back on the bed and went to the last sex scene.

"He slowly removed her panties from her body, making sure to leave a wake of desire and lust with each precise glide of his fingers, which ran down her delicate, creamy skin."

I proceeded to do exactly what she just read aloud. Her eyes caught mine and she seductively smiled, knowing what I was leading to. Once her panties were removed, I tossed them aside and waited for her next direction.

"He spread her open and watched in awe as her face flushed from the forwardness of his actions. She didn't speak, but she didn't have to, her pussy spoke for itself."

I inched her legs to open for me and licked my lips in anticipation of what was to come. "I agree…your pussy always communicates with me, she's actually quite shameless, always juicy and waiting for me to stick my cock in her," I groaned.

She giggled. *"Her arousal was evident on her parted folds and when he placed the palm of his hand to her throbbing nub, she let out a soft moan."*

My hand crept up her thigh to her tight cunt and I pressed forward, pulling back the hood to expose that perfect red clit as she bit her bottom lip.

"Keep reading," I taunted.

"His hand glided forward and backward, her wetness making it easy for him to do so. You could hear the moisture that pooled for him and only him. With his other hand, he used his middle and ring finger to push inside her warm and welcoming heat."

I never stopped moving my hand as she read the next passage and her voice started to break. When I pushed in my fingers, she let out the most incredible moan.

"Keep going, Ysa."

She let out a breath. "He began to fuck her ever so slightly while he manipulated the little bundle of nerves, driving her to the brink of insanity. And then he slowed down his motions, making her wild with need."

I followed her direction and then slowed when she told me to, she whimpered in disappointment.

"He did this a few more times until she couldn't take it anymore and her back arched off the bed as she found her release."

I moved my hands simultaneously, until her walls would grasp my fingers and then I would pause. Every time I did that, her breathing hitched and her body would tremble.

"Do you want to come?" I taunted.

"Yes..."

"Should I let you come?"

"Yes..."

"Why should I let you come?"

"Because I love you."

Well, who could say no to that?

My pace quickened as her juices spread and my hand was soaked by the time she came. She threw her e-reader aside and freed my cock from my gym shorts. She deep throated my dick so far to the back of her throat she gagged, going back and forth, creating a tight suctioning as she went. Her spit gathered quickly and she twisted her hand up and down my shaft as she sucked me off.

"Jesus...Ysa..." I growled.

I gripped the back of her head and watched as she lowered her hand to her clit. She played with herself and sucked my cock like a goddamn vacuum. I could tell she was close to coming with her movements getting heavier and urgent.

"Fuck yes...just like that…suck just like that, baby."

She moaned and that was my undoing. I held her head in place as I spread my seed; she groaned and shook as she came, swallowing every last drop of my come.

"So now tell me…" I panted. "It's not porn, right?"

She laughed.

Y

Sebastian was gone most of Monday at Yachting Enterprises. I hung out with Devon at his bar. He told me he had some urgent situation he had to take care of and that's why he left the island so abruptly. Sebastian and I met on South Beach for dinner and he let me know how his day went. They accepted his offer and were buying him out; he had to return the next morning to finalize all the paperwork so he was gone most of that day, too. I spent the day at the spa and it was perfect. By Wednesday, I was getting anxious because I knew I needed to confirm with Brooke on what the plans were. While Sebastian went to get a workout in, I called her.

"Hey, Bella," she answered.

"Hey, doll, how are you?"

"I'm great, how are you?"

"I'm good."

"Have you been able to get everything taken care of?"

"Sebastian has been working on it and so far so good."

"Awesome! How did meeting the parents and family go?"

"Oh God! It was…I don't even know. But get this…Anthony is dating Julia," I informed.

"Shut the fuck up! My Anthony?"

"Well, I hope he's no longer your Anthony."

"Oh yeah…I haven't seen him in well over a year. That's quite a coincidence."

"I know right…"

"Well, he does have that sexy Latin thing going for him and shit…when he spoke to me in Spanish, it was panty dropping."

"Did it make you want to sit on his face?"

She laughed. "I always want to sit on someone's face."

I chuckled. "So…I've been thinking maybe we could meet for lunch tomorrow?"

"Yeah! Tomorrow works, do you want me to call Madam?"

"Umm…no … I'll call her."

"Okay great! I'm sure she will clear her schedule for you. But listen, doll, I gotta go. I have someone's face I have to sit on tonight and I need to get ready."

I chuckled again. "All right, good luck with that."

"You know it."

I hung up and took a deep breath before hitting the call button.

"Bella Rosa," she greeted.

"Hi," I apprehensively responded.

"How are you, darling?"

"I'm great, I'm actually in town."

"Oh yes, Brooke mentioned some things about that. How does it feel to be home?"

This is no longer my home…

"It's nice," was all I could reply with. "Brooke and I are meeting for lunch tomorrow and I was hoping you could meet us as well."

"Of course, I'll have to switch some things around, but I'll always make time for you," she added.

"I know, let's say around noon. I'll text you the restaurant."

"Perfect, I'll see you tomorrow at noon, looking forward to it." And with that, she hung up.

I stared at my phone for a few minutes contemplating what I had just done.

One thing was for sure.

I wouldn't tell Sebastian.

CHAPTER 13

Y

I sat there in pure panic; Brooke and I decided to meet at eleven so that we could have some time alone before Madam arrived. We discussed her life and I tried to pay attention, although, in reality, I wasn't. I felt awful that I had lied to Sebastian…well, I didn't really lie; I just omitted the truth.

That's not a lie, right?

I couldn't tell him why I was seeing Madam–he wouldn't understand or he would want to come with me. I didn't know which one would have been worse. Madam arrived promptly at noon, she looked exactly how I remembered her, not a hair out of place, her makeup was flawless and she wore a black pantsuit. I paid extra attention to my appearance that morning; for some odd reason, I still wanted to please her. I wanted her to think I was still beautiful and I wanted to make her proud. I even straightened out my hair; Sebastian had called me out on it immediately. I just told him I wanted to look nice for Brooke; she didn't know curly hair Ysa. He seemed to buy it.

"Bella Rosa," Madam addressed, pulling me into her arms.

Her hug reminded me of the same embrace I had with Sebastian's mom.

Maybe she really was like a mother to me…

She pulled away to look at me, still holding my arms in place. "God, darling, you are so strikingly gorgeous. Your hair is so long, I love it! Your skin is so tan and those clothes make you look like a Caribbean princess. No wonder your bar does so well," she praised.

I would be lying if I said it didn't make me feel more at ease. I was happy that she was still taken with me. She shared a similar welcoming with Brooke and we sat down to eat.

We talked about nothing in particular…at first.

"Bella Rosa, tell me everything, how are you and Sebastian?" she asked, making Brooke smile.

"Umm…we're great, perfect actually. I have never been happier."

"Really? Everything is going smoothly? No concerns or cause for complaint?"

I shook my head. "Not at all." I lied.

There was no way I could tell her.

She cocked her head to the side. "Huh?"

"Yeah…nothing to complain about. Our relationship is amazing, everything just sort of fits. It's like we left the past in the past and all that matters is that we're together. We trust each other and there's so much love it's…just…perfect," I exclaimed.

She took a sip of her mimosa and nodded.

And that's when I knew…

"I call bullshit," she announced.

M

As soon as Brooke told me that Ysabelle would be in town, I knew it was only a matter of time till she called me.

I'm never wrong.

When I saw her name appear on my phone, I silently cheered.

Tick tock...

I knew my girls better than they knew themselves. That's what made me The Madam. As soon as I heard her say hello, I knew there was trouble in paradise. I accepted her offer to lunch, even though I had to change my entire day for it. It didn't matter, nothing mattered other than her.

Mine.

I saw her sitting with Brooke as I parallel parked my car. They were sitting outside, right near the street. She looked disheveled, even from far away I could read her. The time had come…I had waited almost two and a half years to get to that point and I had to creep slowly. She was like a scared little kitten and I had to play nice, even though I wanted nothing more than to drag her back to The Cathouse where she belonged.

Home.

She was still picture-perfect, immaculate in every way. We had casual conversation until it was time to put on the show, from both our parts. She was going to play the role of the loving and devoted girlfriend while I played the role of the concerned and sympathetic Madam.

"Bella Rosa, tell me everything, how are you and Sebastian?" I asked, making Brooke smile.

My Brooke, always the eternal optimistic; I truly loved that about her.

"Umm…we're great, perfect actually. I have never been happier."

My…my…darling…your nose is growing.

"Really? Everything is going smoothly? No concerns or cause for complaint?" I coaxed.

She shook her head. "Not at all."

Liar…liar…panties on fire.

I cocked my head to the side. "Huh?"

Bella Rosa could never lie. Maybe she could to other people; I'm sure Brooke bought every single word. I knew better.

You reap what you sow.

I needed to tread lightly.

"Yeah…nothing to complain about. Our relationship is amazing, everything just sort of fits. It's like we left the past in the past and all that matters is that we're together. We trust each other and there's so much love it's…just…perfect," she boasted.

And then I was on…

3…

I took a sip of my mimosa and nodded.

2…

She looked right at me and knew. See…Ysabelle could read me, too. Except that I knew how to perform any role that I set myself in. The Madam can be anything you want her to be and right now, she needed to be understanding.

1…

"I call bullshit," I declared.

"Excuse me?" she asked, taken aback.

"Ysabelle…my Bella Rosa…my darling, beautiful girl…since when have you ever been able to lie to me? I can't tell you that I am not a little offended and hurt by your ability to boldface lie to me; however, I understand. Relationships are a personal thing and I completely respect that." I grabbed her hands and held them in my lap, in a comforting gesture.

"I love you like a daughter, that will never change. I also know you like a daughter. You're confused. Now, please, let's try this again. How are things? Tell Madam."

And *the walls came tumbling down…*

She sighed. "I don't even know anymore. I love him so much and he loves me equally the same. I just…it's just…" she stammered.

"Yes, I know, but all relationships are hard and take work. Anything you love in this life takes work, darling, especially a man."

Her eyes widened. "Wow, I wasn't expecting you to reply like that."

I half-laughed. "How did you expect me to reply?"

"I thought you would say I told you so or something along those lines," she admitted.

Oh…trust me. I am biting my fucking tongue.

"I want what's best for you; that's all I've ever wanted," I honestly replied. "Do you trust him? Are you scared?"

"I'm terrified, Madam; I don't want to get hurt again. It's this paralyzing fear that I have in the back of my mind and as much as I try to steer it away, it always comes back. I can't get away from it. It mocks me."

This is just way too fucking easy, like taking candy from a baby.

"That's natural. You're a strong woman. You control everything and anything about you. That's how you're made."

My blood runs in your veins.

"Love is a scary emotion."

It makes you fucking weak and brings you to your knees. I know, I live it.

"You love him and he loves you; everything else will just fall into place."

And that place is…and will be…you sitting at the throne, in The Cathouse.

The Madam.

It's only a matter of time.

Tick tock.

S

Call it intuition or a sixth sense, but the second I saw her step out of the bathroom with straight hair and completely made up, I just knew. When I asked her where she was going and she replied that she was having lunch with Brooke, it added fuel to the fire, but I gave her the benefit of the doubt. I asked the concierges where the driver had dropped her off and I found myself driving toward the restaurant before I gave it a second thought. I saw her immediately and my heart dropped.

She lied to me.

I waited at the suite for her to return, trying desperately to control the anger that was rising. I needed to give her another chance; she had given me so many that I had lost count. When she walked into the room, I pretended like I wasn't suffocating inside.

"How was lunch?" I casually asked, changing the channels on the TV.

"It was great; how was your afternoon? I missed you," she stated, laying her head on my lap and looking up at me.

I played with her hair, which usually relaxed me. Instead, it brought back painful memories; I hadn't seen her like that in what felt like forever.

"I missed you, too. I got everything done I needed to. How's Brooke? Anything interesting happen?"

I could see it in her eyes; her eyes always held the truth. She contemplated what to say to me. She wanted to tell me. It was screaming and blazing through her mind.

Please don't lie to me.

"Same ole, same ole. We're going to have dinner with her and Devon Saturday night."

I nodded. "Okay. Did she say anything to you about Madam?" I impatiently inquired.

Her head jerked back. "Why would you ask that?"

"Just curious. You're in Miami."

"Oh." She hesitated. "Sebastian…I ne—"

The phone rang, cutting her off, and I irritably answered it. "Yes? Yes. Thank you for confirming." I hung up and looked back at her. "You were saying?"

And just like that, it was gone.

"Yeah…no, I haven't talked to Madam, and Brooke hasn't said anything." She lied.

She fucking lied to me.

I needed to get away from her. I couldn't be near her right then. I didn't know what I would do and it physically destroyed me inside. I wanted to shake her, I wanted to yell at her, I wanted to hurt her. I hastily removed her off me and told her I was going to the gym. As I ran on the treadmill, I thought about everything.

Was this my punishment? Was I getting a taste of my own medicine? Is this how Julia felt every time I lied to her?

I hated myself.

And it was the first time since I made my way back to her.

In that moment…

I hated her, too.

CHAPTER 14

S

I didn't sleep a wink last night and I sensed that Ysabelle didn't, either. Maybe bringing her back to Miami wasn't the best idea, but I couldn't hide her from her past—it always catches up with you when you least expect it. Although, I had assumed that we were done with all of that.

Hadn't we paid our dues?

I never thought she would lie to me. I also thought we were passed all of that.

Apparently, I was wrong…

I tried to understand why she would even have lunch with Madam–the woman was no good. She ruined her and took advantage of her. There was no love. I didn't understand how Ysabelle could interpret anything that involved The Madam as anything more than a scam. I could see right through her from the very first day. The woman loved power, control, and money. She manipulated Ysabelle in every sense of the meaning.

I was her family.

I was her future.

Mine.

If she thought for one second that Ysabelle was going to be a VIP again or be involved in anything to do with that business…

Did Ysabelle miss it? Was she thinking of going back? Was I interpreting this all wrong?

I desperately sought answers and I knew I wasn't going to get them from Ysabelle. I had to go to the source…with or without her consent.

Ysabelle came in the suite from her run as I was buttoning my shirt.

"Hey," she addressed.

"How was your run?"

"Great! Definitely what I needed. Where you going?"

"I have to meet Julia, we're going to discuss Christian."

"Oh…I thought…umm…never mind." She turned away and I grabbed her arm.

"Say it," I ordered.

My patience with her lack of communication was wearing thin.

She looked down at my grip on her arm and I instantly let go, and then she looked up at me. "I just thought I was going with you, is all."

We had enough problems and drama going on; I didn't want to pile on anymore. That's why I decided to go by myself.

I smiled, trying to break the tension that I created. "I don't want to bore you with family legal stuff. Go shopping and enjoy Miami or go see your friends; I know how you miss them."

Her eyebrows lowered in confusion. "Okay, I guess."

I forcefully grabbed her by the back of her neck and pulled her toward me. My mouth caught hers urgently, I kissed her like I hadn't seen her in years, I kissed her like a starved man needing food, I took out my frustrations and insecurities in that kiss. And when I pulled away, her eyes were sated.

My girl.

She grinned at me and I pecked her one last time before making my way out the door.

Y

What the fuck just happened?

One minute he's telling me he wants me to be a part of the decision-making process and then the next, he's telling me that he doesn't want to bore me with the details. I knew he was restless last night when we were laying in bed. Was it because he changed his mind and didn't want to tell me? Did he want to spend time alone with Julia? Had seeing her brought feelings back for him?

That didn't make sense. Sebastian loved me. I knew that.

But…

What if?

S

I followed the man dressed as a butler up the stairs into an office. The walls were lined with shelves of books and a desk with two leather wingback chairs sat dead center. It was the focus of the entire room. There was a sitting area near the right side with white leather couches facing opposite of each other, a black granite table separating them.

"Welcome to The Cathouse, Mr. Vanwell."

I turned and saw Madam standing there, leaned against the doorframe with her arms crossed and one leg over the other. She was wearing a red pantsuit with a shit-eating grin that I wanted to slap off her face. I've never wanted to hit a woman, but The Madam was no lady.

"You know…this office means a lot to me." She contemplated what she was saying and cocked an eyebrow. "It's where I was born. It's also where Ysabelle was born. You see that couch over there?" She nodded toward it. "I witnessed firsthand how much she was created for a life of privilege. I have shaped several VIPs throughout the years, but none of them can measure up to Bella Rosa." She pushed off the doorframe and slowly walked over to the couch. "VIPs are chosen, that's what makes them so precious and valuable." She sat on the couch and crossed one leg over the other, placing her arms on the back of the settee.

"I am sitting in the exact place that Ysabelle proved herself to me, in more ways than one," she stated.

In an instant, the TV that was sitting on the dresser in the corner turned on and *my girl* appeared on the screen. She was wearing a white silk robe that was open in the front, her tan skin and luscious body exposed. Brooke was at her side.

"Spread your legs, Bella Rosa." I heard Madam's voice demand on the screen, and she did as she was told.

"Your pussy is sweeter than I thought it would be, you're just the right shade of cream. It's a nice surprise that you don't have any tan lines. Your caramel skin color is natural. That pleases me," she added.

I recognized the look on Ysabelle's face immediately. She was aroused. She wanted it.

She turned to Brooke. *"Do you know that you have a deep erotic smell about you? It's addicting,"* Ysabelle stated, before grabbing the back of her hair and pulling.

I could see Madam looking at me through my peripheral vision. "You see…that little move...although it's small and miniscule, with that little action, she proved to me that she was born for this," she gloated. "Bella Rosa doesn't wait for what she wants, she goes after it, she controls the situation, she governs the room. They're not made; they're born. She's a motherfucking VIP."

I tried to ignore every vicious word she spewed, but I couldn't tear my eyes off the goddamn screen.

I watched as *my girl* seduced Brooke.

I watched as she kissed her.

I watched as she caressed her neck and breasts.

I watched as they fucked each other on their legs.

I watched as *my girl's* eyes screamed for need and want. They always told me everything I needed to hear.

I watched as Brooke got down on her knees and had her beg to come, exactly how I have done so many times before.

I watched *my girl* shamelessly come apart.

And when it was over…

I watched *my girl's* eyes…want more.

Madam's clapping took me out of my daze and I looked over at her. She was smiling like a Cheshire cat.

"I never get tired of watching that video. Now…Sebastian, I can call you Sebastian, right? I mean, we are family," she mocked, deviously laughing. "You tell me, honestly, do you think you can fully have your Ysa? Do you think that you can satisfy her or make her happy? Does she look happy to you? Huh? Or is she putting on a show? Trust me, darling, I taught her everything she knows. Ysabelle will be whatever you want her to be. It's how she's made."

She placed her finger on her lips in a thinking gesture. "See…I am not an evil woman, contrary to what you think. I actually love her, more than I have ever loved anyone. I want her to be happy, but unlike you, I know when she's faking it. I bet she didn't tell you she went to lunch with me." She grinned.

"Though you already know that or else you wouldn't be standing here. Would you like me to tell you what we talked about? I don't mind sharing." She paused. "All right…I'll take your silence as a yes. She confided in me that she thinks you're going to hurt her again. She doesn't trust you. And she doesn't think she ever will." She shrugged her shoulders. "I could be being biased but…given your track record with women, Sebastian, hmmmm…I can't blame her. You said you loved Julia and you fucked Ysabelle behind her back…ouch…you know?" she ridiculed.

She shook her head as I slowly walked over to her.

"It's only a matter of time before she's back at The Cathouse where she belongs," she emphasized.

I stopped when I was standing over her and she looked up at me.

"This is her home. She's mine," she vowed.

I didn't think and just reacted. I snapped and lunged forward, catching her off guard, and gripped on to the front of her neck; her eyes widened. It was the first time that I've ever seen fear in her eyes and then it was gone. I clutched on harsher until her breathing slowed and her face paled. I used all my body weight to shove her into the back of the couch.

"Listen to me, you sadistic fucking cunt! Are you FUCKING LISTENING?! Nod your pretty little head if you're paying attention, be a good little demon," I baited.

She subtly nodded and I gripped harder, making her mouth slightly part for air.

"I am not one of your fucking pawns. Don't for one goddamn second think that I don't know what the fuck you're doing. You can't manipulate me," I sneered, grasping harder.

"If you for one minute think that I will let her walk back into this house for anything more than your motherfucking funeral, then you're crazier than I thought. I will kill you before you have your hands on her."

Her vein was beating rapidly and she was trying to suck in air. I didn't let her, I held on tighter.

"Now. Do. You. Understand?" I snarled through gritted teeth.

She started wheezing and I lowered my mouth to her ear.

"I could fucking kill you right now and no one would know it was me. You would die in the office that you love so much. It would be your beginning and ending. How's that for irony?" I whispered.

I maliciously held on to her neck firmer and watched as her eyes glazed over and her head leaned sideways.

Against my better judgment…

I let go and walked away. I heard her instantly gasp for air.

"Thanks for the pep talk," I stated, not stopping to turn. "You have yourself a great fucking day, Madam," I shouted.

The truth was…

I meant every last word.

CHAPTER 15

S

I tried to calm down before I met with Julia–she was already waiting for me when I was seated.

"Sorry I'm late," I greeted.

"Not a problem, I was just looking over my notes for this case," she informed, not looking up at me.

The waiter arrived. "What can I get you to drink, sir?"

"I'll take a whiskey neat—actually, make it a double."

He nodded and excused himself. Julia finally tore her eyes from her document. "Wow, double?" She looked at her watch. "It's only one o'clock, you got that 'it's five o'clock somewhere thing' down, huh?" she teased to no avail. "Hey…" She placed her hand on my arm. "What's wrong?"

"I don't even know where to fucking start, Julia. Plus you're definitely not the person I should be talking to about this."

She cocked her head to the side. "You know, Sebby, before we were married and together, we were best friends," she reminded.

The waiter brought back my drink and I took it down in one gulp before he was even done taking Julia's order for a glass of wine. I ordered another double.

"Feel better?" she cautioned.

"It certainly helps."

Once we ordered our food and I was about done with my second drink, I started to feel more at ease.

"You ready to share now? I'm a good listener, I'm also a woman and from what I know, most women can relate to other women. It's like a girl gene or something."

We laughed.

"Ysabelle," I simply answered.

"Yes…I'm aware of that part. What about her?"

"It's like I'm losing a fighting battle that I never had a chance to win in the first place. I feel like she's slipping away from me, and the more I try to hold on to her, the worse it gets. I thought bringing her here to Miami with me would be a blessing, and now I feel like it's been a curse. Her past is here and I never even took that into consideration. I thought she was done with it. Come to find out, it's very present. I am at my wits end with it all and she won't talk to me about any of it."

"Have you tried to talk to her?" she questioned.

"She's not like that, Julia. She doesn't open up like normal women do; she actually hates fucking talking about feelings and shit. Sometimes I can get her guard to come down and she will tell me how she feels, but only when she's backed into a corner," I explained, taking a sip of my drink.

"That must suck for you," she giggled. "You're Mr. Communication."

"Yeah…well…I grew up with my best friend being a girl and if I didn't tell you how I felt, you would cry until I did. It was the only way I could get you to shut up."

She gasped at first, then shrugged it off, grinning. "Maybe…"

"She had a rough upbringing and to go from that to VIP, it's left her jaded and fucked up. Then add what I did to her, it's like icing on the cake, you know?"

"You can't blame yourself forever, Sebby. I know you lied—trust me, I hated you for a while—but when I think about it…I'm to blame, too. I knew you loved me; hell, I still know you love me. And although the love that you feel for me now is exactly the same love you felt for me then, it's the same love you've always felt. I pretended that you were *in love* with me when I knew in my heart you never were. I took advantage of that and that's not right. So I got what I deserved, too. We both did."

"Julia, wow, I don't even know what to say."

"You don't have to say anything. We're in a much better place than we have been since we got married. I married my best friend and I tried to make him my lover and husband, and for a while, it worked. In reality, if it weren't for Ysabelle, it would have been something else. I don't blame her and part of me is thankful to her because it made me see the truth that I tried to hide since the beginning. You're a good man, Sebastian, you always have been. What you did was wrong but no one's perfect, and it looks like your paying for those mistakes now." She hesitated.

"I feel guilt for allowing you to sacrifice so much for me…first with Oli, I knew, Sebby…I always knew you loved her and I knew she loved you, too, and I used both your devotions to me as a ploy for you not to be together. And as for Ysabelle, she absolutely adores you; she loves you. I think even a blind person could see that. However, women are fickle beings and when you hurt us, it's hard for us to forget that. We hold grudges and we analyze everything and make a problem out of nothing. You just have to be patient…she'll come around. Just keep doing what you're doing. It might take her more time to realize it, but she'll get it." She smiled.

"As for Christian we have a handle on it. This co-parenting thing will be easy; even though you're miles away, we'll make it work."

"Thank you, Julia."

"I love you, Sebby."

"I love you, too."

Y

"How was lunch?" I asked, looking up from my e-reader.

"It was surprisingly great."

"Oh yeah? What made it so great?"

He removed my e-reader from my hands and laid his head there instead.

"I missed you."

I smiled. "I missed you, too."

"Lunch was exactly what we needed. We've never discussed anything prior or during the divorce. So…I guess it was somewhat like closure. We'll figure out Christian along the way."

"That's awesome."

"How are you?" he questioned.

"I'm good, just been relaxing. Devon stopped by for a little bit and we had lunch downstairs. You actually just missed him."

"I've been thinking that we haven't enjoyed ourselves and maybe you would allow me the pleasure to wine and dine you tonight."

"Really? And to what do I owe that honor?"

"I'd like to take my girl out for dinner and drinks."

"I think she can oblige." I flirted.

"Perfect. I think that we should shower. Together."

He effortlessly lifted me off the bed, making me giggle, and threw me over his shoulder, spanking my ass and making me shriek as he carried me into the shower. We spent the next hour "showering" and then I started to get ready. I dressed in a white fitted cocktail dress that rested right below my knees and red stilettos. I added product to my hair to make it curlier and did smoky eyes with red lips to match my shoes. I finished it off with silver hoop earrings, a bracelet, and a gaudy ring on my left middle finger. I had sprayed some Armani Code, Sebastian's favorite perfume, before I walked out into the living room.

Sebastian was on the terrace, admiring the view, and I couldn't help but remember St. Barts. It was exactly what he was doing while I was getting ready, except this time, he wasn't dressed in casual attire. He was wearing black slacks, black leather dress shoes with a black button down shirt, and a black vest. He looked good enough to eat. He turned around, catching me gawking at him.

"Well, hello there, handsome. Are you my date tonight?"

"I'm your date every night. You look breathtaking; I don't think I've ever seen you with red lipstick before."

He came right over to me and wrapped his arms around my waist, pulling me toward him, and then leaned in and breathed into my ear. "How am I suppose to kiss you if your lipstick is cock blocking me and you're wearing the perfume that makes my dick hard from across the room. You're teasing me, Ysa," he murmured.

"Who me? Never," I snickered.

He playfully spanked me and I yelped.

"Let's go before I decide to eat you for dinner instead."

"You can eat me for dessert," I chimed in.

We were seated immediately at one of the new restaurants Devon was telling me about. Our booth overlooked the water and our table was separate from everyone else's.

"How did you get reservations here? Devon said that the waiting list is full for the next several months."

He grinned. "You aren't the only one that knows people."

We both ordered lobster and steak and he asked for one of the most expensive bottles on the wine list, three thousand dollars. The server opened the wine and Sebastian tasted it before approving, and then he poured us both a glass.

"Are we celebrating something I'm not aware of?" I questioned.

He lifted his glass. "To new beginnings. I think it's safe to assume that we're *both* leaving behind our pasts and moving forward, together."

I smiled and nodded, lifting my glass. "Absolutely."

By the time the food arrived, the wine was almost empty and I was feeling tipsy. We ate and enjoyed each other's company all evening. We went to a bar for some after-dinner drinks, and once we made it back to our suite, I was drunkity, drunk, drunk. I couldn't stop laughing and I'm pretty sure nothing was really funny.

"You're drunk," he stated.

"Hmmm…maybe a little bit, does that mean you're going to take advantage of me?"

He chuckled. "It's not taking advantage if it's yours."

"Let's go swimming," I randomly yelled, running into the bedroom to change before he had a chance to reply.

I wore my new bikini I bought on Ocean Drive and had to duck his advances to get out of the room. He followed me upstairs to the rooftop pool and had to pay off the security guard to let us go swimming since it was closed. He jumped right in and I followed suit.

"Oh! This feels amazing. We need a pool. A great big infinity pool that looks over the water, just like this one," I said, wrapping my legs around his waist and my arms around his neck. "What do you think about that?"

He nodded, laying soft kisses on my neck. "I'll give you whatever you want."

I giggled as he backed me up against the sidewall.

"What do you want?" I coaxed.

"You."

"How much?"

"Big much."

"What do you want to do with me?"

"Everything."

I smirked. "What do you want to do with me right now?"

He arched an eyebrow and kissed the tip of my nose. "Fuck you."

"Then what's stopping you?" I grabbed the back of his neck and kissed him, he tasted like wine, whiskey, and Sebastian. Our tongues did a sinful and alluring dance as he lowered my bandeau top and kneaded my nipples.

"Oh God," I moaned into his mouth when I felt his dick at my entrance.

The water made it challenging for him to get fully inside, but once he did, he stopped to enjoy the sensation. Water sex was definitely more for the guy, seeing as it was hard to feel the friction through the splashes. It didn't matter, though; I still loved the feeling of having him inside me. Nothing compared to Sebastian.

He fucked me up against the wall, completely enclosed by him, and his arms rested on the sides of the pool. We looked into each other's eyes as I bounced up and down on his shaft. I leaned my pelvis forward so that the front tip of his cock hit my g-spot. It was the most sensitive part for him and it made him come almost instantly.

"Fuck…Ysa…the things you do to me," he groaned, kissing me and coming apart as I rocked my hips to prolong his orgasm.

He growled and roughly grabbed me around my waist, placing me on the edge of the pool. I looked down at him in confusion.

"You know I hate it when you don't come. I take care of what's mine."

His mouth attacked my clit in a forceful sucking motion and I immediately fell back onto my hands. I watched in ecstasy as he devoured my pussy like a starved man, his head moving up and down.

"Jesus, Sebastian…you're going right for it," I panted, never taking my eyes off what he was doing.

Our stares locked when he pushed in a finger, aiming it directly and precisely on the spot that drove me wild. It didn't take long for the tingling sensation to develop all over my body. And when his head moved side-to-side, my head fell back and I came all over his face.

CHAPTER 16

S

We spent most of the morning in bed, making love and then eating breakfast. I wasn't nervous about seeing Devon; meeting Brooke, on the other hand, was going to be interesting to say the least. Ysabelle never disclosed any information about her past, I knew what being a VIP entailed, but I never imagined that…I didn't even know. I needed to play it off like I hadn't seen *my girl* and her best girlfriend going at it. The evening fast approached and we met Brooke and Devon at a restaurant on South Beach. Ysabelle looked gorgeous as usual with her curly hair running wild and a tight black dress short enough that I had to make sure I was standing behind her or she would've given a show. Brooke and Devon were already there when we were seated.

It looked and felt as if we walked in on something and we both picked up on it immediately.

"Bella, I love that dress. Where did you get it?" Brooke asked.

"I'm not quite sure. I bought it on the island, so it's not designer."

She cocked her head to the side. "What are you trying to say? I don't wear anything that doesn't have a label on it?"

Ysabelle rolled her eyes. "That's exactly what I'm trying to say."

Brooke shook her head, blowing it off. "I was just telling Devon here how he should come by The Cathouse and maybe see about getting a membership."

Ysabelle choked on her drink. "Oh my God, Brooke! I told you to behave."

Brooke shrugged. "I am…this is me behaving."

The night proceeded with the girls chatting while Devon and I observed. Brooke and Ysabelle had an amusing dynamic; Brooke definitely was a wildcard and I could tell she was down for anything, anywhere. I didn't know if that was who she really was or if it was her being a VIP. We ate and when the bill arrived, Brooke literally snatched it out of my hands, insisting that she was paying. She said it's a welcoming present. I'm not quite sure what that meant; however, I went with it.

We walked down 7th Ave to a bar slash club as Brooke called it. There was a line around the corner and Ysabelle and Brooke didn't falter, they both smiled and nodded toward the bouncer and he let us right in. Devon and I followed them up the stairs to a private and secluded area that observed the entire dance floor; there was a bottle of Moet and Grey Goose on the table with mixers, glasses, and ice. A circular white leather couch surrounded us. The bottle hostess introduced herself immediately and stated that she was our private hostess for the entire night. She said she would get us "anything" we wanted with a nod and a wink.

"Why are you looking at me like that?" Ysabelle chuckled.

"Just observing."

"Sebastian, this is Miami, and Brooke still works as a VIP. Not to mention, I was one for a very long time, which leaves me the open card to do whatever I want…especially in this town. They know us. I told you Madam runs everything," she informed.

"I see that."

"Would you have preferred to have waited in line and been standing at the bar waiting for a bartender to take your drink order? Because if you'd rather, then by all means, I'll follow you down there, though I guarantee you that when one of the bartenders sees me, I'll be attended to immediately."

Brooke bounced her way over to us and handed me a drink and Ysabelle a glass of champagne. "It's vodka and soda water," she added. "Why are you guys over here not having fun?"

"Sebastian is a little taken aback with our pull I think, and I find it adorable."

She looked back at me. "Awe! Sebastian…Ysabelle's never taken you out in Miami before? This is nothing." She paused. "You guys want any party favors?" She wiggled her eyebrows.

"Jesus, Brooke; it's one thing after another with you."

"Well…I mean, when in Rome. Anyway, I need to talk to you about something. Let's go to the bathroom."

Ysabelle kissed me and they went on their way. Devon was leaning over the balcony with a drink in his hand, nodding his head to the music. I stood beside him.

"Any particular reason you didn't tell Ysabelle about our confrontation?" I asked, looking straight ahead.

"I could ask you the same thing. I love her and as long as she's happy, that's all that matters to me."

"Well then, we can agree on that."

"We're going to be in each other's lives, Sebastian. I'm not going to take her away from you, I'm not going to fight for her, I'm not a threat to you. But…I will *always* be here for her."

I turned to look at him. "Man to man, Devon, I don't fucking like you and I'm not going to pretend like I do. If it were up to me, you wouldn't be in her life, and if I were an asshole, I would tell her so…I'm grateful that you protected her and looked out for her when I wasn't there, but I'm here now and I'm not fucking going anywhere. Let's agree to disagree and be civil for her sake."

He nodded and we both went back to ignoring each other.

The night progressed with the girls drinking, dancing, and laughing. It was like they were in their own little bubble. The crazy part about that was they truly did govern a room; all eyes were on them, men and women. There was this energy that radiated off them that you didn't see from other women. They didn't have to try–it was just there. I always thought Ysabelle put on a façade, a performance, a mask she wore for everyone. The portrayal of a VIP, but she didn't.

It was inherent, it came naturally, they were vixens. They thrived on it; it was a game, a game that they always won. It was never about the client, the money, or the sex. It was about the control and the power. They lured you in without so much as a hello; it could be a look, a smile, a subtle touch, a slight movement in their body. It didn't matter because it was captivating, and the worst part of it all…is that they fucking knew it. It was a drug to them, a high that compared to nothing else in this world. Ysabelle was mine, but that didn't stop her from receiving attention. They exuded sexuality, a magnetic pull that forced you in without you even realizing it.

In that moment, as much as I tried to ignore the thoughts hovering, I couldn't. I remembered Madam's words about VIPs being born, not made, and until that night, I never took the time to observe what she so precisely stated and informed.

They were made for sin. The way they talked, the way they moved, the way they interacted with others. It was addicting to watch; they were like a drug. You knew it was bad, however, you couldn't control it because it controlled you.

One more time…

One more taste…

I promise…

It was all bullshit because you were hooked from the second you saw them, everything else was just an added bonus. It consumed your thoughts, actions, and decisions.

As I watched Ysabelle start provocatively dancing with Brooke, my mind immediately went to the video. They were just dancing like all other girlfriends do when they go out, but it was different. Something about it yelled familiarity.

Was it because I watched them fuck each other?

I'm a man; of course, the idea of Ysabelle being with another woman turned me on. I would be lying if I said watching them on video wasn't stimulating for my cock. That being said, I knew it was tied back to VIP and ultimately Madam, and that made me sick to my stomach.

But…

Was Madam right? Was I enough for her? Was she putting on the mask for me, not the other way around?

Did I truly have Ysabelle or did VIP…

Y

"If you're dragging me in the bathroom to do drugs with you, Brooke, I'm going to slap you."

When she said she had to talk to me, that was usually code for, "I have something you know you want."

"Eww…no. I want to talk about Devon," she said as I looked at her reflection in the mirror.

"What about Devon?"

"I don't know; you've never talked about him before. Why have you kept him hidden?"

I laughed and shook my head. "I didn't keep him hidden, I just didn't want him to know what I was doing."

"Why is that?" She cocked her head in the mirror.

"Well, for one thing, Madam was adamant about our friends and families not knowing what we did."

She finished applying her lipstick and turned to face me. "Okay…so tell me about him now?"

I chuckled. "Devon is really not your type, he's not like other men. He's probably one of the last nice guys left on this earth. Who would never be okay with his girlfriend being a VIP."

"Bella, I'm not talking about dating him, I'm talking about fucking him. Is he amazing?"

I shook my head. "I don't know."

"You've never slept with him?"

"No."

"Oh…huh…why?"

"Because he's my best friend and a brother to me."

She frowned. "I thought I was your best friend?"

I grinned and rolled my eyes. "Okay…he's my best guy friend. Better?"

She smiled. "Much. How would you feel if I took him for a ride? Literally. I mean, didn't you say he just got done with a divorce or something? I would totally take one for the team and help him to relieve some sexual tension, and trust me, he's backed up."

I jerked back. I hadn't expected that. "Ummm…yeah, I guess."

It wasn't that I was jealous—I was far from it. I knew Brooke and she ate guys like Devon as an appetizer. I didn't want him getting hurt and God forbid fall for her and then blame me or something when it didn't work out. I couldn't lose him.

I wouldn't.

I watched them closely for the rest of the night. She was coming on strong and it seemed like Devon accepted each and every advance. When they left together, I almost stomped my foot like a child throwing a temper tantrum.

"You've been quiet the whole way back. You okay?" Sebastian inquired as I took off my jewelry and placed it in my travel bag.

"It's just Devon and Brooke…I mean, it's really bothering me."

"Why is that?" he questioned.

I straddled his lap when I heard his agitated tone and his hands went to my ass. "It's not what you're thinking, silly man. I don't want him to get hurt, and Brooke will do that and think it's funny."

"He's a big boy, Ysa; he doesn't need you to be looking out for him. Besides, he looked quite content all night."

"I'm aware. He's also just divorced his cheating, money hungry whore of a wife and he's lonely and I don't want him to make a rash decision based on how he's feeling."

He laughed. "Let me let you in on a little secret. Men fuck. They actually prefer to fuck with no strings attached. I think Brooke coming his way is the best thing for him right now."

I shoved him harshly, he was pissing me off and he instantly flipped us over with him being on top of me.

"Want to try that again, Ysa?" he taunted with a certain edge to his voice.

"I know how men operate, Mr. Vanwell, trust me. I made a living off it. What you aren't aware of is that a VIP isn't like any other woman. He could fuck any other woman, be fine, and I would pat him on the goddamn back. He will fall for her and not even realize it."

He narrowed his eyes, contemplating what I was saying. "How do you know that?"

You want honesty…well then here it is. "Because we're made to be the fantasy. It's an illusion. And even if she's not getting paid to fuck him, it's who she is. We don't say no…to anything."

I could see the pain in his eyes. I didn't mean to hurt his feelings, but he was offending me by making me feel like I didn't know what I was talking about. I would fuck with guys like Devon because I could and then laugh about it when I was done. It was a game. He was an easy target, plain and simple.

His eyes glazed over and his demeanor changed. It felt as though he had been thinking about VIP all night, like it plagued him.

Now…who's the one who's not being honest…

He urgently grabbed my wrists and held them firmly above my head, caging me in. He wanted me to feel like he was in control and I gladly gave it to him. The truth was, he was. He always is. He had no idea how much control he had over me. And for a woman like me…it was everything. It was more than just my heart and soul. See…control and power were my heart and soul. It is who I am and he owned it now.

I gave it to him the second I told him my name.

He had to know that, right?

“Is that how you saw me? Was I a game?”

It came out as a question, but it was more like an accusation.

What is going on in your head? What are you thinking?

“No, Sebastian, you were different,” I simply stated. “I didn’t understand you from day one. I never had anyone look at me the way you do, I still don’t.”

His other hand grazed my throat. “How do I look at you?” he inquired with an intense stare.

“Like I’m you’re everything. Like you would die for me. Like I belong to you.”

“Do you?”

I didn’t falter. “Wholeheartedly. I’m yours. I have been since the minute I fell into your arms. Here’s what you don’t understand, I will always be a VIP, except it’s for one person now. YOU. A leopard can’t change its spots, but they can adapt. I pretended to be whatever was requested. I’ve never pretended with you. I’ve never wanted to and that’s what makes you different.” I paused to let my words sink in.

“I love you, Sebastian.”

The penetrating gaze subsided and the storm was gone.

For now…

CHAPTER 17

S

We woke up early the next morning to go look at a 40ft Cabo Open Bridge fishing boat. It had a front room master bedroom with bath and a spacious living space. The deck was made out of dark teak with two leather fighting chairs stationed side-by-side. All the fishing equipment came with the purchase and there wasn't anything that needed to be added or done.

"I'll take it," I said to the dealer.

"Awesome, let me write her up for you."

"Do you guys do lettering here?"

"Absolutely, what would you like to name it?"

Ysabelle raised her hand in the air. "I have a name."

"What?" I asked.

She smiled. "Keeping Her Wet."

I shook my head and we both laughed. "You heard the lady."

"Perfect. It will be done by this evening and she will be sailed over first thing tomorrow morning. She should arrive in two to three days, give or take."

Ysabelle needed to get back to the bar, and although her GM said everything was fine, she was itching to get back. So we decided to have someone else sail her back.

We landed on the island mid-afternoon. She spent most of the day looking over receipts, payroll, and getting everything in order for the holiday season that started in a few weeks. The high time for tourism was October through May, but November through the end of January she was slam packed. The snowbirds wanted to leave the cold and people overseas took holidays for a month due to their employment being closed.

To keep the crowd coming in daily, she set up different themes each day; sink or swim, two for one, happy hour, etc. The girl knew how to throw a good time, that was for sure. The waitresses dressed in bikinis and performed dances on the bar at different times of the day. They'd throw confetti in the air and really get the crowd going. It was like an all day party and that's what vacationers wanted.

"You about done, Ysa?"

"Yeah, just trying to work out the profit from the substance sales."

"What's that?"

"The drug sales."

"What the fuck are you talking about?" I roared.

She peeked up from her paperwork, surprised by my drastic change in tone. "What are you talking about?"

"You're selling drugs here?"

"No, I mean not really. I barely make any profit off it. Why are you looking at me like that?"

My eyes widened. "Ysabelle, please tell me you're fucking kidding."

"I wouldn't have said it if it weren't true."

"Why?" I demanded, trying to keep my temper at bay.

"Why what?"

"Your bar brings in a crazy amount of revenue as it is. Why the fuck would you involve yourself in that?"

"I don't, I don't supply it. I don't look for it. I'm the middleman. I have nothing to do with it, other than letting the one guy come around and see if anyone wants anything."

I couldn't believe what she was saying. I couldn't believe what I was hearing.

"It's mostly just weed and shit." She dropped her pen on the desk in a frustrated gesture. "Come on, Sebastian, don't look at me like that. People on vacation want to have a good time. The crowds I bring in are looking to let go and just have fun. Marijuana is legal for recreational use in two states, it's only a matter of time till it's legal everywhere else. Don't be so straight-laced."

"Is that all your selling?"

"I'm. Not. Selling. It."

"What if he asks the wrong person, huh?"

"Seriously…these guys know what they're doing. They make a living off it, long before I even arrived. This isn't the States. This is an island where the government makes money off tourism. They get caught, they pay them off. Nothing is tied back to me. End of story."

"I don't want you to do it anymore," I demanded.

She cocked her head to the side. "Excuse me?"

"I'm serious, Ysa, it ends."

She folded her arms over her chest. "I'm sorry, I don't remember asking you for permission to run MY business. I know what I'm doing and I don't need your input."

I placed my hands on the edge of her desk, hovering over her and she didn't cower down. Not that I expected her to.

"Is that all you sell?"

"What do you mean?"

"Don't play dumb, Ysa. Is that all you sell?"

She rolled her eyes. "No. Sometimes they buy blow and molly…very rarely, though."

"And you think that's okay?"

"I don't think anything. It's not my business to care about what other people want to do on their vacation. I supply a good time." She pointed to herself. "That's my job. I'm not backing down from this, Sebastian. There are a lot of things I'll give you and meet you halfway on, but this is not one of them. I'm a businesswoman, and if there's a demand, then I supply. Trust me…I'm not the only bar or even restaurant on this island, or any other island for that matter, doing the same thing."

I backed away and left, slamming the door behind me.

For the first time since I met her…

She reminded me of The Madam.

Y

It was late by the time I made my way upstairs. I was exhausted from looking at numbers and getting everything ready for the chaos of the tourist season. I tried not to think about the shit show that awaited me when I walked in. The place was quiet other than the dim lighting that came from the TV in our bedroom. There was a plate of food on the dining table with a paper towel placed over it. I picked at the plantains and some of the vegetables and then threw the rest out. I didn't have much of an appetite. I hated fighting with Sebastian and I knew that was the cause of not wanting to eat.

I contemplated what he would say to me when I walked into the bedroom, and part of me wanted to sleep on the couch or in the guest bedroom just to avoid it. I figured that would only be adding fuel to the already lit fire and piss him off more.

I understood where he was coming from, however, that's how I had done things since the beginning. He couldn't come into my life, expecting me to change everything about how I ran things. That's not fair. I didn't think I was doing anything wrong, it was a stupid argument and I should have just kept my mouth shut. I definitely didn't expect him to react like he had; I mean, he had done molly with me. People are allowed to make their own choices in life and I'm not responsible for that. He was blowing it way out of proportion.

I rubbed at my temples from the migraine that was lurking. I took a deep breath and made my way into the bedroom. He was lying with his arm behind his head, watching TV; the sheet was low on his waist and his toned core was showing with his muscular arms on display. I wondered if he had done that on purpose and tried to hide my smile.

"Care to share what you're thinking, Ysa?"

I frowned. "Not thinking anything, just admiring the view," I teased to no avail. "Oh, come on, Sebastian, this is such a stupid argument. Why don't you trust me? I know what I'm doing."

He lowered the volume on the TV and sat up. "This has nothing to do with not trusting you."

"Then what is it?" I asked, sitting on the edge of the bed.

I could sense that this was much deeper than what I originally thought.

"It's not the drugs, Ysa. It's your demeanor about it."

"I'm not following."

He sighed. "I understand that you know what you're doing. Trust me…I know more than anyone that you are capable of doing anything you set your mind to. What I don't like is your blatant disregard for doing something dangerous or something that could possibly get you into trouble. You don't fear anything and that's what scares me."

My eyes widened and my mouth dropped. I didn't expect him to say that to me. I had no idea how to even respond to that.

"You're one hell of a woman and sometimes I worry that you don't know right from wrong."

"Jesus, Sebastian," I gasped and reacted. "You want to talk about right from wrong? Right is not cheating on your fucking wife, right is not fucking me and going home to her, right is not stringing me along, right is not having me as your whore, right is not breaking my fucking heart and making me crawl to pick up the pieces."

I regretted the words as soon as they left my mouth. He didn't move, his face remained neutral with no emotion at all and I started to wonder if he had heard what I so viciously spewed. I didn't know where it came from, it just came out.

"You're right," he murmured. "Everything that I did was wrong and I take full responsibility for that. I've told you time and time again that I fucked up. I hate what I did to you. I hate what I did to us. I have to live with that for the rest of my life."

I bowed my head. "I'm sorry, I have no idea where that came from."

How did we go from one thing to another?

He scooted forward and grabbed my chin to make me look at him. "I think the closer we get, Ysa, the more things are going to come to light. I'm not upset with what you shared. I'm actually kinda grateful that you're opening up to me, even if it's at my expense."

"I don't know what to say to you…I can't argue the fact that part of what you're saying is right. I have done some really shitty things. I know that. I can't sit here and dwell on them any more than I already have. I've moved forward with what I know, from what I've been taught or from what I've seen. I adapt, Sebastian, that's what makes me a survivor."

His eyes bared more emotion than I had ever witnessed before. I didn't understand how women loved talking about their feelings. I hated being weak.

"You're not alone anymore. I'm here and I'm not going anywhere. I'll always take care of you." He paused. "What? Tell me? I can see it in your eyes, they never lie to me. Say what you're thinking. Please…" he urged.

I swallowed the saliva that pooled in my mouth. "I want so desperately to believe you…you have no idea how much I want to believe every word. My heart believes you. It always has. But my mind…it's trying." I shrugged. "I'm sorry, I wish I could give you more than that. I wish I could give you everything." I placed my hand on his heart. "This. It's yours…and…"

"I understand," he interrupted me. "Ysa, I know you think that you have a family in VIP, and I know you see The Madam as a mother," he said through gritted teeth. "You have no idea how much it physically pains me for you to associate that demon with anything more than filth and scum. She's a parasite, a waste of space. I will never let her in our lives. Please tell me you know that."

I nodded. "I do."

"I would kill her before she ever got her hands on you again."

"I know."

"I'm your future now and you're safe with me. I promise you that. I won't ever hurt you again. You're mine and I'm yours."

"I know."

And I did.

CHAPTER 18

S

Two months went by and it had been almost seven months since I found her on the island. Christmas was right around the corner and we planned to spend it in Colorado. It took a few weeks for all the paperwork and permits to get approved for my charter business. Ysabelle helped immensely since she already knew what needed to be done. She also had a great marketing idea to have the clients bring in their catches of the day and her cook would prepare them, free of charge. She said she would make money with the alcohol they purchased and so far it worked like a charm. I was taking families, bachelor parties, guy trips, and couples out daily. $500.00 for four hours and if they wanted the entire day it was $1,000. I provided alcohol, snacks, gas, the fishing gear, and bait. I was booked solid for days at a time and couldn't have been happier.

I was living the dream.

"Hello," I said, answering my phone.

"Hey, Sebby," Julia greeted. "How are things?"

"They're better. We're still working out some stuff, but it seems to be getting easier. My business is thriving and everything else looks like it's falling into place."

"That's great. I'm happy to hear that. I'm actually calling to talk to you about Christmas. Are you guys doing anything?"

"Yeah, I'm taking Ysabelle to Colorado."

"Awesome. Listen…I hate to be doing this to you, but Christian has been acting out in school. I mean, I guess I've seen a little bit of a change in him and I just thought it was normal boy stuff. I just left a conference with his teacher; she says he's been talking back and not listening."

"That doesn't sound like Christian at all."

"I know. I think everything finally clicked for him; the divorce, you moving, me dating…it's a lot for a kid."

"I agree."

"So...I was thinking…I know you wanted to take Ysabelle away, but maybe you guys could take Christian. I know he misses you terribly and I'm sure you do, too. Ysabelle hasn't really been around him and I think it would probably do them some good to get to know each other. He might see her as the enemy right now. He's been giving Anthony a hard time, too. I've tried to talk to him about it, but he blows me off. I think he's embarrassed, you know…I'm the mom. You could probably get more out of him."

"I think so, too. I would love to spend Christmas with him and I'm sure Ysabelle won't mind."

"Great! I'll tell Christian then. Shoot me an email letting me know dates and times. I'll take care of everything else."

"Julia, I got it handled. I'll buy his ticket tonight and let you know."

"Okay, sounds good! I can't wait to tell him; he's going to be so excited. Talk you soon, bye."

Ysabelle was cooking dinner when I walked in.

"It smells amazing," I groaned into her ear.

She giggled. "You smell like fish."

"I thought you loved my manly smell."

She turned and put her hands on my chest. "I do, but not when I'm all clean. You need to go shower; dinner is almost ready."

I kissed her and smacked her ass before making my way into the bathroom. Dinner was set and she was pouring wine into our glasses when I once again came up behind her, wrapping my arms around her tiny waist and pulling her into me. I loved how petite she felt in my arms. I could pick her up and throw her around where I wanted her, which I completely intended to do.

"I missed you today." I kissed the side of her neck, laying soft kisses like I knew she loved.

"You just saw me this morning."

"I know. It's been too long. I think you should come with me on the boat and be my first mate."

"I know nothing about offshore fishing. I'd be lying on the bow all day reading."

"Yes…but then I could see you in your bikini and it would make me very happy."

She shook her head laughing, trying to get away.

"Where do you think you're going, Ysa?"

"I'm hungry!"

"So am I, you should feed me."

"After dinner."

I picked her up and she squealed as I carried her over to the couch. I pushed her body forward and she immediately stood on the tips of her toes, falling over the back of the sofa with her ass in the air. I slowly removed her panties and kicked them aside, pausing for a few seconds to admire her perfect, round ass. I spread her cheeks to find her welcoming pink heat. My fingers stirred, wanting nothing more than to touch her most sacred place. I slapped her ass cheek instead and she yelped. I did it until it was red, bright, and warm. She alternated her footing to try and relieve the ache that I created. I then softly and lovingly caressed the rosy imprints while her breathing leveled.

"I've bent you over the couch and spread you open. Why do you think that is?" I probed, never letting up on rousing her.

"To tease me?" she taunted.

"No…try again."

"To spank me?"

"Getting warmer."

"To love me?" She grinned, looking back at me.

I raised an eyebrow. "Where?"

She bit the side of her lip.

"Where, Ysa? Tell me where I'm going to touch you, lick you, and then fuck you?

Her eyes dilated.

"No words? Nothing to say? Let me see if I can fix that."

I pulled out her bottom lip and replaced it with my index and middle finger, gliding them on her tongue to gather spit.

"Here? Do you think it's here?"

I saw it in her eyes, the little vixen wanted to bite me so I shoved my fingers down her throat, making her gag. I swiped the saliva and quickly positioned my wet fingers on her clit.

Her eyes widened.

"What should I do now, huh? Still nothing to say? What if I moved my fingers like this?" I slid them forward and backward. "No? Okay…what about this?" I slid them side-to-side and then in a circular motion and her mouth parted, breathless.

"That feel good?"

Her hips started rocking and that answered my question. I removed my fingers, skimming them to her opening, pressing just the tips in.

"What about here?" I tormented, making her whimper. "Should I fuck you here?"

She sucked in her bottom lip, knowing what I was leading to.

"If you don't answer then I'm just going to do what I want." I walked my soaking fingers up to her anus and pushed in slightly.

"Because I want it here. This is where I want my cock to go…do you want my dick in your perfect, tight little ass hole?"

She made her booty bounce and I spanked her. Hard.

She didn't make a sound.

Y

This was a game I loved to play and he knew it. I think it turned him on as much as it frustrated him. I was a little shit at heart. I didn't want to tell him what to do, where's the fun in that? He could do what he wanted with me, I trusted him. Nothing is better than a forced orgasm. Plus, it turned me on to have him take me and throw me around like I was a ragdoll, and I knew that he would if I gave him just enough incentive to keep going. He loved my ass; it was his favorite asset, no pun intended. When he placed me over the couch, I immediately knew where he wanted to stick his cock and I eagerly awaited it.

Anal sex is a tricky thing…there needs be a lot of foreplay and preparation for it. It's not something you can take on command; you have to wine and dine it first, and that meant I would get more attention. What girl doesn't want that? When he plunged the tips of his fingers in my anus and told me what he wanted to do, I bounced my booty to both provoke and piss him off.

He spanked me, hard, and I bit my tongue from screaming out, so he did it again and again until I finally screamed mercy.

Bastard.

"I win," he mocked, so I swayed my ass back and forth to relieve the burn and taunt him.

"Are you going to be a good girl, now?" he coaxed.

"I'm not a good girl, Sebastian," I goaded.

"You're right about that one." I watched as he got down on his knees to spread me open, still looking up at me. "But you're my girl," he added with possessiveness before he dove his tongue right into my ass hole.

My body simultaneously fell forward, making my ass stand at attention and allowing him to lick and devour my private area. I knew most women wouldn't be caught dead in that position, with their significant others tongue up their ass, but I'm not most women and it felt fucking amazing. His fingers started to torment my clit while the other ones finger fucked me from behind, never letting up the delicious friction his tongue was giving. Within minutes, I was close to falling apart and he sensed it, his movements slowed.

Damn him.

Sebastian had his own game he loved to play, always three steps ahead of me. He wanted me to beg for it. He wouldn't give me what I wanted until he had me say the words.

"Ysabelle…" he said in a singing tone. "Why don't you want to play with me?" He pushed in another finger and moved them in a come-here motion. My eyes rolled to the back of my head, but I didn't make a sound. His fingers massaged my clit as he continued to lap at my anus. I kept as quiet as I could, trying to enjoy the sensations without giving away that I was close to orgasm.

"I know your body…" He paused and licked. "I know the way your skin glows…" He stopped and pressed his fingers in deeper and further. "I know how your back perspires just slightly…I know how your breathing teeters from heavy to still…" he arrogantly stated. "Tell me what I want to hear and I'll let you have what you so desperately want."

I gasped when he removed all his fingers and his tongue found my clit from behind immediately. I was on the tips of my toes, trying to get the most stimulation possible. He was unrelenting with taking me to the edge and then slowing down. I clenched my jaw and subtly swayed my hips.

He smacked my ass and laughed. "No cheating," he ordered.

"Fuck!" I frustratingly yelled. I hated losing.

He attacked my nub with more determination and I couldn't take it anymore.

"Please…please…please…" I shamelessly begged.

I knew he was smiling.

"Please what?" He licked in slow torture.

"I love you," I whispered.

"And…" he groaned in between sucking.

"God…that feels good."

The fucker started humming and the vibrations were indescribable.

"Please…Sebastian…please make me come…please…"

He mumbled something about my pussy tasting fucking amazing and he finally gave me what I wanted. I screamed out his name and he prolonged my orgasm by never letting up on his desire to taste me. I started to shake from the sensitivity and he stood and kicked off his gym shorts to coat his dick with my arousal.

"Spread your ass," he ordered and I did as I was told. "Now that's a fucking view," he growled, smacking my ass.

My wetness pooled everywhere. He used his fingers at first, opening and preparing me. Once he knew I was ready, he slowly thrust in his cock. I felt minor discomfort until his head was in and then breathed through the rest. Once his balls hit my pussy and his hips pressed against my cheeks, I knew he was all the way in and I took several deep breaths.

"You good?" he asked.

"Yeah…" I moaned. "Go slow."

He gently inched in and out; the burning sensation subsided and was replaced with the craving for more. My reactions stirred and I started to meet him for every push and pull.

"Touch yourself," he groaned.

I lowered my hand to my throbbing clit and manipulated the bundle of nerves. I gritted my teeth from the impending orgasm that was looming.

"Jesus…fuck me…how do you get this tight…" he growled, gripping on to my hips harder.

He shoved all the way in and stalled. I knew what he wanted; he wanted to watch me dance, as he called it. I rotated my hips up and down, giving him the show he craved. Women truly are fucking you on the dance floor with their asses on your cocks. I felt his dick harden more and I knew he was close, as was I. Sebastian leaned forward and laid sloppy kisses all along my shoulder blades, breathing on me and that was enough to have me coming apart again. Wetness dripped out of my pussy as my ass milked him clean.

Just another normal Tuesday evening.

CHAPTER 19

Y

I had to take another shower, but it was worth it. Sebastian was sitting at the dining table with a huge smile on his face.

"I warmed up your food," he said.

"That's so thoughtful of you."

"I'm a thoughtful kinda guy."

I rolled my eyes. "Anyway, I was starving before you decided to violate me."

He shook his head and gave me a cocky grin. "I didn't hear you complaining; it was actually quite the opposite."

I laughed. "I never turn down a good time."

"How was your day?"

"It was great. I'm so looking forward to Colorado and spending some time alone with you," I stated, taking a bite of chicken.

"About that…I talked to Julia today and she's having some issues with Christian."

"Oh wow, what's going on?"

He sighed. "I guess he's been talking back and not listening to her or his teachers. She thinks it might be from all the changes in the last year."

I nodded. "Yeah, that is a lot for a kid to take in."

"She suggested that we bring Christian with us to Colorado and I said yes. I think it would be good for us. I want him to get to know you better and vice versa."

"Oh," I replied.

"What?"

"Nothing."

"Seriously? You know that bullshit isn't going to work with me."

"I don't want to argue; let's just drop it."

"No. You not telling me is going to make us fight. We've made so much progress, Ysa, just tell me what's up."

"Fine." I resigned. "I'm a little taken back and caught off guard with Christian coming to Colorado, not that I don't want to spend time with him and get to know him. I just thought I would have been part of the decision-making process…or at least been asked how I felt about it."

He winced. "I'm sorry, I had no idea. I thought you wouldn't have had a problem with it."

"I don't. I have a problem that you didn't include me, and you and Julia decided for us. That's all. It doesn't matter." I shrugged. "It's already done."

"I can call—"

"No! Don't you dare! Then I'll just be the bitch and she will hate me even more."

"Julia doesn't hate you."

I narrowed my eyes. "Sebastian…she hates me and she has every right to."

He cocked his head to the side. "You know, Ysabelle, the only person that hates you for what happened…is you."

I wanted to argue with him, but I couldn't because he was right. I did hate myself. I blamed myself for hurting her and breaking up his family. It didn't matter how many times he told me that it would have happened regardless. I couldn't change the fact that I fell in love with a married man. And all those thoughts lead right back to my other clients.

How many marriages had I broken up? How many men had fallen in love with me? How many women had I hurt?

I held so much guilt for not only Julia but for all the other women's marriages I destroyed. It never bothered me before, and I never thought about it until after I left.

That was the part of VIP I hated.

To fuck with no remorse.

With no heart.

With no conscience.

It ate at me…

"I want to include you in everything and I apologize if you feel like I didn't, that wasn't my intention. I was absorbed and concerned with the behavior issues of my son, as any parent would. I miss him so much and to get to spend Christmas with two of the most important people in my life…seemed perfect," he acknowledged.

He always had a way with words to make me feel at ease and safe. Christian was his only child and I knew he gave up a lot for me by moving. I wanted to get to know his son, but I had no clue what to do with a kid. It scared me to realize that they were a packaged deal. He was a father…I didn't just break up a marriage.

I broke up a home.

"What are you thinking, Ysa? It's written all over your face, your mind is spinning."

I smiled. "It doesn't matter. So…" I clapped my hands together. "Christian, tell me everything I need to know. Should I go buy toys or something? I mean, does he eat special foods?"

He chuckled, trying to hide the disappoint he felt from me not sharing. I couldn't. He would want to make it better.

Maybe I wanted to punish myself…

"Christian is an amazing kid. You're going to love him and I know he's going to love you."

S

Ysabelle had demons, I knew it the second I laid my eyes on her. She was the strongest woman I had ever met; she's also the most stubborn. Her thoughts and feelings were racing as I casually continued our conversation about Christian. Although she pretended to pay attention, I knew she was somewhere else. Lost in her own battlefield. I often wondered if the flag would ever go up. It's so easy to be able to communicate with someone, it's casual conversation where you talk about it and work things out. You reach common ground and in turn, the relationship gets stronger and better. That's normal. That's a relationship.

She wasn't like that.

The damaged, broken, and scared woman before me owned my heart and soul. I wanted desperately to put her back together. When we first got together, I thought she was feisty. I thought she kept herself at arms length because that's what she was trained to do. I couldn't have been more wrong. Learning about her upbringing, her mother, Madam, and everything in between has left her frail and guarded. Our situation obviously didn't help. I assumed over time that things would parallel each other; we would establish some sort of order. A hierarchy so to speak; communication, love, sex, safety, and trust, standard stuff to someone who grew up in a normal environment where they received and gave love.

She didn't.

At times, she would open the door…though she'd never let me in. I would stand there until she slammed it in my face, and I would once again wait for her to open it. Each time she did, I got to see a little more of what was inside, but as soon as I stepped in, she shoved me right back out. The endless cycle was repeated.

How do you put something together when you're missing the pieces?

You couldn't.

But I would die trying.

Y

A few days later and Thanksgiving was here! I had never experienced a normal Thanksgiving or ate a turkey and I wanted it to be perfect. Sebastian's parents were due to land in a few hours and I had woken up at five AM to get everything ready. I researched different styles of turkeys and ingredients for days until I found the precise one. Sebastian said I spent a small fortune on food, but I didn't care.

"What time is it?" he asked, coming out of the bedroom with bedhead, shirtless, and fucking adorable.

"It's six thirty."

"Ysa, it's crazy early."

"So why are you up?"

"I rolled over and you were gone. Come back to bed."

"I can't, I have so much to get done before your parents get here. The turkey is in the oven and it looks beautiful, if I do say so myself."

He came up behind me, nuzzling my neck.

"Hey! Stop that," I said, moving away.

He held me firmer. "But I'm up."

I laughed. "I can feel that. I'm serious, stop!" I pushed out my ass, bumping him backward and ducked under his arms to turn around.

I held up the potato peeler that was in my hand.

"What are you going to do, Ysa? Scrape me to death?"

"Oh my God! Go do something, stop being so needy." I smiled. "Or you can help me?"

"Hmmm…I'm going to go take a shower. But first…"

He was over to me in two strides, pulling me in to passionately kiss me. When his hands started trailing from my waist to my breasts, I shoved him.

"Be good! I have shit to do."

He left to go pick up his parents around ten, and by the time they made it back, it was almost noon. I was checking the turkey when they walked in.

"And there she is…where she has been all day," he informed, making his mom hit him in the chest. "Ow!"

"Sebastian, she has been cooking all day, you stop picking on her," she reprimanded.

"I'm sorry, I'm still a mess. I thought I'd have enough time to shower before you guys got here. The time just got away from me."

"Oh, honey, don't worry about it. I completely understand. If Sebastian is anything like his father, I'm sure he has been sitting on the couch."

I nodded and laughed, and then she slapped him again.

I went and showered, dressing in a casual maxi skirt and tank top. I opted on minimal makeup with some mascara, blush, and lipgloss.

Sebastian closed the door behind him as I was putting on my sandals.

"Mmm…you smell good, and you look so pretty," he groaned into my ear from behind.

"You don't look so bad yourself."

"I missed you today. Come here," he whispered, turning me to grope me.

"Stop. Your parents are right outside."

"It's fine, my mom's on the phone with a friend and my dad's watching football. We have time."

My eyes widened. "Are you insane? I am not having sex with you with your parents less than twenty feet away. Stop," I demanded, fighting off his frisky hands.

"I don't want to stop. Since when do you ever deny me?"

"I'm going to hurt you. Stop."

We went at this for a few more seconds, him trying to touch me everywhere and me blocking every advance. I finally broke down and started laughing, and he took the opportunity to carry me over to the bed, lying on top of me, and caging me in.

"Shhh…I'll be really fast. Don't make any noise."

"No. Stop," I urged, moving every chance I got.

"Shhh…just let it happen."

My stomach hurt from laughing. When he wanted in, he was getting in.

"Ysabelle," his mom said, knocking on the door.

"Yeah?" I yelled, giving him the death look.

"I think the turkey might be ready to come out. Your timer went off while you were in the shower. Do you want me to take it out?"

"No! I'll be right out! Get off."

He laughed and rolled over and before I could jump up, he grabbed my face and kissed me.

"I love you. And it's on later, Ysa."

I rolled my eyes and went to deal with his parents while he took a few minutes to get his hard-on under control.

Unbelievable.

CHAPTER 20

Y

His mom helped me set the table and get everything in order. We nonchalantly talked about nothing in particular. She was the sweetest woman, so caring and gentle. I loved her immediately. She showed me some tricks and family secrets, as she called them, for marinating the food. She also told me about Sebastian's favorite foods and I made a mental note.

"Sebastian, would you like to say grace?" his dad asked.

"Sure."

He leaned over to grab my hand and everyone else followed suit. I was confused. I had never been a part of anything like that. They bowed their heads and closed their eyes and I did the same.

"Dear Lord, thank you for this food that we are about to eat. Please bless everyone at this table and our loved ones who couldn't be here with us today. Thank you, Heavenly Father. Amen."

We all looked up and they did this cross thing in front of them.

"I'll start with what I'm thankful for," his dad said. "I am thankful for my beautiful and amazing wife who I have had the honor of being married to for the last thirty-seven years. I am thankful for my son, I couldn't have asked for a better gift. I am thankful for my career that has given me the opportunity to help people in need all around the world. Thank you, Lord, for all your blessings."

He kissed his wife and Sebastian squeezed my hand.

His mom went next. "I am thankful for my husband, who has always provided all my needs and wants and who gave me the greatest blessing of all, which is my son. I am thankful for my grandchild and hoping for many more in the future," she added, looking right at me and winking.

Oh man...

Sebastian followed. "I am thankful for my amazing parents who have always supported and loved me unconditionally. I am thankful to have found the love of my life, Ysabelle." He smiled at me. "And I am thankful for my son."

All eyes were on me. "Umm...I am thankful for meeting such beautiful, welcoming people. I have never felt more love than I have at this table today. Thank you for letting me be a part of that."

His mom frowned. This woman barely knew me and she was sad for me. It warmed my heart.

I locked eyes with Sebastian. "I am thankful to you. Thank you for loving me." I blinked a few times to clear the tears that were at bay. I didn't know what came over me, but I had the sudden urge to cry, not from sadness, but from happiness. I had never felt that before.

"I can see why my son is taken with you, Ysabelle."

I shyly smiled at her and we all went on to eat.

S

The next few days we showed my parents around the island and doing tourist things. They loved Ysabelle's bar and my mom and her seemed to be getting along great. I took my dad out offshore one morning.

"Hand me another beer, son."

I grabbed two from the cooler and handed him one.

"So tell me about the girl?"

"Where do I start?" I laughed, sitting back on the leather fighting chair.

"Your mom really likes her; she thinks she's good for you."

"She is."

"So where do you see this going? You guys talk about the future?"

"Not really. I know where I'd like things to go, though. I'd ask her to marry me tomorrow if I thought she would say yes."

"A woman who doesn't want to get married. They exist?"

We laughed and I nodded. "Apparently. She didn't have the best upbringing and then how we met…that whole disaster."

"I see."

"Trust me, Dad, I'm not proud of what I did. I never wanted to be that man. You raised me better than that. The heart wants what it wants. You know?"

"I'm going to share something with you because I think this will help. People aren't perfect, especially men. When you were two years old, your mother and I were having some issues. I was working seventy hours a week and she was stuck at home; her whole life changed when she got pregnant with you. It was a difficult adjustment for both of us. We worked through it, though. However, it was touch and go there for about a year. I was sleeping in the guest bedroom and there were nights I thought maybe we wouldn't make it. We went to therapy and over time, it helped. The reason I'm telling you this is because relationships take work, even the best ones."

My parents always looked like they had the best marriage, it surprised me that they went through hard times.

"It took us a while to get back to where we were before we had you, but once we did, it was better than it had been before. Men are selfish and I wanted to keep running my practice and have her at home with you. I never imagined she needed me to be around as well. Not that I didn't want to be, I just thought she could handle everything on her own. From then on out I made it a point to be home for dinner and be able to tuck you into bed and spend some alone time with her. I forgot how much she needed the adult interaction and our time together."

"Is that why you didn't have more children?"

"No. We just decided that one was enough for us. You always seemed to be happy being the only child, though I'm sure having Julia around helped." He took a sip of his beer. "How is Julia? How are you guys dealing with the changes?"

"At first, it was terrible, but over the last few months, it seems like we are back on track. She seems happier, if that makes any sense."

"Completely. Julia always was an independent spirit. When you were younger, your relationship was very much brother and sister. It surprised us when you guys started dating. Not because we didn't love her as our own, but you were very different and that sometimes can be a huge problem."

"Julia was my safe spot, and at the time, that's what I needed."

He nodded. "What do you need now?"

"I have everything I want." I hesitated. "I just hope it stays that way."

Y

"Here, I brought us some frozen margaritas," I announced, handing Sebastian's mom one before lying back on my lounger.

"Now this is the life…beautiful view, great company, and fruity tropical drinks. Maybe Steven and I need to look into getting a timeshare or a property here. I mean, I know we're going to want to spend a lot more time here once Sebastian's dad retires."

I nodded, looking at her.

She turned to smile at me and raised her sunglasses. "And maybe after some grandchildren." She smirked and raised an eyebrow. "What do you think about that?"

I opened my mouth and then quickly shut it. Not knowing what to say.

What the hell do I say to that?

She righted her sunglasses back on her face. "You know, Ysa?" She paused. "Can I call you Ysa?"

"Of course."

"You remind me a lot of myself."

I chuckled. "I highly doubt that."

She shook her head. "I don't. You don't say much, but you really don't have to because it's written all over your face. Even though you guard your emotions, you still wear them on your sleeve. It's normal to be scared of things you don't know. Trust me. When I first had Sebastian, I had no idea what to do with him. His father was always working and I was stuck at home playing homemaker and mother to a small boy that I loved with everything I had. Julia's mom and I are best friends; we have been since high school. She had Julia shortly after we had Sebastian. I remember how much she loved being a mother and a wife."

I hadn't stopped staring at her as I listened carefully to everything she was sharing.

"I loved it, too. However, I wanted more out of life. I had worked as a nurse for my husband for a little over a year before I got pregnant. I loved it. So when Sebastian came, I hadn't realized how much of my life would be turned upside down by someone who weighed ten pounds." She laughed, reliving what she was saying.

"I often thought there was something wrong with me because Julia's mom seemed perfect. They tried for a baby almost immediately and they could never conceive again. I learned quickly that looks can be deceiving, not everything is as perfect as it seems. You," she stated, pointing to me, "seem perfect, and that worries me a little bit. I've never seen my son as happy as he's been since he's been with you. Now don't get me wrong, I love Julia, she will always be like a daughter to me. But I knew from the second that they got together it wouldn't last. You see…my sweet girl. He loved her…but he wasn't in love with her. It's very easy to mix the two." She sat up and grabbed my hands.

"My son is in love with you, Ysa. He wants a future with you. I know you love him, too. I also know you're terrified of the future. I know how you met and I know why he got a divorce. Shit happens."

My eyes widened.

"Pardon my language, but there's no other way to say it. People aren't perfect. We make mistakes; his first mistake was marrying Julia. And my mistake was allowing it to happen…but as mothers, we stand by and support any and every decision, even if it's wrong. He's where he's supposed to be now…I feel it in my heart and I see it in the way he looks at you."

She pulled me in for a hug. "And I know you are, too. It's just going to take some time to realize that. But all good things come to those who wait. I'll be sure to tell you *I told you so* when the time is right."

I shook my head, laughing, and hugged her back.

I prayed that she was right.

CHAPTER 21

S

A month later and it was Christmas. I grabbed Ysabelle's suitcase and placed it with the other three by the door, only one of them belonged to me.

"You know we're only going for a ten days, right?"

"Yes!" she shouted from the bedroom.

"You couldn't tell with the amount of luggage you've packed," I replied, walking into the bedroom and laying on the bed with my arms behind my head.

"Two of those suitcases are presents."

My mouth dropped open.

"What?" She folded her arms. "It's my first Christmas…with both of you, and I wanted to make it special and memorable." She shrugged.

"I can understand that."

I was over having this conversation and had other things in mind. I grabbed her around the waist and threw her over my shoulder, dragging her into the shower with me.

"I'm not done packing," she shrieked, giggling.

My parents' visit might have been the best thing that happened to us since I had found her on the island. Her demeanor had changed; she looked happy and content. There was a certain peace about her that hadn't been there before, and I had a suspicion that it had something to do with my mom. Though neither would divulge any information. I had even caught Ysabelle talking to her on the phone a few times.

Our flight to Colorado left on time, as scheduled. Christian was taking another flight from Miami. I made sure to let the airline know that a child would be flying first-class by himself. They assured me that he would be in good hands. Our flight arrived thirty minutes before his, so it gave us plenty of time to walk over to his gate to pick him up.

Ysabelle had been quiet the entire flight and I knew it was from nerves. She held my hand reassuringly as we waited for Christian to walk through the terminal.

"Dad!" he shouted, running over to me.

I immediately picked him up and hugged him with everything I could muster.

"Hey, buddy."

I placed him back on the ground and took a look at him. "Wow! You've grown. I barely recognized you."

"Really?"

"Absolutely."

I turned to Ysabelle, who was closely observing our interaction.

"Christian, you remember Ysabelle."

He nodded. "Hi."

"Hey, Christian, I hope your flight was okay."

He nodded again. "It was fine."

"Oh great. Do you want me to help you with that carry-on?"

"No, I'm fine. So, Dad, Mom says you have a really cool big boat," he exclaimed, turning his attention back to me.

I winked at Ysabelle and put my arm around Christian's shoulder as we walked side-by-side.

Y

I knew nothing about kids other than that they talked a lot. Christian hadn't stopped talking or asking questions since we picked him up from the airport. Sebastian had rented an SUV and I sat in the backseat to let them catch up. He had high energy and everything he spoke about was as exciting as the last thing that came out of his mouth. He already had another question before Sebastian answered the previous one. He wanted to know everything about his new life and Sebastian happily obliged.

"Ysabelle has this really cool bar that she owns. We get to meet lots of new people all the time."

"That's awesome, Dad. I can't wait to come visit. I'm sure Mom would love to visit, too. You remember when we used to take the boat out every Sunday and Mom didn't like to go in the water so you would carry her in?"

There was a certain tone in his voice that I couldn't quite pick up on and it made me hesitant.

Sebastian nodded.

"That was really funny. I bet Mom would love the island. Do you remember that time that she pushed you in the water and you lost your new sunglasses?"

I could feel Sebastian's eyes on me through the rearview mirror, but I ignored him.

"Hey, bud, check out the house!" he said, changing the subject.

"Wow! Is this where we're staying! It's huge," he said, getting out of the car.

"Yep, this is home for the next ten days. Ysa, why don't you take Christian inside and show him the place while I get our bags."

I was about to say yes when Christian said that he wanted to help with the bags, too. Sebastian told him he had it under control and he reluctantly came with me. The fireplace was on and there was food in warming trays on the kitchen island. The cabin was breathtakingly beautiful with a big open area that had stairs leading to a kid's playroom and another few bedrooms. We took off our coats and scarves and I hung them up on the rack by the door.

"Want to see your room?"

"Yeah!"

"Well, there are a few of them that you can choose from so you can pick wherever you'd like to sleep."

We walked into the second room and it was decked out with toys and a flat screen.

"I'll take this one," he stated, sitting on the bed.

I smiled. "I think this room is perfect."

He nodded. "What room are you taking?"

"Oh," I replied, taken aback. "Ummm…the downstairs one."

"But that's my dad's room."

"Right…it's…my room…too."

His eyebrows lowered. "But you aren't married. My mom says that only married people sleep in the same room."

Oh my God! Someone shoot me…where the hell is Sebastian?

"Yeah…she's…she's ummm…" I stuttered.

Sebastian pushed open the bedroom door, holding all of Christian's luggage. "This is…" He looked around, placing the bags by his bed. "…a good choice." He looked back at me and mouthed, "What's wrong?"

"Yeah, Dad! This is my room. Ysabelle said she's sleeping downstairs in your room," he reiterated. "I think she's confused…you aren't married and only married people sleep in the same room. Right, Dad?"

His eyes widened and I jauntily smiled at him.

"Yeah…bud…that's true."

"See, Ysabelle, there're three other rooms. The one with all the pink might be a good one for you. Mom loves pink."

"Yeah…I can sleep in that—"

"Ysabelle," Sebastian interrupted, taking a seat next to him on the bed.

Is there a hole in this room? Maybe I could hide in the closet?

"Why don't I leave—"

"Ysabelle and I are sleeping in the same room, buddy," Sebastian chimed in, knowing that I was about to flee. "Remember, I told you that we live on the island together and we have a place above the bar. You know this."

"I know. But I thought you guys had your own rooms. Mom never lets Anthony stay the night because she said only married people sleep together."

And if the earth wanted to open up at any point in time, do so…right now!

"I can understand why your mom would say that; however, things are different for us. We live together."

He nodded, looking back between us. "Oh, does that mean you're getting married?"

Of course…that would be the next question…God hates me. I'm his personal comedic relief for the afternoon.

"Hello!" Someone shouted downstairs.

Oh, thank you, random stranger that's in our cabin!

"I'll go handle that. You guys...you do this..." I pointed to them and got my happy ass out of there as fast as I could.

S

"All right, let's have a man-to-man talk. How do you feel about that?" I asked.

"I'm okay with it," he agreed.

"You know Ysabelle is my girlfriend."

He nodded.

"And you know Mom has a boyfriend."

He nodded again.

"The only difference between my relationship and your mom's is that I live with Ysabelle. And since we live together, it's different than it would be if we were dating. Do you understand?"

"Kinda."

"What is confusing?"

"I don't know...I don't understand why you guys aren't together anymore. I know Mom said that it was grown up problems and it had nothing to do with me..."

"And it didn't, it still doesn't," I reaffirmed.

"Do you think that maybe you guys will get back together? Because my friend Jacob's parents got a divorce and then got back together."

I placed my hand on his back. "No, bud, we aren't going to get back together."

"Are you sure, Dad?"

I shook my head. "I'm positive. We will always care for each other and we will *always* love you."

"Okay..." He bowed his head.

"I know it's confusing for you right now because so much has changed, Christian. I'm sorry that you've had to grow up a lot in the last few years. Sometimes parents try to do what's best for them and their family, and what's best for us is that we are no longer together. I love your mom and she feels the same way about me. One day you will understand the difference between a friendship and being in love."

"Yeah...Mom said the same thing."

"Is that why you've been acting out in school and giving your mom a hard time? You know that's not acceptable."

"I know. I'm sorry. I guess Anthony is okay…he's nice."

"Ysabelle is really nice, too. I think you should try to get to know her."

"I guess I could do that."

"I'd really appreciate it if you would. You know you're my main man and your opinion is very important to me."

He peeked up at me and smiled. "Yeah, I guess we could be friends. She's really pretty."

I laughed. "She is very pretty. I agree. Are you okay?"

"Yeah."

"Great. I'm going to go help Ysabelle. Can you unpack all your stuff and meet us downstairs in a half an hour for dinner?"

"Okay."

I kissed him on the head and closed the door behind me before I made my way downstairs.

To the other problem…

CHAPTER 22

S

"Hey," she greeted as I walked down the stairs. "So that was the caterer, it was really nice of you to have this food for us tonight. I guess it makes it easier and now we don't have to go grocery shopping tonight. But I can do that in the morning and you can hang with Christian."

I wrapped my arms around her.

"I mean, unless you want us to go together, which is probably better so that he picks out the food that he wants to eat. I mean, I don't really know what kids like to eat, it wouldn't be hard, though; I'm sure I could just ask someone—"

"Ysa…shhh…take a second to breathe," I murmured and she laid her head on my chest.

"He hates me," she confided.

"He doesn't hate you."

"Maybe I should just sleep in one of the other rooms. It's not that big of a deal."

"It's a big deal to me. He needs to learn, and he will. Just give him some time. He's a kid; it's confusing for him."

"Maybe I should give him a present?" she encouraged.

I pulled away from her and cocked my head. "Is that why you went crazy with the presents?"

"No…" She looked everywhere but at me. "I mean…maybe. I don't fucking know." She backed away from me. "I mean shit…I mean damn it…" She placed her hand on her forehead. "I can't do this, Sebastian."

I laughed. I couldn't help it. Seeing her all frazzled was adorable. Especially for her, I loved witnessing more of her walls coming down.

"You're laughing at me now?"

I put my hands up in front of me in a surrendering gesture. "Calm down…if you took a step back and looked at yourself right now, you would be laughing, too. I used to cuss all the time, so did Julia. It takes time, Ysa, it's not going to happen overnight."

She sighed.

"Are you okay?"

She nodded.

"I'm going to go shower before dinner. You think you can manage for about ten minutes?"

"Yeah…"

I kissed her on the forehead and left. I knew she needed to regroup and it was better if she did it by herself.

Y

How did I find myself in this situation? I'm not someone's parent. I hated having intense conversations. We had just arrived and we were already having one. What if something happened while Sebastian was gone? How would I handle it by myself? I would have given the kid anything just to stop where the conversation was leading to...parents don't do that.

They have their shit together all day, every day. Sebastian jumped in, head first, without a care or concern for the world. It was natural to him. I was ready to jump off the balcony. My heart was beating rapidly and I couldn't stop the anxiety that crept into my being. I never wanted to be a parent…I was never one of those women who looked at babies and felt all warm inside. They seemed like a burden more than anything else.

I really was my mother's daughter.

All of those years that I had blamed and resented her were for nothing because I was exactly like her. That's why she hated me; she never wanted me in the first place and had me so that she could receive more welfare from the government. I was a pawn. It made me sick to my stomach to feel anything other than hatred for that woman. However, I stood there and felt sympathy and understanding. I related to her. We were one and the same.

Madam's words echoed in my mind.

"Ysabelle, I've been doing this a very long time. You'll come back, you'll get bored, you'll need excitement; you'll be back. Women like us are made like that, it doesn't just stop because you want it to, it's in our blood."

"I want more, Madam, I want it all."

She chuckled, "You want the white picket fence, the 2.5 kids, and the husband. Jesus Christ, Ysabelle, have you learned nothing these last few years? I mean how many married men have you been with? Have you ever seen a happy marriage?"

What if she was right? What if I'm not made for this? It was just the tip of the iceberg and I was ready to jump ship.

I sat down on the couch and placed my head on my lap to take a deep breath.

"Ysabelle…you love Sebastian. Its been a rocky start, but everything will be fine. Stop being an asshole and get your shit together. You can do this. He's a small child. You love Sebastian. There is no life without him. You know that…just calm down," I spoke to myself.

I looked up and Sebastian was leaning in the doorway, looking at me attentively. His eyes said everything I needed to know.

"I love you," he simply stated.

It was the first time that I needed to hear those words.

And for some reason…they helped.

S

"That wasn't so bad," I said as we finished putting away the groceries.

"I thought he would have wanted more sugar."

"Julia was pretty adamant on having him on an organic, healthy diet."

"I see that."

Christian raced down the stairs. "I'm ready!"

We were going to hit the slopes; she was going to ski while we snowboarded because apparently, skiing was for girls and snowboarding was for boys.

"Let me get my suit on, I'll be out in a few minutes."

"Dad, look at my board, it's got skulls on it."

We waited for Ysabelle and she came out looking like a snow bunny. I had an instant hard on.

"I'm ready."

"Yeah! Let's go!"

I had grabbed her around the waist before she exited the door. "What are you trying to do to me?"

She giggled. "Christian is waiting. Come on."

I groaned.

We hit the easy trail at first and worked our way up to the intermediate. Christian made some friends and asked to go hang out with them. I gave him my cell phone and told him we would meet up at the lodge in a few hours. Ysabelle said the trail was too easy and she wanted to go try the advanced. The lift was high and the takeoff was rough.

"I changed my mind," she blurted.

"No way, we're already up here."

"I don't want to anymore."

"Nope, the only way back down is on the trail."

"No! Did you see all those people who biffed it coming off the lift? I don't want to eat shit."

I laughed. "You're fine."

"No I'm not. I'm taking it back down."

"No you're not. Now come here and get ready."

She shook her head back and forth instantly. I grabbed her by the waist, trying to support her weight and slid her off.

"Ahhhh!" she screamed until she glided down the stoop and then turned. "Oh! That wasn't so bad. Sebastian? Sebastian, where did you go? Why are you on the floor?"

"I sacrificed myself for you."

She chuckled. "It wasn't that bad."

"That's because I pretty much carried you off."

She smiled. "Awe! Let me kiss and make it better," she teased.

She was a great skier, kept up with me the entire time. I was surprised. I had been doing it since I was a kid and I knew it hadn't been more than a few years for her. I'm assuming it was associated with VIP, but I didn't want to know. She was picking up great speed and somewhere along the turn, I lost her. I started to panic; these trails were dangerous if you didn't know what you were doing.

"Ysa!" I yelled. "Ysabelle?"

No answer.

"Ysabelle, this isn't funny." I unlocked my boots from my board. There were miles and miles of snow ahead of us, but there were some trees scattered. I was terrified she might have gotten wrapped around one.

I started running toward that direction and an icy shot to the head stopped me.

"Now that's funny," she laughed and I turned following the sound of her voice.

"Oh…Ysa…it's on," I warned.

"Bring it!"

I took off running and she shrieked, ducking to the massive pile of rolled up snowballs she had in front of her. She hit me with one right after the other and it slowed me down. Once I got closer to her, she sprinted in the other direction, taking a few snowballs with her.

"You can't catch me!" she shouted.

She was hysterically laughing and lost her footing. I tackled her to the ground, catching myself before I crushed her with my weight. We fell into a pillow of ice.

"Hi." She smiled. "I win."

"You cheated."

"It doesn't matter how you win or lose, Sebastian, it's how you play the game."

"Oh yeah?"

I grabbed a pile of ice and smashed it in her face. She squirmed, kicking and twisting to try to break free.

"Why are you freaking out? What's going on?" I taunted, piling more and more snow on her face.

"Okay! Okay! Okay! I cheated. You win."

I immediately brushed off all the snow and her face was bright ass red. I felt bad.

"I can't feel my nose."

"Awe! I'm sorry." I placed my hands on the sides of her face and blew warm air. "That better?"

She nodded, grinning. I leaned in and kissed all over her face until I reached her mouth. The kiss started off innocent enough, but it quickly became heated and passionate.

"I love you, Ysa. I love you so much. You're my whole world."

"I love you, too," she moaned into my mouth.

I kissed her one last time and pulled myself up, dragging her with me. She stumbled, trying to find her balance.

"Whoa, I'm a little lightheaded."

I held the woman that I wanted to marry in my arms.

And it took everything in me…

Not to ask.

CHAPTER 23

Y

Two days went by and it was Christmas. I had stayed up till late the night before wrapping all the presents and piling them under the tree. I hoped my gifts were better than the food I was picking out for him at the grocery store. Everything I thought he would want to eat was wrong. There is no sugar or sweets in this kid's diet. I would pick something out and place in the cart and he would look at me like I was crazy, then he would remind me that his mom knew everything and he never had to go to the grocery store.

"My mom doesn't buy that. My mom wouldn't let me eat that. That's not how my mom cooks it."

I gave up and just started to grab Sebastian's and my stuff.

"My dad never ate that before. My mom used to cook that for my dad. Oh, that was my dad and mom's favorite food. Dad used to love the way my mom would make that." It was a shit show.

"Dad! Wake up! It's Christmas," Christian yelled from the living room. It couldn't have been later than six in the morning, I felt like I had just gone to bed.

"Oh man…how is he up right now?" I groaned.

"Welcome to the world of kids and Christmas. They wake up ass early." He yawned. "They also do this on birthdays."

"Dad! Come on!"

"I'm coming, bud!" he yelled. "Hey…" he whispered, nuzzling my neck. "Merry Christmas, Ysa."

I peeked my eyes open. "Merry Christmas," I repeated.

"Dad!"

"Let's go before he starts foaming at the mouth."

We brushed our teeth and changed into some casual clothes. Christian had all the presents split up by name and I couldn't help but notice there were quite a few presents with my name on them. I looked up at Sebastian and he winked at me. Christian said the gifts needed to be opened by age so he got to go first, me second, and Sebastian last.

He opened everything with the same enthusiasm as the first. It didn't take him long to finish.

"Thanks, Dad, can we hook up my new PS3? Mom got me all these games! Let's go play them."

"Yes, but Ysabelle picked out a lot of these things, including that PS3."

"Oh." He walked over to me, and it was the first time I saw that he was hesitant and shy, a big difference from the kid who was just bouncing off walls.

"Thank you, you can play the game first if you want."

I chuckled. "Nah, that's all you. I'm glad you liked everything."

"I loved everything. Ummm…can I give you a hug?"

"Of course."

We both leaned into each other at the same time. I looked over at Sebastian and he mouthed, "I love you."

"Okay, now it's your turn," Christian reminded, pulling away from me and going to play with his new toys, not paying us any mind.

I nodded, trying to hold in all the happiness I felt. I opened a few presents from Brooke and Devon; Sebastian said that they had mailed them over and he had hid them in his suitcase. There was a card with just my name on it with one of Brooke's gifts. I recognized the handwriting immediately and decided to open it later. We had also decided that we would open our gifts in private, and Sebastian wanted us to wait till New Years Eve. I was confused but went along with it.

"Dad, don't forget to open all Mom's gifts. You know she always buys the best presents," he said, looking right at me.

We spent the rest of the day lounging around and helping Christian set up all his new toys. They had played PS3 for hours at a time as I watched and read. It was nice. The more time I spent with Christian, the more I learned about him. He was shy and reserved if it was just the two of us, but the minute Sebastian came back in the room, he'd light up. I could tell that his dad was his hero. He admired him. It was endearing to watch. It was also overwhelming; he would throw comments here and there about Julia. The woman could do no wrong. She seemed like the perfect mom and wife when they were together. There was no way I could ever measure up to that.

Why would he leave her for me?

The days went by quickly and we spent most of them on the slopes or inside watching movies. I found it interesting that most "kid movies" had such adult and somewhat vulgar humor in them.

It was New Years Eve, and I was laying on the couch reading while they were upstairs playing PS3. I looked up to find Sebastian coming down the stairs and he came right over to me. He grabbed my legs and I winced.

"I'm so sore. I don't think I can ski anymore."

"Well then, we definitely need to try out that hot tub outside. Christian won't make it till midnight, he'll be passed out within the hour. We can celebrate in private with the champagne bottle I stored in the freezer."

"That sounds perfect."

He sat down, placing my legs on his lap and massaged them. "I know we haven't been able to get much alone time in since we've been here."

"It's okay, I know you wanted to spend time with him. I understand."

"I'll make it up to you later, I promise."

"I'm going to hold you to that."

It was eleven by the time we made it into the hot tub. I went in first and he followed shortly after, setting up the champagne on ice and placing the strawberries on the table next to the hot tub.

I moaned. "This feels amazing. We're sitting in a hot tub while it snows all around us. It's like a Christmas card."

"Why are you so far away?"

I smiled. "Because I'm trying to relax and if I sit near you…I won't be relaxing."

We sat there for a few minutes just enjoying the view.

"Are you ready for your gifts?" he asked, breaking the silence.

"Of course, you're lucky I've made it this long."

He handed me two wrapped presents and told me which one to open first. I wiped my hands on the towel that he just used to wipe his own and scooted up to open my first gift.

It was a key.

"This isn't something cheesy like this is the key to your heart," I teased, half-serious.

He shook his head no, grinning. "No…open the other one."

I opened the next present and it was a document; no, it was a contract with both of our names on it.

"Oh my God."

"Calm down. Nothing is set in stone."

When his parents were in town, they wanted to go look at houses one day and we went along with them. There was this house that wasn't far from the bar and I had told him that the pool reminded me of the one in Miami. It was oceanfront property with an infinity pool, four bedrooms, a study, two living rooms and a kitchen that would make my chef jealous.

"If you want it. It's ours."

My mouth hung open, I had no idea how to respond.

"Just think about it," he stated, reading my mind. All I could do was nod.

I reached over the ledge to grab his present and handed it to him, still shaken from the unexpected surprise. He quickly opened it. It was a framed picture of the morning after we were intimate in St. Barts; I was a VIP and he was still married. I remembered thinking that I wanted a memory of our night together. I had never taken a picture with any man before and I wanted his. Ours. We were still in bed and I had grabbed my phone and taken a picture of us just as we were.

"That's the only thing I kept from our time together."

We locked eyes.

"It used to make me really sad when I looked at it. I kept it hidden under my mattress. When you found me on the island, we moved forward that day. That night I pulled it out for the first time since I put it there when I moved. I kept that photo because it was the first time I had ever made love and that's why it made me sad to look at it. When I looked at it that night, it made me smile…I thought maybe I hadn't imagined it all and we really did share something."

His eyes were wide with shock and grief.

"I want you to have it," I added, trying to hold back the tears.

I had never felt more vulnerable and exposed than I did in that moment.

"I believe everything you say about you loving me since day one. The look on your face now is the same look you gave me then, I just didn't realize it. I wracked my brain for weeks trying to think about what to get you for Christmas. You have everything. So I figured I'd give you the truth." I paused; his intense stare was agonizing. "Sebastian, please say something."

He looked back down at the picture, like he was envisioning everything I had just shared. When his piercing stare caught mine again, there was more emotion than I had ever seen before and he looked deep into my eyes.

"Marry me."

It wasn't a question. My eyes widened and my hand went to my mouth, shocked.

S

I couldn't believe what just happened. She kept the picture of the first night we shared together. I remembered that morning as if it were yesterday, her taking the picture and me going through her phone, realizing that I was the only man on it. I knew it was the first time she had ever made love to someone and I had no business taking that from her. It didn't stop me, though.

I wanted to be her first. To know that we shared something that she hadn't with anyone else. I needed to own her in a way that no other man ever had the privilege of claiming.

Mine.

"I believe everything you say about you loving me since day one. The look on your face now is the same look you gave me then, I just didn't realize it. I wracked my brain for weeks trying to think about what to get you for Christmas. You have everything. So I figured I'd give you the truth." She hesitated. Her glossy eyes and words almost brought me to tears.

"Sebastian, please say something."

I didn't think and I just reacted on pure impulse.

"Marry me."

Her eyes widened and I heard a slight gasp as her hand covered her mouth.

"Ysa, you're it for me. You always have been. Marry me and make me the happiest man on this earth. Be my wife and the mother of my future children."

She hadn't moved or made a sound. I wanted to keep my eyes on her, but the small shadow in the corner caught my eyes before I ever heard him.

"NO!" Christian screamed, making Ysabelle jolt and turn. "She's not my mom! She will never be my mom!" His stare moved from me to her and it was like everything progressed in slow motion. "You will never be my mom! I hate you! You ruined my family! I heard…I heard my mom tell my grandmother that you're a whore! That you broke up my family! That it's all your fault! You're a bad person! I hate you so much! Do you hear me? I hate you!" he screamed and then ran back inside.

"Fuck!" I shouted, jumping out of the hot tub and grabbing my towel. "Ysa," I called out to no avail. She sat there, motionless and in shock.

"Ysabelle!" I yelled.

She shook her head in a daze and looked at me.

"I'm going to go talk to him. Are you okay?"

"Yeah…yeah….I'm fine…go," she said, barely above a whisper.

"I love you. Ysabelle, do you hear me? I love you; this doesn't change anything. Do you understand?"

She barely nodded.

"Ysa, tell me you understand."

She blinked a few times, taking in my words.

"I understand," she said with no emotion whatsoever.

I feared that she thought I was leaving her behind. That I was choosing him over her but what was I supposed to do? I had to calm him down and explain.

I took one last look at her stunned and baffled demeanor, begrudgingly leaving her to chase after my son.

Y

Have you ever seen your life flash before your eyes? People say it happens in seconds. That there are these picture images that run through your mind like a movie reel, one right after the other. Nothing makes sense, and then there's this moment of clarity. Where everything just seems to fall into place. For one second, it all clicks and the voices are gone and you are alone with the truth.

She is ugly.

She is vicious.

She is you.

My worst nightmare, my deepest insecurities, my truths that I so desperately tried to ignore, and wanted nothing more than to bury and hide, were thrown in my face by an eight-year-old boy. It all came tumbling down on me like a force field and I was hanging onto the ledge by one finger.

The reality of my fairy tale was that I was going to say yes…

I wanted everything he had just promised. The marriage, the family, the children, the future. The happily ever after wrapped in one big bow with the simple response of a *yes.*

I stepped out of the hot tub and walked into our bedroom, closing the door behind me. I opened my drawer and grabbed a pair of black panties, and there before my very own eyes was a red envelope with my name on it. The same envelope that I hid on Christmas morning, I reached for it and brought it with me as I sat on the edge of the bed. I moved in autopilot, opening it. It was a black postcard with VIP etched on the front and I flipped it over to read the back.

Bella Rosa,

Merry Christmas my beautiful girl. I hope the New Year brings many revelations for you. Always remember that you have a family here and nothing will ever change that. A toast to you and finding your way back home.

Love,

Madam

My eyes caught the clock in the corner.

12:00am.

Happy fucking New Year.

CHAPTER 24

S

I changed into some dry clothes and then knocked on Christian's door before walking in. He was laying in bed with his back to me and the sheet pulled over his head.

"Christian, I know you're not sleeping."

He didn't answer.

I took a deep breath, grabbed the chair, and faced it next to his bed. I slouched forward, placing my elbows on my knees.

"You know, when you were born I was scared shitless. We had tried for almost a year to have you and when your mom finally told me she was pregnant, I was thrilled. The entire pregnancy I couldn't wait to meet and hold you. When we were at the hospital and they put you in my arms, I remember thinking, 'Shit! He's really here and I'm really a dad and I have no idea what's going to happen.' It was real then."

He started to stir a little.

"Not knowing what's going to happen in the future is difficult. It doesn't matter if you're eight, thirty, or sixty. The unknown is scary. The older you get, the more you realize how short life really is and how you need to make every day count as if it were your last. I don't know what you know about our divorce, and one day when you're old enough, I will happily tell you. I hope that you will learn from my mistakes. Just because I'm a dad doesn't mean I don't make them. I make them every day; the only thing I can do is try to learn from them."

His body turned to face me, but the sheet was still over his head.

"I love your mom. And Ysabelle will never replace your mom in your life. Ever. That I can promise you. However, she can be a friend, a confidant, someone you play with…but she definitely needs to be someone that you respect, and then maybe, somewhere along the way, the feelings, the affection, the love part…might come. And I'm not saying it's going to happen tomorrow or next week, or even next year for that matter."

I could see him playing with his fingers under the blanket.

"I love her, bud. I love her a lot. The way you reacted, I can understand, but it was hurtful to Ysabelle and she doesn't deserve that. She's not the villain. You're not going to treat her like that. I'm very upset about it. I'm sorry that I didn't discuss the future with you, but to be honest, the proposal just sort of came out. You ever said anything that you didn't think you were going to say and it just comes out?"

He nodded.

"Well…it was kinda like that. Your mom will always hold a place in my heart. Always. The thing about hearts, though, is that they have an enormous amount of room. It's endless. There is no limit. I love you so much, Christian. I loved you even before you were born and your mom told me she was pregnant. I would never want to hurt you, and the fact you're hurting right now…kills me."

He pulled the sheet off his head and tears fell down his face.

"There's going to be so much more change in your life. I can promise you that I will always be there, though. So will your mom. We're parents to you, forever. Nobody I marry or she marries can ever come between that."

He sniffed his runny nose. "I guess I could try."

I smiled. "That's all I ask."

"Is she crying?"

"She's not really a crier." We laughed. "But I'm sure she's very upset."

He looked down at his hands. "I heard Mom say that to Grandma a really long time ago. I didn't even understand what it meant, but Mom caught me listening and she explained to me that she was upset and didn't mean it. Mom told me that she's happier now than she has ever been. It makes me sad because I miss you." He shrugged. "I just miss my family, that's all. Anthony is nice and so is Ysabelle."

"It makes me happy to hear that. Are you okay?"

"Yeah. I'm better."

"Okay." I stood and kissed him on the head. "I love you, bud."

"I love you, too, Dad."

I closed the door behind me and propped my head on it. I knew that this conversation was much easier than the conversation that awaited downstairs. If I could even get her to talk…

I walked into the bedroom and she was packing.

"What are you doing?" I calmly asked.

"I need to get out of here," she replied, putting more things in her suitcase. She made no sense–she was still wearing her bathing suit.

I kicked the door closed behind me. "Are you fucking kidding me? You're leaving me?"

She shook her head, blowing me off. "No…I just need some space. I changed my flight and you'll be home in two days. It's not that big of a deal."

I yanked her by the arm to turn her to me and she closed her eyes.

"It's a big fucking deal. I'm am so sick of you running every time something happens. Is this what you're going to do for the rest of our lives?" I scolded.

She immediately opened her eyes and I didn't recognize her. I grabbed onto her other arm, holding her in place in front of me. She didn't falter, nor did she show any emotion. It only pissed me off further. The walls were back up and I was exhausted of playing this cat and mouse game.

"Talk to me. I know what just happened wasn't easy for you. He's a kid, Ysa. He doesn't know what he was saying. I'm sorry he hurt you. You know that I would never want that to happen."

"Let. Go. Of. Me," she replied through gritted teeth.

"No." I shook my head, holding on harder. "Listen to me! Just fucking talk to me; for once, tell me how you feel. It's me, Ysa," I reminded, slightly jarring her to emphasize who I was. "Do you have any idea what this does to me? Do you even fucking care? This isn't just about you; it's about us. I can't keep fighting a losing battle, you have to help me."

"It doesn't matter!" she screamed right in my face. "None of it does. He's right, Sebastian. I did break up your family. Not just yours, I've probably broken hundreds. Do you have any idea how many men I've fucked?" she sadistically said.

"I can't believe what I'm hearing spew out of your mouth."

I was disgusted and it took everything inside not to react to her hateful words.

"How are we back here again?"

"Maybe we never left."

"You don't believe that," I reaffirmed. "You're just trying to hurt me. You're trying to run away and the only way you can do that is by causing me pain." I pulled her closer to me and she had to step forward to catch herself.

"I know you, Ysa. Your eyes speak everything to me every fucking time. You forget that."

She lifted her to chin in defiance. "Come on, don't tell me you've never thought about it. You know Julia is right, somewhere deep inside, you know I was a whore. I've made millions on giving my body to people. I told you since day one that I preferred the married ones. It was a fucking game to me. I'm not a good person, I never was. You deserve better. You deserve someone like Julia, who is a perfect mother and was the perfect wife. I'm never going to be like that. Ever! Don't you see that? I'm not made like that. Why do you think your kid hates me? Because he knows. He can sense it."

"That couldn't be further from the truth. I've never seen you that way. Not once. You were never Ysa with them. Ever. Julia isn't perfect, she's so far from it and Christian is a child, he's just reacting. He knows nothing. You can try to deny it all you want, but I know the truth. I'm fully aware of what you did and I don't fucking care. Don't you understand that I will take you any way that I can have you?"

She looked away and closed her eyes. I knew I was getting to her. I held her closer and kissed all over her face. Her eyes were so tightly shut that it wrinkled her face.

"Where's Ysa? Where's my girl? Open your eyes and look at me, let me see you," I demanded, watching her internal struggle. "I love you. I love you with everything I have. You know that. I don't care about your past, I'm your future and that's all that fucking matters and you know that," I shouted, hoping that it would sink in.

Tears slipped out of her closed eyes and it shattered my heart. I hated seeing her like that–if I could switch places with her, I would. I wished I could take away all her pain and self-loathing. She finally opened her eyes, but they were still cold and distant. It didn't matter that she was crying. She wouldn't give in and I was starting to get to my wits end. I was teetering on the sidelines with her, waiting for the direction she would take us. I would follow her anywhere. It didn't fucking matter.

She didn't hesitate. "Sebastian, I'm not fucking around. Let go of my arms," she roared.

I cocked my head to the side and narrowed my eyes. "Or what? Huh? What are you doing to do, Ysa?"

Her pupils dilated and her eyes widened. She looked crazed. The next thing I knew, she drove her knee up and I had to let her go to block her from trying to kick me in the balls. I stumbled backward and she came at me.

"Fuck you! Why would you do this to me!" she screamed, pushing and punching me in the chest over and over. "I was fine! I was fine before I met you! Why did you come after me! Why did you find me! This is all your fault! Why couldn't you have just left me alone!" she yelled, never letting up on hitting me.

I didn't know what to do; I was stunned. I left my hands in the air, allowing her to take out her frustrations on me. When my back hit the wall, she didn't stop.

"I don't know who I am anymore! I don't know if I ever did! Why do you want to be with me? I'm so fucked up!" she openly wept, unable to control her turmoil.

"I know who you are!" I shoved her hands away and roughly grabbed her face, bringing her toward me. She whimpered as if my touch caused her agony. "Look at me. I know who you are. You're mine! And I'm yours. I couldn't leave you alone because I can't fucking breathe without you." I kissed at her mouth. "You're my air, you're my life, you're my everything."

"I'm so fucked up!" she bawled, shaking her head back and forth, trying to move away from me. "I'm sorry I can't be better for you! I'm sorry you have to deal with me! I hate myself for what I put you through. I ruin everything!"

"Never. You're my girl."

She frowned and slid to the floor. I went right along with her. I pulled her into my arms and she let me, holding her as tight and close as I could.

"I'm not a good person…I'm not a good person…" she repeated.

"Shhh…it's going to be okay…shhh…just breathe, baby…" I whispered, kissing her all over her head.

I never thought I would see the day that she would break down and fall apart.

How did I not see this coming?

Y

He held me until I had calmed down and my breathing steadied, and then carried me over to the bed. I panicked when he moved away from me, but he reassured me that he was getting the blanket because I was shivering. It was then that I noticed that I still had my wet bathing suit on. He sat up against the headboard and I hugged him, lying across his lap with my face buried on his stomach. He pulled the covers up to my shoulder and rubbed at my arms.

"I'm so sorry," I whispered.

"You have nothing to apologize for," he emphasized with sincerity and hurt in his voice.

"I'm fucked up, Sebastian, and I think I've always been like this. I'm scared I'm never going to find out, though." I took a deep breath. "I can't marry you," I said, holding him tighter. "I do love you. I love you so much that it petrifies me; I lose more and more control every day that I am with you and I am beginning to wonder if that's the reason that I'm losing it."

"Ysa, I'm not letting you go. I've known since day one that you are your worst enemy. We'll work through it together. I don't care about anything else as long as you're by my side."

I nodded.

"Just know that I talked to Christian and he feels badly about what he said. It's my fault, not yours. I'm sorry that I put you in a situation where you got hurt. I just didn't think. I'm not going to lie and say that I don't want you to be my wife because I do. I want it so bad that it hurts, but the way I feel in my heart surpasses any piece of paper. I don't want you to be Julia; I would still be with her if I wanted that. I want you. Just you."

"I wish I could give you everything that you wanted," I murmured.

"You will. I know you will."

We didn't speak after that. I think we both had said enough. I listened to his breathing and heartbeat till it lulled me to sleep.

That night, I didn't dream about the past. I dreamt about the future.

And for the first time…

It terrified me.

CHAPTER 25

Y

I was the first to awake the next morning. I was lying on Sebastian's chest with a leg on top of him and his arms were wrapped around me. I slowly removed myself from him so that I didn't wake him. I changed into sweatpants and a sweater. My head was pounding; I needed coffee with a possible splash of Baileys.

Christian was eating cereal on the kitchen island and there was another bowl of cereal next to him. He poured in milk when he saw me coming.

"I know you like this kind of cereal so I made you breakfast."

I grinned. "Thank you."

I sat down next to him and we ate in silence for a few minutes.

"Do you still have that dog?"

"I do."

"My mom says I've met you before, but all I remember is your dog. Maybe I can meet him again."

"That would be cool."

"My dad looks really happy when you're around."

"You think?"

He nodded. "I know. I'd like to see him more. I miss him a lot."

"He misses you a lot, too."

"Maybe I could come visit him?" he asked, peeking over at me.

"I'm sure that wouldn't be a problem."

"I could see your dog again, too."

"Definitely."

He bit the corner of his lip. "Maybe we could hang out or something. You know, whatever." He shrugged.

"I'd like that."

"Okay."

He grabbed our empty bowls and cleaned them out in the sink. He dried them and then put them away and walked back over to me.

He looked down at his feet. "You want to go play PS3 or something?"

"I don't really know how to play."

He looked up. "It's okay, I can teach you. We'll just start from the beginning," he added.

For some reason, I knew that meant more than just the game.

We were playing for about an hour when Sebastian walked in. The look on his face was priceless and I winked at him.

"Hey, Dad, I taught Ysabelle how to play Black Ops, she's pretty good for a girl."

"Oh yeah?"

"You want to play, Dad? I could set up another player."

"I'd love to play."

He came up behind me and kissed my cheek, taking a seat right in the middle of us and I put my legs on his lap.

We spent the New Year playing Black Ops and made love later that night. The next day, we went home.

S

Two more months went by. We never talked about New Years Eve again. We both jumped back into work when we came home and everything returned to the way it was.

I was on the phone when she walked inside.

"Yeah, Jen, I really appreciate you holding onto it this long. I should have called you sooner, but I think we're going to pass on the house."

She was pretending to look through the mail, but she was really eavesdropping.

"Yeah, I understand, it's a hell of a deal. It's not the right time for us."

I could see her mind spinning as she stirred from foot to foot and then she started to bite her nail on her thumb.

"Yeah…no, it's fine. Maybe next time and don't worry you'll be the first—"

"Tell her you'll call her back," she interrupted. "And tell her not to do anything yet."

My eyebrows lowered as I spoke into the phone. "Jen, let me give you a call back and don't do anything yet. Okay, bye."

"Was that about the house?" she immediately asked.

"Yeah."

"Were you telling her to put it back on the market?"

"Yes."

"Why?"

I laughed. "What do you mean why?"

"I thought you wanted the house?"

"I do."

"Then why are you asking her to put it back on the market?"

I arched an eyebrow. "Ysa, why are you asking me this? It was never my decision, it was yours."

She nodded. "I didn't tell you I didn't want the house."

"You also didn't tell me you did."

Her eyes wandered all around the room and then back at me. "I want the house," she simply stated.

"You do?" I questioned, caught completely off guard.

"I think so…but I want both of us to buy it, together."

"Ysa, it was my gift to you for Christmas. Your name will be on the title, it will be our home. I'd like to buy it for us."

"Well…I'd like to help. I mean we've been living together for ten months now. This place was completely paid for so we didn't have to discuss bills and stuff. Maybe we should do that."

"Okay…"

She sat down on the other couch with nervousness and anxiety radiating off of her.

"I don't think this needs to be said, but I'm going to say it anyway. We both have a lot of money. I mean, I have more money than I know what to do with. I'd like to invest in the house as well. They're asking three million dollars and we could split that and not have a mortgage. The bills could be split evenly as well."

"I don't know how I feel about that. I want to take care of you."

She sighed. "I really appreciate that. Honestly I do. But I don't need you to take care of me, at least not in that way. I would feel like a freeloader or something if you paid for everything, and I don't like that. I want us to go into this together, I'm not saying I want a joint bank account; your money is your money and so is mine. Though we can have an account that we each deposit money into every month to cover our bills."

My eyebrows leaned in together and my mouth curved.

"I know what you're thinking and it's not because I don't trust you or anything like that. I've given you a lot of me. I pride myself in being financially stable. I never had been growing up and I can't give that up. So please don't ask me to. We're partners. Buying a house together makes me feel like I'm bringing something to the table and so are you. Can you give me this?"

As much as I wanted to fight her on it, I couldn't. I had won half the battle and it was going to have to be good enough. For now.

I reluctantly nodded and she tackled me, wrapping her entire body around mine.

"I love you! Ahhhhh! We just bought a house! Call her."

I called her and she told us to meet her at the house to go over everything and to bring our checkbooks. We signed all the paperwork and we each wrote her a huge fucking check. She handed over the keys and said she would bring the title, along with the rest of the paperwork in a few days. We hugged her goodbye and walked her out.

The house was officially ours.

Y

"Now what?" I goaded, spreading my legs on the stairs.

"I have something in mind. Get up," he demanded.

I arched an eyebrow. "Why?"

He pulled me into his lap, my back to his front. "If you won't move then I'll do it for you." He bit my shoulder. Hard.

"Ow! What was that for?"

He softly kissed the bite mark, not saying a word, and placed a few more kisses along my shoulder blades. Then he bit me again. Hard.

"Ow! What are you doing?" I asked, trying to move away, but he held me firmer.

I could feel him smiling, though he still didn't say anything. He repeated the process a few more times, leaving bite marks from one shoulder to the other and then tenderly kissed every last one, trailing kisses back up to my ear.

"My girl."

I smiled and nodded.

"You know what I want?"

"Hmmm..."

"I want to fuck you on these stairs. I don't want to be soft or tender, I don't even want to be sweet."

I looked back at him and he kissed along my jawline.

"You want to know why?"

"Yes," I breathed out.

He grinned as his hands reached around to remove my dress. He tossed it aside and I was left in nothing but panties. He kneaded my breasts and my head fell back on his shoulder.

"Where are you right now?" he asked with a certain desire and edge to his tone.

"Home," I instantly replied.

"Where am I?"

I peeked over at him, knowing what he wanted. "Home."

"And where are we?"

"We're home, Sebastian, our place, together."

He smiled and slapped the side of my breast. I whimpered in pleasure as his nails started raking up and down my torso until he dug his thumbs in the sides of my panties. I leaned back onto his body and he slid them down, I kicked them off when they reached my ankles.

I rocked my hips on his hard-on and he jerked my head back by my hair.

"Are you wet?" he murmured into my ear.

I moaned in response and rested my hands on his thighs to open my legs further, provoking him to check. He took my silent plea and his fingers crept to my clit.

I cunningly smiled.

"You're always so fucking wet," he groaned into my neck.

He alternated using his palm and fingers to manipulate my nub and I moved my hips in the opposite direction that he stimulated. My clit was overly exposed from the angle and it didn't take long for my wetness to pool.

"That feel good, Ysa?"

There was something animalistic in his voice that I had never heard before. I sucked in my lower lip and he let up on my hair, opting to grab the back of my neck instead and geared me sideways into his lap. We were face-to-face now and the expression on his face was primal. When his fingers slipped into my opening, my head wanted to fall back, but he wouldn't allow it. He held me firm in place, where he could watch my face come apart. He finger fucked my g-spot like a man possessed and on a mission to prove something.

My mouth parted, my breathing escalated, and when my eyes started to roll to the back of my head, he yanked my neck forward so that they would stay open.

"Jesus…Sebastian…please let me come…please," I begged.

"Pull out my cock," he demanded and I did.

He sat me on his dick before I even saw it coming, and he effortlessly thrust up while I slid down his shaft in one plunge. I came on the spot. My body trembled and my come dripped down his balls. He didn't give me any time to recover as he turned our bodies so that we were closer to the railing, and I grabbed a spindle to support my weight.

"Lean forward," he huskily ordered.

I did as I was told and he gripped my hips. Hard. I knew there would be markings all over my body when he was done having his way with me. He forcefully and urgently made me bounce on his cock as he slammed into me with his own movements.

"I'm climaxing so hard, your dick feels fucking amazing."

He growled and clutched my hips harder, standing us up.

"Jesus…Sebastian, what's gotten into you?" I panted, trying to find my bearings.

He put one of my legs on the other railing and leaned my body forward on the other. I started to shake from the awkward angle.

"I got you, you're not going to fall," he stated, reading my body.

I nodded and he swiftly thrust back inside me.

"Fuck…" we said in unison.

He stood sideways in between my legs, slamming in and out of me, holding my hips and body weight the entire time. My noises grew louder and louder the closer I got to release.

"Oh my God, Sebastian, I am going to come so hard. Please…please…please…make me come."

He fucked me harder and faster, mercilessly pounding into me.

"That's it…squeeze my cock with your tight pussy that I can't get enough of. Fuck…you're pulsating, so tight."

The slapping sound of our skin-on-skin contact echoed in the room.

"Yes…yes…yes…" My body shuddered and I almost lost my balance from my intense and overpowering orgasm.

He didn't stop, his hands moved to my shoulders and he continued to slam into me. I tried to keep his pace, barely done with one release and another hit.

"Fuck yes...do it, do it, do it," he urged. "Keep coming on my cock." I fell forward, clenching onto his cock and he made this roaring sound as we came together.

We both panted profusely, trying to catch our bearings and he kissed all over my face, not removing himself from deep inside me.

"Are you okay? Did I hurt you?"

"I'm fine…I'm fine…" I repeated, looking up at him.

"Welcome home, Ysa."

And he had just fucked me like he meant it.

CHAPTER 26

Y

It didn't take long for us to move in since we decided to keep my place above the bar as it was, just in case we wanted to stay there for whatever reason. All we had to move were clothes and stuff like that. We ordered everything online together and our style was Caribbean chic. It took two weeks for everything to be delivered and then another week to get it all situated, it had been three weeks since it was ours. I had never decorated a house before, and there was 4,500 square feet. That didn't include the lanai.

"Are you really moving that again?" he asked.

"I don't know. Do you think it looked better where it was before?"

"Yeah, I do, considering there's already holes in the wall where it was."

I narrowed my eyes.

"Kidding…put it wherever it makes you happy."

"Sebastian," I said, stomping my foot.

"Ysabelle," he mocked, stomping his foot.

"You haven't helped at all and every time I ask you for your opinion you don't care."

He smiled. "You're right, I don't."

I glared at him.

"Ysa, I have a dick, which means I don't give a fuck where anything goes. Do what makes you happy."

I placed my hands on my hips. "That's stupid! And makes no sense."

"Listen, feisty woman. Unless you want me to make you come on the painting, then I don't care."

"All you ever think about is sex. I can't even get a straight answer from you for five minutes because you just want to get your dick wet."

"I didn't hear you complaining this morning and again this afternoon," he shouted, walking away from me.

Damn him.

"That's because you keep making me have sex with you everywhere!" I yelled back.

He was adamant on us christening every corner. I'm not kidding.

Who has sex in a pantry?

We do.

S

Julia's number appeared on my cell phone.

"Hello," I answered.

"Hey, how are you?"

"Great, we're about settled. Ysabelle might be going crazy, though."

She laughed. "She's nesting, Sebastian, it's what we do."

"Mmm hmm…so much fun. How are you?"

"I'm good. Christian's spring break is coming up."

"Wow, I can't believe it's already almost into April."

"I know; can you believe you've been there for almost eleven months?"

"Time flies. Are you planning anything for spring break?"

"I am. That's why I'm calling. What do you think about us coming to visit for spring break? I can take some time off and so can Anthony. Christian won't stop talking about your boat."

I laughed. "Yeah, he's been like that on Skype, too. Let me talk to Ysabelle and see what she thinks and I'll get back to you."

"Okay, sounds perfect. Let me know ASAP because I have to let my partners know and Anthony needs to request the time off as well."

"No problem. Talk soon, bye."

I found Ysabelle in the exact same place I had left her, except this time she had down another damn painting.

"Have you come out of hiding so you can help me?" she asked, half-serious.

"Not at all. I just talked to Julia."

I saw her tense immediately.

"Christian's spring break is coming up."

"Okay."

"She wants to come and visit."

"Oh."

"With Anthony," I added.

She relaxed but still seemed cautious.

"What do you think about that?"

"Umm…yeah…I guess that would be okay. I mean, we're going to have to be in each others lives, might as well start now, right?"

I smiled that she reflected that much into it.

"I agree."

"When is spring break?"

"Two weeks."

"Wow. Soon."

I nodded. I could tell that a lot was weighing on her mind. I wanted to ask her, but I knew I wouldn't get the answers I sought. I was profusely in love with the woman in front of me and I wanted so badly for her to let me in. We were coming up on our year anniversary of me finding her and still no change.

Would she ever let her guard down? Was this who she is? Will there ever be a change?

"Where are they going to stay?" she asked out of nowhere, catching me by surprise and taking me away from my thoughts.

I shrugged. "I don't know. I'm assuming a hotel."

I could see her mind reeling, like she was debating on whether or not she should say what she was thinking.

"Maybe they should stay here," she stated, unsure.

My eyes widened in surprise. "Are you sure?"

"No," she nervously chuckled. "But I'm never sure about anything. We have this big house, you know? It would be silly for them to stay somewhere else."

"Ysa, we don't have to do that. We're not responsible for where they decide to stay," I affirmed.

"I know that, but maybe it will do us some good. Maybe I can learn something."

I cocked my head to the side. "Learn something? What are you talking about?"

"Never mind. You're right, they can stay somewhere else." She hastily turned to leave and I grabbed her arm.

"No. Tell me what you meant."

She inhaled. "It's not a big deal."

"Try me."

"I just thought that…that…you know, she knows everything and maybe I could pick up a thing or two. That's all," she whispered, bowing her head.

I grabbed her by the chin to make her look at me. "Are you talking about Julia?"

She frowned. "Yeah. Julia, Sebastian…you know, your ex-wife. She knows everything about you and Christian so I thought it could help me. I could learn how to be a better person or something…I don't fucking know…" she mumbled, shaking her head.

I didn't even know what to say or how to respond to that.

"Please don't look at me like that. I hate it when you look at me like that. This is why I don't like to talk about my feelings and shit because I get that look and it makes me feel weak and out of control and insecure. Everything I fucking hate. That's not who I am or want to be so just drop it. I don't know what I was thinking."

I pulled her to me and she buried her face in my chest.

"Ysa, I have no idea how your mind can even think that. I don't know what it's going to take for you to understand that Julia is not what I want. I want you. Just you. You have this image of her in your mind of this perfect person that she's not. I've known the girl my whole life. Trust me, I know."

"I know you want me and I know you love me," she said into my chest.

I just held her. That was one thing that she would always let me do. I comforted her the only way she would allow. The longer I was with her, the more I learned how truly damaged and broken she was and it just made me hate Madam more. I despised the woman with every last fiber in my body. She was pure evil. Satan in the form of a human being. I should have strangled her to death when I had the chance. It didn't matter—Ysabelle would never go back to her.

At least I knew that much to be true.

Y

I always felt safe in his arms like nothing could hurt me when he was holding me. I knew he loved me, I could never deny that. The longer we were together, the more real things became. We owned a house together now and I knew soon marriage would come up again and then babies. Just the mere thought of it all scared the shit out of me. I didn't know if I even believed in marriage; if it's not broken then why fix it. We were fine as we were, at least for me. I knew Sebastian felt differently and I didn't know how long he would let it slide, giving me time that he desperately thought would change things.

I knew better.

I had slept with endless amounts of married men and they never took their goddamn ring off. They didn't even think twice about. I'm not the marrying kind. I'm not the mothering kind, either. Bringing a child into this world would be the biggest mistake I could ever make. I wasn't maternal. What if I had one just to appease him and I turned into my mother? It would destroy him and he doesn't deserve that. I want to be the woman that he envisions; I just knew the fantasy would not measure up to the reality.

I could never be Julia and I knew somewhere deep inside he craved that, even if he didn't admit it.

So in the meantime, we would continue to play house with a deck of cards and hope it didn't come crumbling down.

CHAPTER 27

Y

They were due to arrive any minute and I was a nervous wreck. I had mentally tried to prepare myself over the last two weeks, but the more I thought about it, the worse it got. I wanted her to like me. How asinine is that? I fucking stole her husband. I was literally the whore that took him away from her. I never once thought about her feelings when I was sleeping with her husband for a year, and here I am hoping that she cares about mine.

I waited in the kitchen and made sure that all the food was perfectly placed on the island. I had my chef prepare some authentic island food and then displayed it nicely for them. I hoped they were hungry. I had spent the last two days cleaning the house from top to bottom and made sure that the guestroom was immaculate. Christian's bedroom was finished and I decked it out with everything he said he liked during Christmas.

When Sebastian suggested to Julia that they stay with us, she jumped right on it. She said she thought it was a great idea and it would give us time to get to know each other and show Christian that we could all be a family. I'm not going to lie, it gave me anxiety that she was being so nice. I couldn't help but be reminded of Madam always saying to keep your friends close and your enemies closer, maybe that's what she was trying to do, or maybe that's what I was trying to do.

I heard the garage door open and I took one last look around, and then at myself in the mirror. I dressed in a maxi dress with some wedges.

"Dad! Wow! Your house is huge!" Christian yelled, walking in with everyone following.

Chance immediately darted toward them, jumping all over Julia's white dress.

Shit!

"Chance!" I scolded. "Get down!"

She waved me off. "Oh no, don't worry about it; we have a dog, too. It's fine."

Christian got down to his level and Chance licked him all over his face, making him laugh.

"I'm sorry, he has no manners. Sebastian's always telling me I need to discipline him more, I guess he's right," I embarrassingly justified.

She kindly smiled at me, and I thought for a second I saw something behind her eyes, but just as fast as it appeared, it was gone.

"Wow! That's a lot of food. It's beautiful, Ysabelle, where did you buy all those serving trays?" she asked, looking it all over.

"I actually got them online. I do a lot of online shopping; it's easier for me. The bar and Sebastian keep me busy."

She nodded. "Oh yes, I remember needy Sebastian."

I raised my eyebrows, feeling somewhat uncomfortable.

"Is this what you guys are going to do the entire time?" Sebastian asked, laughing.

"Awe! Sebby," she sympathized, patting his back and looking back at me. "He's very sensitive. I'm sure you already know that."

I shyly smiled. "Yeah," I lied.

"Can I see my room?" Christian chimed in.

"Of course," I replied. "Come on."

They all followed me toward his room, admiring the house as they went.

"This is really beautiful. Sebastian has finally found someone who loves the water as much as he does. He wanted to decorate our house with all this Caribbean feel."

I smiled, feeling a bit more relaxed.

"This is your room," I announced, standing aside so everyone could walk in.

"Wow! This looks awesome. Dad, you did a great job."

"Actually, bud, this was all Ysabelle."

Julia looked at me with glossy eyes and it surprised me. "Thank you," she said with sincerity.

"It's not a problem. I remember him saying all the stuff he liked in Colorado, I have a good memory."

"You didn't have to do all this. Thank you so much for including Christian in your home."

"Of course," I replied.

"Christian, what do you say?" she scolded.

He walked over to me and smiled. "Thank you."

S

I gave them a tour of the house while Ysabelle got dinner ready. She said she had to warm up some of the food that was brought over earlier.

"This is quite a house you got here, Sebastian," Anthony stated, looking at the water from the lanai. Julia was unpacking in the guestroom.

I handed him a beer.

"Thanks, I can't really take credit for it. Ysabelle picked out the house."

"She has good taste," he said, taking a sip of his beverage.

"She does."

"How do you like living on the island?"

"I love it. It's great. I'm living the dream, you know?"

"Yeah, although I doubt I could ever get Julia to move somewhere like this."

I chuckled. "Good luck with that. I used to have a hard time getting her to go in the water."

"I really admire how you guys are handling this whole co-parenting thing. You know most divorced people fuck everything up for each other. I'm a divorce attorney so I would know."

"Right…Julia had said something about that."

"It's admirable, man, seriously. I respect it."

"I appreciate that. We seem to have a good grasp on it so far. It's been fairly easy. How are you guys doing?"

"Can't complain. She's a great woman."

"She is. You're a lucky man."

I heard someone clear their throat and we turned around to find Ysabelle standing there. She looked sad and I didn't understand why, but she quickly smiled, trying to hide the fact that I noticed it.

"Dinner's ready."

We sat at the table. Ysabelle was being overly quiet and I never wanted to know what she was thinking as badly as I did at that moment.

"Dad, when can you take us out on the boat?"

"Oh my God! If I hear about this boat one more time, Sebby, I'm going to kill myself," Julia dramatically claimed. "That's all he talks about, isn't it Anthony?"

"She's right, he's a bit obsessed."

"He really is your child, he's more and more like you every day. I'm just going to start calling him Baby Sebastian."

"Mom." He rolled his eyes. "I'm not a baby."

"You'll always be my baby." She blew him a kiss. "I'm serious, though; do you remember that thing you used to do when we were kids? You know what I'm talking about, right?"

I snapped my tongue in my mouth, making the sound that used to annoy the hell out of her.

"Yes! That! He does it, Sebastian! I don't know where he would learn it? You haven't done it since Olivia—" She looked right over at Ysabelle and I followed.

The look on her face was unrecognizable. I had never seen it before and it worried me that I couldn't read her.

Where was my girl?

She casually smiled. "You were saying?"

Julia shook her head. "Never mind."

"So, man, tell me about this boat that I keep hearing about?" Anthony asked, clearing the air.

I grabbed her hand under the table and she let me, squeezing it back in reassurance.

Y

"Sebastian, go hang out with the guys, Ysabelle and I can clean up," Julia suggested.

Please don't make me look bad...

"Ysa, you okay with that?" he asked, looking over at me.

Damn it.

"Why wouldn't I be?" I nonchalantly responded.

"See! Go!" she insisted, patting his chest.

Dinner was eye opening to say the least. They shared so much of their lives together, as children and now as adults. It was hard to watch the familiarity of the way they spoke and acted around each other. I thought I knew him pretty well, but I realized that I barely knew anything. She had his past, and in a way, she would have his future, too. Christian tied them together for life, and part of me knew that it wasn't just Christian. There's this history between them that I will never be able to touch or even come close to, realizing that was a brutal awakening. They shared a love for each other that I couldn't begin to understand.

"Ysabelle," she said, taking me away from my thoughts.

"Yeah, I'm sorry, did I zone out?"

She smiled. "Yeah, you okay?"

I nodded, grabbing the plates off the table. "Thanks for helping me clean up, but you don't have to; I can handle it."

"Oh no, I know what it's like to have to clean up by myself."

Of course, you did. You had him first.

"Sebastian tells me that your bar is amazing. That's inspiring that you started it from nothing."

"It wasn't really that hard. Tropical Island, vacation spot, alcohol, food, girls…it brings them in the door."

"Your bar was voted top three places to visit in the Caribbean–that's not nothing."

"Yeah, I guess you're right," I responded, loading the dishwasher.

I was confused when I saw her look under the sink.

"Do you have any cleaning supplies so I can clean off the table?"

"Oh yeah…umm…I keep them in the laundry room…but yeah, I should probably keep them under the sink. It would probably make it easier for cleaning the kitchen."

She smiled. "I'll go get it."

Way to go, Ysabelle, you don't even know where to put cleaning supplies. This is why Sebastian thinks that Anthony is a lucky man.

"Did it take you long to find this house?" she questioned as she wiped down the table.

"It's actually pretty random. His parents were looking at properties and we sort of stumbled upon this house."

"Oh, that's right, Mom did tell me that."

"Your mom?" I asked without thinking.

Her eyes caught mine and she looked like a deer in headlights. "No…I mean Sebastian's mom, I'm just so used to calling her *Mom*. We've been calling each other's parents *Mom* and *Dad* since we were kids. It's silly really." She lowered her gaze to the table, continuing to wipe it down and I returned to loading the dishwasher as if I didn't feel like I just took a bullet. "It's a beautiful house. It must have cost a small fortune."

"It did but we split it so it would have been a lot worse if it was all on him," I informed, wanting her to see that I wasn't a gold digger, that I had my own money.

"Oh…and Sebastian was okay with that?"

"What do you mean?"

"He's just always been the provider and he takes that role really seriously."

Fuck…was I wanting to buy the house together making him feel like he wasn't a man? Had I fucked that up, too?

"I'm just surprised is all…not that it's a bad thing or anything. I'm not saying that at all," she mumbled and it was the first time I saw her nervous. "I mean…I think it's awesome that you're an independent woman. Sebby definitely needs a woman like that."

"Why do you call him Sebby?" I asked, trying to change the subject.

She laughed. "Our parents said I couldn't pronounce Sebastian when we were babies. I started calling him that and it's just stuck. I should probably stop doing that. He hates it."

"You guys have shared so much of your lives together."

She nodded. "We have. He's a good man, Ysabelle. You're very lucky to have found each other."

I couldn't tell if she was being sincere, but it didn't stop me from hoping that she was.

CHAPTER 28

S

Three days went by and I took everyone out on the boat. We had spent the last couple of days sightseeing. Christian was in love with the island; he said he wanted to move there when he was eighteen and be my co-captain. Anthony was a nice guy; I sensed he was in love with Julia and I think she was, too. They looked happy. I didn't remember the last time I had seen her so content, she was usually all over the place when we were married. She looked like she had slowed down and started to enjoy life and it made me wonder what she learned out of our time together, and out of our divorce. I wondered if it was similar to what I had.

Ysabelle remained distant and with each day, it seemed to be getting worse. She talked less and interacted fewer. I could see that Julia was trying to make her feel comfortable, but she was too stuck in her own head to notice it. I thought the trip would have made them closer or even us closer and now I feared it was the exact opposite. I wanted to make everything better and I knew that there wasn't anything I could do to accomplish that. At some point, I knew we would have to discuss everything, but I didn't want to do it with them being in the house. There was enough tension on her behalf and I didn't want to add to it.

It was a beautiful day outside and the weather was perfect; there were no waves, just solid flat surface. Ysabelle was laying out on the bow and I think she fell asleep. I watched her beautiful hair blow in the wind and her perfect figure get darker by the minute. I was so in love with her I couldn't see straight. I wanted to make her my wife, to have her take my last name. As a man, we have this primitive desire to claim what's ours and part of me felt like I wouldn't truly have all of her until we were married.

The urge to want to see her belly grow with my child grew with each passing day as well. I wanted nothing more than to have a family with her and to be husband and wife. I wanted to look deep into her gorgeous green eyes that showed me the world and say my vows that I felt so deeply in my soul. I thought when I found my way back to her that it was going to be enough, that if I gave her time, she would see everything that I hold so strongly in my heart.

She hasn't.

I was starting to think that she never would. She was blinded by whatever demons she couldn't surpass and I couldn't help her. I never could. The mere thought of it could almost destroy me, but I'd pick myself back up again. I'd remember that she was in my arms and that was good enough for me. Nothing else mattered when I was holding her. The world stopped moving and time paused. It was just us.

She stirred and then looked over at me with her pouty sleepy face.

My girl.

I would give you the world if you would let me.

I had taken them to a private island Ysabelle and I frequented. We decided to grill out and spend the day relaxing under the sun in seclusion.

"Dad! You want to throw around the ball?"

"Of course!"

"I'm in, Anthony fell asleep," Julia said, standing up and brushing off sand.

"Ysa?"

"No, I'm okay," she responded.

We spent the next hour throwing around the ball.

Y

I pretended to be reading, but I couldn't tear my eyes away from the scene before me. It was like a car accident that I knew I needed to look away from because it was going to cause me pain, but I couldn't help myself. My eyes were glued to the image before me. I stared at the family that was in front of me. They looked perfect together, playing with the son that they both adored and were devoted to.

How could I have destroyed something so beautiful?

They fit flawlessly. It brought back the memory of when I saw them at the dog park. The day my world and illusions came tumbling down on me like a ton of fucking bricks, suffocating me and making it hard to breathe.

Had I ever really resurfaced?

I could still feel the love and devotion as much as I did that day. It radiated off of them. The easiness of how they worked together was blowing in the wind and I was inhaling it into my bloodstream. They laughed, smiled, and played like they had been doing it their entire lives, and the truth was, they had. They shared a life before me and they would share one after me. I was the odd man out in this equation.

The way Julia catered to Christian, the way she knew each and every mannerism, how it effortlessly came to her, like she was born to be a mother. I knew in that moment that it would never be me. I took care of myself since I was a child, my mother stripped away every last shred of my innocence the second I was born. I hated her. I was raped and my virginity was stolen from me because she wanted more money.

Who the fuck does that?

Someone's whose blood runs through my veins.

I felt all the color drain from my face when Christian fumbled the ball and Sebastian and Julia tackled him. They rolled around in the sand and Sebastian picked Christian up, throwing him over his shoulder as Julia ran behind, holding on to his arms. They were cheering and singing. They were the family that I always dreamed about.

I was not a good person.

I ruined Christian's life, the life that I so badly wanted when I was a child. I needed to get my shit together before I started to cry.

When did I turn into this weak woman?

Who am I?

M

"I need the job done within the next few weeks. It needs to look like an accident," I ordered.

"Madam, with all due respect, do you have any idea what you're asking? How dangerous it could be?"

"Pablo, did I ask for your opinion?"

He shook his head no.

"I didn't think so. Now, either you get the job done or I'll find someone who will."

"Madam, we have known each other for decades now. What would possess you to want to fake an attack that could get you killed?"

"It's none of your fucking business. And, am I paying you to think? No. You're getting paid so that I don't have to worry about dying. If something happens to me, guess whom it will fall on? Any guesses? Here I'll give you a hint, he's standing in this room and he's acting like a pussy."

He stood up straighter. "How bad does it have to be?"

"You have to almost kill me." I sat back in my chair and crossed one leg over the other. "Trust me, darling, I will be high as a fucking kite, I won't feel a thing." I smiled.

"Jesus, Madam, have you lost your goddamn mind?"

"I think you need to remember whom you're talking to. Where are your fucking manners? I'm a lady," I said, placing my hand on my chest. "Now, get the fuck out of my office. You have two weeks."

The time has come.

Mine.

Tick tock.

S

"Come here," I groaned, grabbing her around the waist and placing her in front of my body. We were lying sideways in bed and I wrapped my entire body around her. I loved feeling her petite frame under me.

"You've been so quiet these last few days. What's up?" I asked, nuzzling the back of her neck.

"Nothing, I'm fine," she argued, kissing my arms around her shoulders.

"I find it interesting that you still don't think I know when you're bullshitting me."

"And I think it's hilarious that you still call me out on it when you know I don't want to talk about it."

"What if I turn off the lights? Hmmm...we'll lay here and just see what happens. Want to try that?"

She shrugged and I took it as a yes. I turned everything off and saw her faint shadow as I wrapped myself around her again. We laid there in comfortable silence and after a while, I thought she had fallen asleep and I closed my eyes.

"Sebastian," she whispered.

"Mmmm..."

"Are you sleeping?"

"No."

"Are you tired?"

"No."

"Tell me the best memory you have."

I smiled, opening my eyes. "I have a lot of great memories."

"Give me the best memory you have from childhood."

"Why?"

"Just tell me."

"Okay," I sighed. "When I was...I want to say nine, I think, my dad was always working and never went to any of my baseball games, my mom was always there, though. All the players on the team had their dads at every game and I said something to my mom about it. Later that night, I heard shouting coming from their bedroom. It was the first time I ever heard them fighting. At the next game, I remember looking up in the stands to wave to my mom, like I did every game, and my dad was there. Sitting right by my mom with the biggest smile on his face. After that, he was there for every game, never missed one again."

"That's an awesome memory," she murmured.

"Yeah...I learned that day that men will do anything when they love someone, and behind every great man, there's a strong woman."

She took a deep breath. "I don't have a best memory from childhood. At least I don't remember any...I used to pretend that I had this perfect family somewhere in the world and that they were looking for me. That my mom had stolen me from someone and that one day, they were going to find me and take me away from her."

"Ysa…" I coaxed.

She restlessly chuckled. "You have a really nice family. You, Julia, and Christian were everything I wanted as a kid. Christian's really lucky. Julia is an amazing mom. You can tell that she was born to be one."

I didn't know what to say. I knew she was physically there with me but emotionally and mentally she was somewhere else entirely.

"My Mom used to have sex all around the house. I learned what sex was when I was…fuck…six maybe. I can't tell you how many times I accidentally caught her fucking some random and she never stopped. They just kept going. She gave me a doll once and I loved it so much. It was the only thing she ever gave me." She paused, her voice started breaking.

I held her tighter and kissed her shoulder repetitively. As much as I hated hearing about her childhood and her piece of shit mother, I wanted her to tell me everything. It's not healthy for anyone to hold that all in and I knew that she was telling me something she had never told a soul.

She cleared her throat and sniffled. "I had done something at school, I don't even remember what it was, but she was pissed when I got home. She took my doll and burned her right in front of me. She said it was my punishment for being a bad girl." She shook her head, trying to push away the image I was sure. "It was the only toy I ever had. I fucking hated her after that. How do you hate your mom when you're seven years old?"

"Ysa, she was never a mom. Not one day," I reassured her, hoping she believed me.

"She's the woman that gave me life. I wouldn't be lying here with you without her. I think that makes her pretty important."

"That's the easy part. She didn't raise you."

"Yeah…" she pondered. "What's your worst memory from childhood?"

Fuck.

"Ysa, I don't want to talk about this anymore."

"You don't have to. You just answered it. It's when Olivia died, isn't it?"

I nodded.

She looked like she was contemplating what to say next.

"Mine was being raped," she blurted, like she was telling me about the weather. "For the longest time, I thought about what I could have done differently. I didn't do anything…I laid there and let him do whatever he wanted to. I didn't make a sound, I didn't move, nothing. I made it easy for him," she choked. "It makes me sick to my stomach to even think about…but maybe the reason I didn't react was because subconsciously I liked it? The apple doesn't fall far from the tree, Sebastian. I grew up to be a whore, too. I did it with class, so to speak, but it doesn't change the fact that I grew up to be like her. Like mother like daughter."

I immediately pulled away and she fell to her back. I hovered above her and by the look on her face, I might have scared her.

"Listen to me, I will only say this once. You are NOTHING like her. Don't you ever compare yourself to that vile excuse for a human being again. Fucking animals are better mothers to their offspring than she was to you. She took away your innocence and made you believe it was your fault, Ysa, that's fucking sick. I would kill her if I knew it would take away all these thoughts that you think are so true."

Her eyes widened.

"She's a waste of air. A piece of garbage has more sustenance than she does. You know how to love, Ysa. She doesn't know the meaning of the word. You would never be anything like that to our children. It doesn't matter that she gave you life–that's all she fucking did for you. And it was for pure selfishness. You're a good person in your heart, mind, body, and soul; I know that."

I caressed her cheek. "Baby, you gotta believe that. Please tell me you know that?"

Her eyes veered for one split second, but I saw it.

"I do."

And she boldfaced lied to me.

CHAPTER 29

Y

I didn't sleep at all that night. I hadn't been sleeping for days and I was exhausted. My body felt rundown. I had been thinking a lot about Madam. She was the only woman that has ever taken care of me. A mother figure. Where would I have been if I hadn't met her? Would I have stayed at the bar with Devon?

If I had stayed with VIP, would I still be feeling like I am? I was perfectly fine before Sebastian; I didn't have a care in the world. I loved what I did. As I lay there with his arms securely wrapped around me, I felt safe. He was home to me. I loved him so much that sometimes it hurt to breathe. I think about him all the time. I wanted to make him happy.

But how can something that started off so wrong become something that is so right? It can't. It's already tainted. Did I deserve a happily ever after?

My life had always been a giant puzzle, where I would find different pieces scattered here and there. I thought when I left VIP, I had finally found the last piece. I was complete. Then Sebastian found me and I started to think that the pieces weren't in the right places so I tried to move them around, desperately wanting them to fit somewhere. Except now, I couldn't place them together; the angles were all wrong and they weren't connecting. They're not staying. I'm once again, incomplete.

I thought I needed control and power and that's what led me to VIP. I left because I wanted more out of life. Almost three years later, and I'm more lost than I was when I left. I have turned into a person I didn't recognize anymore. I'm weak, I'm scared, I'm confused.

I thought love was supposed to be easy?

We had spent the next few days relaxing and I watched their interactions like a hawk. The more time I spent with them, the clearer it became. It was Saturday and they left the next morning. I had my chef prepare a five-course meal and I reserved one of the best tables at Chances for us.

"Ysabelle! This is amazing. The food, oh my God, I have definitely gained five pounds off this meal. So worth it!" Julia praised.

"Thank you."

We spent the rest of the night drinking, dancing and trying to have them enjoy their last night on the island. Christian went upstairs to our old place because it was getting late and he was tired. We hung out for a few more hours and it was starting to get late so Julia went to go get Christian and Sebastian went with her to let her in. I stayed with Anthony.

"Thanks for your hospitality while we've been here, Ysabelle, it was really nice of you."

I smiled. "It's not a problem."

"Do you still talk to Madam?" he asked, catching me completely off guard.

I arched an eyebrow. "You do recognize me," I stated.

"I do. Julia also told me about your history."

"Oh. Umm…to answer your question, I do. Sometimes."

"I remember you being a lot different."

"What do you mean?"

"No offense, but you seemed more alive back then. I'm not saying you don't look happy because you do. I mean, it's obvious you guys are crazy about each other."

"We are."

"I assume it would be hard to live a normal life after what you've already experienced."

"Yeah…I guess…maybe." I smiled. "I'm going to go check on them."

He nodded.

I walked up the stairs, trying not to think about our conversation. The door was slightly ajar and I peeked in. They were sitting on the couch, both their backs to me. Christian's head was on Julia's lap and she was playing with his hair.

"I really like Anthony," he said. "He seems like a nice guy."

"He is." She hesitated. "I'm in love with him."

"That's awesome."

"I think he's going to ask me to marry him, Sebastian."

"Wow. Congratulations. I'm so happy for you."

"I know. I can't wait. I want to marry him and have more kids. I'm not getting any younger and I would like to have at least two more."

He nodded.

"What's wrong?" she asked.

My heart was beating out of my chest.

"I can't help but think about Ysabelle. I mean, here you are talking about getting married and having more kids and I am dying for the same thing."

"Oh my God! That's amazing. Why would that make you sad?"

"I asked Ysabelle to marry me on New Years Eve."

"What? You're engaged?"

"No. Christian caught us and it was pure chaos. I'm surprised he didn't tell you."

"Not at all. He told me he had a great time."

"That's good."

"So what happened?"

"Well…I asked her to marry me and for a second, I thought she was going to say yes, but then Christian interrupted; it was a disaster, I had to chase after him."

"Oh my God, I'm so sorry."

"Yeah. I found her after and she was packing to leave. She had a complete meltdown and to be honest, things haven't been the same since. I don't think she's ever going to want to get married and have kids."

"You don't know that, maybe she needs more time."

My heart was breaking to hear his admission.

"Julia, the more I learn about her…" He shook his head. "She's so broken and I want to put her back together, but I don't think I will ever be able to. I can't help her when she doesn't even know what she needs."

"But you're what she wants, Sebby. That's huge."

"I know. I'll take her any way I can."

"But…"

"I can't believe I'm going to say this." He took a deep breath and I swear I was holding mine.

"I've lived my life for everyone else, Julia, you know that. Ysabelle was the first selfish thing I ever did. I love her. I've never loved anyone the way I love her. I know she's my soul mate."

I smiled at his words.

"But I would be lying if part of me isn't terrified that she won't ever want to get married and have a family, that I will be sacrificing myself for someone else again and that I will resent her."

My hand immediately went to my chest and I swear on everything that is holy, I couldn't fucking breathe. The air from my lungs had literally been sucked out of me and my heart was shattering, breaking with shards of glass that were etching their way out of my skin and leaving scars in their wake. Wounds that would never be able to heal. The blood drained from my face and tears came pouring down. I needed to get the fuck out of there. I went into the bathroom and composed myself as best as I could. I told Anthony that I had an awful headache and needed to leave. I got back to the house and stood in the foyer, looking at everything around me. The life I was building, the future, my happiness. The house of cards came tumbling down and I fell to the ground with it, bawling my eyes out with the truth that I tried to ignore.

It finally slapped me in the face.

I just never thought it would be by Sebastian's hand.

S

"But you're what she wants, Sebby. That's huge."

"I know. I'll take her any way I can."

I know in my heart that I'll love her forever.

"But…"

Maybe if I say it…if I let the fear free, then it will no longer haunt me.

"I can't believe I'm going to say this." I took a deep breath, trying to build up the courage. "I've lived my life for everyone else, Julia, you know that. Ysabelle was the first selfish thing I ever did. I love her. I've never loved anyone the way I love her. I know she's my soul mate."

She's all that and more. Words can't explain what she means to me.

"But I would be lying if part of me isn't terrified that she won't ever want to get married and have a family, that I will be sacrificing myself for someone else again and that I will resent her."

"Oh, Sebby," she sympathized. "I don't think that's true at all. Your love for each other can surpass anything."

"I know. Julia, she had the worst upbringing. The things she went through no child should ever experience."

She frowned.

"I know I have to be patient. I'll take her any way I can. I couldn't live without her, I've tried."

"I understand."

"The way she sees herself is mind blowing to me. She would be a great mom, and I already feel married in my heart. I think it's more about the fact that I want her to let me in and I know what it's like to have a child with someone. I want that bond with her. That connection that you created life together and no one can take it away from you."

"Do you think you're going to lose her?"

"No. I'd fight for her."

"Then that's all that matters."

Anthony was talking to some locals when we came back down. I held a sleeping Christian in my arms. He told us that Ysabelle said she had a headache and went home. I would have gone home with her; I called her cell phone, but she didn't answer. It took us a while to get a cab and all the lights were off when we got back to the house. I placed Christian in his bed and said goodnight to Julia and Anthony. The room was dark and I saw her sleeping form under the covers. I took a quick rinse and changed into some gym shorts. I didn't want to wake her. I put my arms around her and she didn't stir.

I swear that I heard her say, "I'm sorry," right before I fell asleep.

CHAPTER 30

S

It was our year anniversary and I had planned a romantic dinner at the house. Ysabelle hadn't been feeling well for a few days and went to the doctor that morning. She called to tell me it was stress related and that she was going to go check on a few things at the bar and would be home for dinner. I knew she was emotionally spent. She had been distant and withdrawn since Julia left. She was pulling away from me more and more every day. I gave her space, hoping that it was the right decision. I didn't want to push her, knowing that it wouldn't work—it'd only make it worse. I wanted to make it a special evening for her. I prepared all her favorite foods and bought the most expensive bottle of champagne I could find.

Chance started barking when he heard the garage door open.

"Hey, Chance, how's my boy?" she greeted, scratching his head. "Wow! What's all this?" she asked looking at the dining room table.

"Come here," I said, pulling her to me. "You never let me hold you anymore, unless we're in bed."

She snuggled into my chest and it was the first time since Julia left that I actually felt her. She embraced me the way she used to, like she didn't want to let me go.

"You okay?" I asked, kissing the top of her head.

"Mmm hmm…"

"I told you I wanted to spoil you tonight for our anniversary."

"Oh yes, I remember."

We ate dinner, laughed and talked. It was great, but there was something behind her eyes that had been there since they left. She hid it well, although I could tell.

"Do you want your gift?"

She rolled her eyes and smiled. "Of course."

God I missed that smile.

I left to go grab her gift and when I came back, there was a wrapped present for me on the table.

I handed it to her. "You first."

She opened it and gasped. "Oh my God, Sebastian."

It was a white gold Cartier bracelet and I had our initials engraved on it.

"The salesman told me there's a story behind these bracelets, you're supposed to give them to someone that you want to be with forever. Once it's locked and screwed in place, your love is eternal."

She looked up at me with glossy eyes. "Thank you."

"Here let me help you put it on." I grabbed her wrist and put in place. "Gorgeous."

She smiled.

"Open yours."

I opened it and it was a Rolex silver vintage watch.

"I bought it for you when we were in Miami. The salesman said that antique watches are supposed to be timeless pieces and given to someone that is forever. Endless."

"Thank you, Ysa, I love it." I put it on. "I guess we had a theme without even knowing it, huh?"

"Looks like it."

I kissed her.

"You did all this, I'll clean up."

I nodded. I wanted to prepare for her next surprise. I finished as I heard her calling out my name down the hallway.

"Sebastian, where did you—" she broke in, walking into our bedroom.

The whole room was lit with candles and there were rose petals all over the place and on the bed.

"Wow, it's like a book scene in here," she added.

"Happy anniversary, Ysa."

"You're going to make me cry."

"Come here."

"Sebastian, let me go change and put on lingerie."

"I don't care about any of that. I want you. Come here."

She walked over to me and stood in between my legs, I was sitting on the edge of the bed, looking up at her.

She gazed down at me with a look I couldn't quite read.

"You're so beautiful. Do you have any idea how beautiful you are?"

She shyly smiled and slid the straps of her dress down her body, leaving her bare with just panties. She attentively watched as I grabbed the edge of her panties to bring her closer to me. I leaned forward and kissed her navel and she sucked in a deep breath, her body trembled as I kissed all around her abdomen. I tried to ignore the prevailing thoughts of wanting to see her pregnant, but as I continued to caress her stomach, I closed my eyes and let my mind wander to what it would be like kissing my child through her growing belly. The child that I put there, the one that we made out of our love.

Her breathing became erratic as I continued to fantasize about a future that appeared to be further away each day. I looked up to her closed eyes and there were a few tears flowing down her face.

Ysa," I coaxed. "What's wrong?"

She slowly opened her eyes with a huge smile on her face. "Nothing. They're happy tears."

She lowered herself to the floor before I could give it any more thought and stared into my eyes; there was so much emotion behind her expression it was hard to follow. I was always in tune with what her eyes shared with me, but in that second, they were indescribable. It was like she was torn with what she was feeling, her mind was spiraling out of control and it was wreaking havoc on her soul. I could actually feel the pained glare on her face. It was a window to what was happening in her mind.

It was more than I could have ever imagined, she had never looked at me like that before. When her delicate fingers caressed the sides of my face, it was as if she was making a memory. I was at a loss for words.

"Sebastian, stop thinking. Just feel, just be with me," she whispered, sensing my apprehension.

She reached for the hem of my shirt and pulled it off. I watched as she started tracing the outline of my bare chest and around my heart that beat just for her. She smiled, reading my thoughts I was sure. Her fingers crept toward my shorts to unbutton them and pull them down with my boxers. My hard cock sprang lose. I held in a breath when she licked along the tip and then her warm lips took me in. She gilded them in a slow, torturous rhythm, taking me deep and then back out. Her eyes never left mine as I closely observed her making love to me with her mouth.

I grabbed her hair by the nook of her neck and brought her lips up to meet mine. I pecked her at first; teasing her with the tip of my tongue along the outline of her perfect, pouty mouth that was slightly swollen from sucking my cock. Her tongue sought mine and our kiss quickly turned passionate, moving on its own accord and taking what the other needed. There was something agonizing about the way we were kissing each other, it was urgent and demanding and all-consuming. We both couldn't get enough of each other and wanted more. Wanted everything.

I carried her up my body, never breaking our kiss, our connection. I gently laid her down onto the bed and placed myself on top of her. She roughly grabbed the back of my neck, bringing me closer, wanting to make us one person and kissing me like her life depended on it. My fingers ran against her cheek and then down to her breasts, as I caressed them lightly, grazing my fingers around her nipples and then along the cup, all while I kept my other hand firmly in place behind her neck.

"Sebastian," she moaned, in a voice I didn't recognize.

Our bodies moved like they were made for each other, nothing ever compared or even came close to when we made love. I knew that's what she wanted. Ysabelle wasn't a making love kind of woman; it didn't matter because it always felt like we were, even when the act was rough. There was something about her in that moment that wanted me to go slow; she wanted to feel like I owned her body, mind, and soul. She wanted to feel safe and worshiped; I gladly distributed it to her, but her body was also burning with a longing for something else that I couldn't identify.

I could feel her rapid beating heartbeat on my chest and I placed my hand on it and she dotingly opened her eyes.

My girl.

The devotion, commitment, love, and adoration were spilling out of her dilated, intensely piercing green eyes that always showed me the world. It was glowing out of her and engraving itself into my heart, right where it belonged. I hadn't seen it in such a long time and I was literally fucking shattering.

Mine.

"I love you, please don't ever think that I don't love you. I didn't know the meaning of the word until I met you. You will *always* own every part of me. It's yours," she expressed with lust and sincerity.

"My girl."

"Yours. Always yours," she reaffirmed.

I tenderly kissed all over her face, along her jawline, her forehead, and on the tip of her nose, placing my cock on her clit. I rested my elbows on the sides of her face with my whole body displayed on top of her. I rocked back and forth on the bundle of nerves in a steady motion, grabbing her by the chin to once again claim her mouth. It started off slow, but my movements became urgent and more demanding, her mouth parted and I felt wetness slipping out of her and onto my balls.

Her eyes widened in pleasure. I effortlessly thrust into her in one plunge and her back arched off the bed and I immediately lapped at her neck and breasts, leaving tiny marks all over, I didn't want to move, I wanted to enjoy the sensation of her pussy clamping down on me and of us becoming one. She started to rock her hips and I took her silent plea, gyrating my hips and making her legs spread wider to accommodate me.

"That feel good?" I groaned, making my way back up to her mouth.

"Yes…deeper…harder," she breathed out.

Her arms reached around me and she hugged me against her body, wanting to feel my entire weight on her. I leaned my forehead on hers and I didn't even have to tell her to open her eyes to look at me. They were already opened, looking lively and thriving and full of love for me. Our mouths were parted, still touching and we were both panting profusely, trying to feel each and every sensation of our skin on skin contact. I swear the pounding of our hearts echoed off the walls. I felt myself starting to come apart and Ysabelle was right there with me, waiting to take the mind-blowing dive together. I put all my weight on my right knee and used the other for more momentum to push in and out. She moved her hands to my ass, holding on tightly, making my dick shove deep within her core.

"I love you, I love you, I love you," she continually moaned, climaxing all around my cock and taking me right along with her.

I shook with my release and kissed her passionately until I was hard again and we continued to make love all night.

CHAPTER 31

Y

I awoke the next morning alone. There was a single rose and piece of paper on his pillow.

I have an offshore trip all day. I won't be back till late tonight. I didn't want to wake you. I love you, Ysa.

Sebastian

I grabbed the rose and brought it to my nose, breathing in its splendor and beauty. I took a shower, trying to clear my thoughts and confusion.

Was I really going to do this?

Part of me was relieved that Sebastian was working all day and that I wouldn't have to see him after last night. The night we shared was passionate and powerful; I wished everything could be that easy. Our sex life was never an issue for us, we didn't have to use words and we were able to express our feelings, thoughts, and emotions that we felt through our in sync movements. It was simple.

It was never about love…that was never the problem.

Love was the easy part.

No one tells you about the other stuff that goes along with sharing your life with someone. How much you have to be on the same page to move forward. The future that is now two people becoming one. It's terrifying. People say that opposites attract. We were like a magnet with different kinetic energy that immediately got pulled together with a force that neither of us could understand. It was greater than knowledge or reason. It was meant to be. I didn't doubt that he came into my life for a reason; I was positive that I came into his for another. We completed each other in a way that I couldn't fathom.

There were underlying issues that I didn't take into consideration until now. Things that I knew would never change for me and also for him. I couldn't continue to be selfish and risk the best thing that ever happened to me. It wasn't fair to him. And I knew deep down he was aware of it. He could see it every time he looked at me. I couldn't hide from him.

I never could.

When you love someone, sometimes you just have to let them go. I did that the first time and he came back to me…

Could I do it again?

We built a life together. A home.

How could I walk away from that?

But how could I stay knowing that we both wanted different things? I blatantly heard him say it, *resentment* is not a bitch I wanted to fuck with. I spent the entire morning and afternoon lying on my patio furniture, looking at my bracelet…spinning it around in a circle. The irony was not lost on me.

The sun was setting as I walked back inside and my cell phone rang.

"Hello," I answered.

"Hey, Ysabelle," my hostess from Chances replied.

"Hey, what's up?"

"Nothing, I was waiting for you to send the comps over for tonight's VIP list."

"Oh shit, I completely forgot. I gave the list to Sebastian and he's offshore till late tonight. Let me check if it's in his office. I'll call you back."

"Okay."

I hung up, making my way into his desk. I searched around the first few drawers.

"Got it," I said to myself, holding a bunch of pieces of paper together. I placed the list on the desk and I was about to put the rest of the sheets back where they came from, but there was the back of a picture at the bottom of the drawer and something possessed me to grab it. I flipped it over and it was Olivia. She was sitting in his old bedroom at home.

I had to sit down because I felt like the ground beneath me was shaking and crashing.

Why would he still have a picture of her? And why would he hide it?

It was all too much. It was like one thing after another.

Boom. Boom. Boom.

My cell phone rang and it took me out of my disoriented daze.

"Hello," I responded, in autopilot.

"Bella," she choked.

"Brooke?" I asked, confused. "Are you are all right? What's wrong?"

"Bella, it's Madam. We're in the hospital and she's been badly injured. I don't know what to do and I need you to come home. I need your help with everything. I can't do this on my own. Please, please tell me you'll come home."

Madam hurt? "What? Is she okay?"

"Yes…but the doctors don't know how long it will take for her to recover and VIP can't run itself. I need you to come home and help me. Bella, we owe everything to VIP. We can't let it go down because Madam is helpless. Tell me you are coming home."

What do I do? "Brooke…"

"Please…for me," she whimpered.

I looked down at the photo in my hand and it made the decision for me. "All right. I'll book the next flight out."

"Don't worry about it. I'll have the jet come get you. It should be there by tonight."

"Okay," was all I could reply with.

"And Bella?"

"Yes."

"Are you coming alone?"

I couldn't tear my eyes away from the picture. "Yes."

"Okay, I love you."

"I'll see you soon," I said and hung up.

I didn't know how long I sat there and I barely remembered packing and leaving. It was like I was having an out of body experience.

I came to when the pilot announced, "Welcome to Miami."

S

I knew the second I walked into the house, something was wrong. I grabbed the letter and read it. It was then that I realized last night wasn't about us making love.

It was about her saying goodbye.

M

Men.

You can't live with them; you can't live without them.

Who the fuck does he think he is…telling me he loves me and has left his wife. *Does he take me for a fool?* Love NEVER fucking prevails. It's a myth. Created by women who have nothing better to do than to fantasize about fairy tales, happy endings, prince charming, and the motherfucking Tooth Fairy.

I learned a long a time ago that you depend on one person and one person only.

Yourself.

I had no time to deal with Mika and his avant-garde performance. Ysabelle was coming home.

Finally.

"Hello," Pablo answered.

"Did you take care of all the loose ends?" I asked into the phone.

"Of course. It's all taken care of; it looks like it was a fluke. Just a random attack. How are you feeling?"

"How the fuck do you think I'm feeling? I'm high on morphine; I'm fucking fantastic. Brooke is on her way back to The Cathouse and Ysabelle will be there shortly."

"You're really going to let them run things?"

"It's a test that I know she won't fail."

"I hope you're right for the sake of your business."

"I'm never wrong," I said, hanging up.

"Jesus Christ, Angel, you fucking faked it?" Mika stated, pulling back the cloth curtain.

Goddamn it.

"Contrary to what you believe, I don't have to answer to you," I argued.

"Stop giving me The Madam bullshit. I don't buy it and I never did. I don't cower to you like your minions do. Now answer the Goddamn question before I make you answer it for me."

I glared at him. "Yes, Mika, I faked it, kind of like I do when I'm with you so you should be used to it by now." I smiled.

He pulled his hair back in a frustrated gesture. He let it grow out again and it was down to his chin.

"Why?"

I arched an eyebrow. "Why what?"

"Don't fuck with me. Why?"

"Can you cut the melodramatics? I've had enough of it today." I placed my hand on my forehead. "God, between Brooke, you, and the staff, I'm ready to sign myself out of this hellhole."

"Have you looked at yourself in the mirror? You look like you were beaten within an inch of your life. You can't even walk, your legs are broken and most of your ribs. Don't even get me started on the other injuries."

I rolled my eyes. "That's what a good plastic surgeon is for. I'm not worried about it. I'll be fine. I don't need you. I never did. Now, can you get the fuck out of my room? I'm tired and I need my beauty sleep."

He shook his head. "I'm not leaving until you tell me why."

"I already told you. She's my granddaughter and I need her back to run VIP. That's all."

"I know everything," he stated.

I cocked my head to the side. "Excuse me?"

"You know, *Lilith*, I have connections, too. You forget who I am? I know it all. I did some digging around and what you have done to this poor girl—"

"I HAVE DONE EVERYTHING FOR HER! She's mine," I roared.

"What are you going to do when she finds out the truth?"

"She will never find out."

"She'll hate you when she does," he affirmed.

"Blood is thicker than water," I stated. "She'll understand."

"You think she will understand about how you were behind her getting raped? How about the fact that she's in Miami because you put her here? She's been your goddamn puppet and doesn't even know it. You gave up your daughter," he vindictively reminded me. "You did that. You can't make it up with her. She's not your child. Your kid is a crack whore, literally," he mocked, "who offered to suck my cock before I even knocked on her door."

My eyes widened. "Get. The. Fuck. Out," I seethed through gritted teeth.

"With pleasure, but this isn't over," he warned, leaving my room.

No one would stand in my way.

Not even Mika.

Mine.

Y

Brooke was outside The Cathouse when my limo pulled up. Chance came barreling out of the car, running toward her.

"You brought the mongrel?" she asked, stepping away from him like he was disease infected.

"Yeah, he's my dog. Chance, leave her alone, she's wearing Chanel," I teased.

She laughed and pulled me into a hug. "I'm so glad you're here. It's been awful, Bella, you have no idea."

"What happened?" I asked as we walked inside.

"I guess Madam was in the wrong place at the wrong time and she got attacked. They beat the hell out of her. She's lucky to be alive."

I jerked back. "Madam? Who would mess with her?"

She shrugged. "Just some randoms, I guess. Thank God they found them and they're behind bars."

"Jesus. That just doesn't sound like something that would or even could happen to her."

We walked into one of the many guestrooms and I placed my luggage on the floor. "Are you staying here, too?"

"I will be on and off, yeah."

I nodded. "Okay."

"It's late. Get some rest and I'll take you to her in the morning."

I nodded again and she smiled. I knew she was dying to ask me about Sebastian but would wait till later to ask. I lay down on the bed and closed my eyes, falling asleep immediately from exhaustion.

Or maybe my mind didn't want to process that I was back in the home that I swore I'd never step foot in again.

CHAPTER 32

Y

I rolled over, looking for Sebastian, and immediately opened my eyes when his side of the bed was cold. I hastily blinked, trying to shake off the sleep and it took me a few minutes to realize where I was. I hadn't dreamt everything and I really was back at The Cathouse. I ignored the migraine that was looming and took a shower and dressed. I let Chance out in the backyard and then found Brooke in the kitchen, pouring coffee.

"What are you wearing?" she asked, eyeing my outfit up and down.

I followed her eyes and looked down at my outfit. "Jeans, a tank top, and sandals," I replied, confused.

"Bella, no offense, but maybe you should change into something more…less…I don't know…what you're wearing," she casually replied.

"Brooke, I don't have any of my old clothes. This is what I wear now."

"No, I understand." She sipped her coffee. "I dig it. Sort of…you have this whole comfortable thing going on. But you're back, for now. Maybe you should dress the part; I mean, we are taking over VIP for a bit. It would probably make sense to wear some heels or run a brush through your crazy ass hair." She shrugged. "Just saying."

I frowned. "I don't have time to go shopping and it's the last thing I want to do right now. And there's nothing wrong with my hair," I stated, pulling it out of my face.

She rolled her eyes. "Do you forget where you are? Madam has three rooms full of clothes. She has her own boutique upstairs for us. Come on."

"Ugh!" I followed behind her.

An hour later and she was grinning all the way up to her ears. "See…don't you feel better? Your hair is straight, you got on some red soles, and you're not wearing something off the rack. You look like Bella again. You can't tell me you don't feel like a million bucks because you sure do look it."

I looked at Brooke's perfect reflection in the mirror and then at mine. She was absolutely right, I did look like Bella, and it was as if I had never left. Except this time, these clothes, this image, this persona standing before me didn't look like anyone I recognized anymore. I didn't know who this flawless woman with the expensive outfit on was. She was a stranger. I left everything behind for a reason, and there it was, staring me in the face.

The dream.

The illusion.

The fantasy.

VIP.

I rode in Brooke's car with her, seeing as I didn't have a vehicle. We walked into Madam's room and there was an older man dressed in ripped jeans and a motorcycle jacket sitting with her. He had long blond hair tied in a ponytail and intense hazel eyes. He was breathtakingly handsome. They looked like they were having a heated argument or discussion. When our eyes locked, I swear his appeared to desperately want to say something. They were screaming at me and I had just met him.

"Bella Rosa," Madam announced, taking me away from his frantic trance. "Darling, come here."

"Aren't you going to introduce me, *Angel*?" he asked, making her eyes glare at him.

Angel? I had never heard anyone call her anything other than Madam.

She turned to Brooke, not paying him any mind. "Brooke baby, can you please tell security that this gentleman is no longer allowed to visit with me. I want him out, *permanently*," she emphasized.

He laughed, not cowering down. "And you think that's going to stop me? Come on, *Lilith*, at least let me stay and watch the show."

No one disrespected Madam. Ever. It was the first time that I ever saw real fear pass through her face and something came over me to want to help. I didn't like seeing her as anyone other than Madam; it hurt me for some reason. It pained me to watch the woman who controls everything, vulnerable and exposed.

It was too real.

I turned to him and our eyes caught. "I'm sorry, I think she asked you to leave. There's the door, you could leave on your own or I could call security. The choice is yours." I sneered.

The fucker smiled. "Wow." He folded his arms on his chest. "Hmmm…" He looked at Madam. "Looks like you've made quite a little soldier. You should be proud, Angel, she's everything you wanted her to be. A wolf in sheep's clothing, just like you."

She breathed out and grinned. "That's where you're wrong, darling…I'm the wolf. Always the motherfucking wolf, dressed in nothing but a pantsuit and fuck-me heels."

He shook his head. "I'll leave, for now. Have fun with your reunion." He looked back at me. "Till next time, *Ysa*."

I jerked back. No one called me that other than Sebastian.

What the fuck is going on?

"Ignore him, darling. What do I always tell you about men? Give them your pussy and they'll want your heart. That's what makes VIP one of a kind. Pay him no mind. Now come here, let me see you. You're glowing. Nice to see you dressed in real clothes again."

I half-smiled, trying to shake his presence and attitude.

"My girls. We're all together, like one big happy family. Just as it's meant to be." She glanced behind me. "Is Sebastian here?"

I shook my head. "No."

"Is he at The Cathouse?"

I peeked up at Brooke and she reassuringly smiled.

"He's not here, Madam."

"Why is that?"

"I left."

Her eyes widened and there was a glimmer of…hope…maybe?

"No…I mean…not like that. At least…I don't even know. I just need some space and you need help. So I'm here."

"What's going on?" she eagerly questioned.

I grabbed a chair and placed it by the bed. Brooke followed suit.

"It's been hard since I last saw you. I love him, Madam. I love him so much that I can't even begin to describe the feeling because it's so powerful. However, we want different things. He asked me to marry him."

"Oh my God, Bella! You didn't tell me! Are you engaged?" Brooke excitingly shouted while Madam lay still, almost like she had stopped breathing.

"I'm not engaged. I said no," I whispered, looking down at my lap. "I don't even know if I believe in marriage. He wants kids and…" I shrugged.

"Bella Rosa, look at me, my beautiful girl."

I did.

"You're a VIP. You're made for more. That's why you can't live a normal life. You're not made like that. You're the elite, darling. Sebastian was standing in your way. Men do that. They're selfish. He doesn't want you to shine, so he thinks he can take that away by making you a wife and mother." She shook her head. "Tsk…tsk…tsk…shame on him. You're perfect the way you are. Why ruin it with a child and a ring? That will wear you down. Don't you see?"

I took in her words.

"VIP is your home. I want you to own it."

Brooke and I both looked at Madam like she had lost her mind.

"What?" I jumbled.

"You heard me. It's yours. It always has been. You're here to prove to yourself that you can do this. I already know the answer. This isn't a test for me, it's a test for you."

"Madam, you don't know what you're saying. I'm here to help, with Brooke. I'm not here to take over. You don't want to step down; you'll be fine after this. Stop worrying," I nervously said.

"You'll see. Once you step into my heels, there's no going back."

"I—"

"All right, ladies, I'm going to have to ask you to leave. We need to run more tests and scans," the nurse said, walking in.

Brooke and I nodded, obviously baffled and stunned by Madam's assumptions.

"You'll find everything you need in my office. I know you will make me proud, both of you," she alleged, only looking at me.

We kissed her goodbye and were quiet for most of the car ride to The Cathouse.

"Did you know?" I blurted, breaking the silence in the car.

My head was spinning; there was no peace and quiet in my mind.

"Of course not. I'm just as puzzled as you are. But you know Madam; she's impulsive. She may not mean anything by it."

I glanced over at her, angling my head on the headrest. "When does she ever not mean what she says?" I justified.

"Is that something that you would want?" she replied, ignoring my statement.

"No…I don't think so. Who was that guy in the room?"

She shrugged. "I think his name is Mika. I've seen him around a few times, every time it's been secretive and random. I don't think he's a client."

"A lover?"

She laughed. "Really? Madam? I don't think so, probably just a partner or a fuck buddy. Lover has way too much meaning for her."

We pulled into Madam's driveway and she put the car in park. I grabbed her arm, stopping her from exiting the vehicle. "Brooke…"

"What?" she answered, knowing what I was about to ask.

"Are you okay?"

She smiled. "Why wouldn't I be?"

I arched an eyebrow. "Brooke…"

She sighed. "I'm fine. Am I a little hurt that it wasn't me that she offered it to? Of course. You've always been her favorite, we all know it."

"Why do you think that is?"

"That's like asking why the sky is blue and the sun is bright. We won't ever get answers, Bella. She does what she wants, that's what makes her The Madam."

I nodded, she was right.

Except, for the first time…

I wanted answers.

We spent the rest of the morning getting everything in order, making phone calls, scheduling appointments, and responding to RSVPs. I never realized how much work actually went into running VIP. Madam had everything organized in perfect order and it made it easier on us trying to make sense of it all. Brooke left around noon, saying she needed to run some errands, and I had the chef bring me some lunch. I was starving.

I kept my mind busy for as long as I could, but the second I let my mind wander to Sebastian, I swear to God, my heart called him.

Not even five minutes later…

I watched him barge through the office doors.

CHAPTER 33

S

I got everything in order with the house and my business. Ysabelle seemed to be one step ahead of me, since everything was being taken care of at Chances. This was premeditated and I couldn't help but wonder how long it had been that way. I took the next flight out. I knew exactly where she went and tried like hell to control my temper, but as soon as I shoved those double-sided doors open into Madam's office…

I was fucking furious.

"Miss Ysabelle, I am sorry. He charged through as soon as I opened the door. I couldn't stop him. Would you like me to call the police?"

I cocked my head at her, daring her to reply with what she was thinking.

She shook her head. "No, Hector, I have it under control. I'm sorry for his rude introduction. Thank you; you're excused," she announced, fitting every part of the role she was portraying.

It made me sick.

It made me want to hurt her. Badly.

"What the fuck do you think you're doing?" I seethed.

"Calm down, okay? I don't want to fight," she argued.

"Well, you have a fucking shitty way of showing it. You leave me a Dear John letter after the night we shared and I'm expected to be fucking ecstatic that I find you in Satan's office, looking like a whore?"

Her eyes widened. "Jesus…Sebastian."

"Explain. NOW!"

"I'm not going to talk to you when you're like this. We can talk when you've calmed down."

I was over to her in four strides and she immediately backed away from me. Frightened.

"What the fuck? You're scared of me?"

"No, of course not. But when you get like this, it's overwhelming and it's instinctual to back away from a bull."

"Oh, you haven't seen anything yet. Now, fucking tell me! Why are you back here? What are you doing?"

"I just needed a break, Sebastian!" she yelled, throwing her hands in the air.

"A break from me? A break from us?"

She urgently nodded. "Yes. A break from everything. I wasn't planning on coming back here—it was a coincidence. Madam is in the—"

"I don't give a flying fuck if Madam is in the goddamn morgue and you're here to plan the funeral."

"Oh my God, Sebastian. What is wrong with you?"

That did it. The fact that she was blowing me off like I was the bad guy was too much to take and I reacted. I pushed her up against the wall and caged her in, with each arm on each side of her body.

"You want to try that again? I fucking dare you."

She gulped. "I understand why you're upset."

"You don't understand shit and you don't respect me. You wouldn't be here if you did."

"She needed help. I'm here to help," she reasoned.

"Help sell your pussy? That's what you're helping with, right? See who the highest bidder is this time? You've been gone for a while, must be great for clients and sales," I viscously spewed.

Her mouth dropped open. "Fuck you!" she roared, slapping me across the face. Hard. "I'm not here to be a VIP. I'm here to help keep everything in order," she said through gritted teeth.

I opened my mouth, swaying my jaw around from her unexpected blow and found her intense stare.

"Just because you call it a VIP doesn't make it anything other than selling your goddamn soul to the devil. You've done it before and you got away, why on earth would you come back to this place? Why?" I raged, wanting answers.

"Because this is my home," she simply stated, knocking me on my ass.

It was like taking a bullet directly to the heart. Nothing had ever hurt me more than those five words. I backed away from her for her sake…and mine.

"Sebastian…" She promptly grabbed my arm, holding me in place. "I didn't mean it the way it came out. You're my home, but this is like my parents' house…okay…can you understand that? She's the only mother I've ever known. I'm here to help until she gets well."

"And then what?" I immediately countered.

"I wish I could tell you. You wanted me to stop running, I am. This is me, not running and being honest. I just need some time," she justified.

My head fell back from laughing. "This is you not running?" I emphasized with my hands in her face. "That's exactly what you're fucking doing. You want to hurt me or else you wouldn't be here."

"That's not true!"

"Prove it. You want space…I'll give you the motherfucking equator; leave here and I'll send you wherever you want to go. You can take your space or your goddamn break, but NOT here. I'll leave you alone, Ysa. I promise you. Please…leave here. I'm begging you. You want me down on my knees, groveling for you to leave here? I'll do it. I'll do whatever it takes. Just go."

She hesitated. "I gave her my word."

"Yeah…well you gave me your heart. So where does that leave us?"

"Please don't do this," she murmured.

I placed my hand on her neck in a possessive gesture, running my thumb up and down her windpipe. "I thought watching you with another man at The Gala was the worst memory of my life. Not Olivia." I paused to let my words sink in. "I let you believe that because I didn't want to talk about that night. I'd much rather have you believe that her dying was my worst memory."

Her eyes watered and her lip started trembling. I moved my hand to the nook of her neck and traced her quivering lip with my thumb. "This. Right now. Me looking at you, dressed like that. Seeing you in this office. Holding you but not feeling you." I pulled her toward me and she stumbled on her heels, placing her hands on my chest for balance. I placed my mouth near her ear. "It's my worst memory," I whispered and she instantly broke down crying.

I kissed the side of her face where her tears were streaming.

And spun around, not looking at her.

I couldn't see what my heart already knew.

She was a VIP.

Y

I bawled my eyes out when he walked out on me. I didn't know how long I sat there on the flooring, crying for it all. He had never walked out on me before and I knew that this time he was serious. I had loyalty to The Madam, why couldn't he understand that? She's the only mother I ever had. I wasn't doing it to hurt him. How could he think that?

"Bella?"

I glanced up at her. I was in my room and Chance was by my side.

How did I get in here?

"Are you okay?" Brooke asked.

"I don't know anymore."

"Sebastian was here?"

"How do you know?"

"Hector said some man was here and that you were upset. I brought you some tea. It's chamomile."

She placed it on the nightstand and sat beside me. I lay down, putting my head in her lap. She rubbed my hair out of my face, massaging it at the same time.

"I'm sorry, Bella."

"It's not your fault."

"What happened?"

"He's pissed that I'm here."

"Yeah…"

We stayed silent for a while.

"Why are you here?" she questioned.

"It all got so complicated. I love him."

"I know you do."

"Brooke, all I know is VIP. That's it. I'm here because it's home to me."

"I understand. It's home to me, too."

I rolled over and looked up at her. "Why are you here?"

Her forehead wrinkled in thought. "What do you mean?"

"I mean…why are you a VIP? You've been here what? Ten, eleven years?"

She grinned. "A lady never tells her age, Bella."

"No, don't do that, don't laugh it off. I don't know anything about you and you don't know anything about me. We're supposed to be best friends and we know nothing outside of VIP about each other. Why are you here, Brooke?"

"I don't need to know about your past to feel like you're a sister to me."

I smiled.

"I love you, Bells."

"I love you, too. Now, answer my question," I reminded.

She scratched her head and rubbed at the back of her neck in a comforting gesture, but didn't respond.

"You're gorgeous. I have seen men fall head over heels in love with you. I know you had a bad taste of love but don't you want more?"

"I have everything I want. I'm here because I want to be," she reassured.

"Brooke, I had the worst upbringing ever. VIP found me," I informed, hoping she would open up to me.

"I had the best upbringing but it doesn't mean shit…it didn't stop things from happening. It's life. You move on. That's what I did. I'm not broken, Bella. I've done what I wanted to do. I love my life. VIP didn't save me…I was never lost."

I nodded, knowing that was all she was going to tell me.

"I want to party!" she yelled out of nowhere. "Let's go out!"

"Brooke…no…"

"Oh, come on! We haven't partied in a really long time. Let's go do something. You want to go to Vegas? You know you want to go to Vegas!" she taunted in a singing voice.

I rolled my eyes and sighed. "Fuck it. Let's go."

She wiggled her eyebrows and called the private plane.

CHAPTER 34

S

"Sebastian..."

"Mmmm..." I groaned.

"Sebastian, get up!"

I opened my eyes, the light shining in was burning my retinas and my head was throbbing.

"Where am I?" I mumbled.

"My guest bedroom. You're lucky Christian didn't see you this morning. He just left for school. You don't remember calling me?"

I shook my head, covering my eyes with my arm.

"You were wasted last night. You called me from a bar. I couldn't even understand what you were saying you were that incoherent. I had to finally talk to the bartender. Whom I left a very nice tip, too, so your wallet is going to be missing some bills. He took away your keys. You wanted to drive."

"Fuck...I don't remember shit."

"Well...that's good. Anthony had to pretty much carry you inside." She sighed. "What are you doing here? Where's Ysabelle?"

"Julia, I don't want to talk about this right now," I hoarsely replied, rolling over.

She pulled the pillow out from under my head and hit me with it.

"Wake up! You need to explain what the hell is going on? I'll hit you again, Sebastian, now tell me!"

"Oh my God, you're so annoying. Stop being so loud." I sat up against the headboard and scrubbed my hands over my face. "Ysabelle is back at The Cathouse. We broke up or taking a break, I don't even fucking know whatever it is, but she's back there and I'm here. That's all I got for you right now."

"Why?"

"Because she's running. What she does best."

"Well, did you chase after her?"

I glared at her. "Of course. It doesn't matter."

"What happened?"

"She hasn't been the same since you guys left. She thinks you're fucking perfect, Julia. She thinks she broke up our family. She thinks she's fucked up and not good for me. I could give you a dozen other answers, but that's the gist."

She sat down on the edge of the bed. "Wow…"

"Yeah…tell me about it. I've been chasing her around for the last year. I'm at a loss and now she's back at the whorehouse."

"She's not…you know…"

"She said she isn't. I guess something happened with the ringleader and she's helping in the meantime."

"Oh. Anthony has told me about her. She's ummm…"

"A cunt? The devil? Evil? Bitch? I could go on."

"Yeah, something along those lines."

"Exactly. The worst part is she sees her as a mother figure. She actually believes that woman cares for her. She thinks she's home, staying at her mom's. It makes me fucking sick."

"I'm sorry, Sebastian."

"What do I do? I have no idea what to do anymore. I want to literally strangle her until she understands what I'm saying. I feel like I'm beating a dead horse. The longer she's there, the more I'm losing her. But the more I push her, the more I lose her. I'm in between a rock and a hard place. Either way, I'm screwed. I just have to sit back and watch." I pulled back my hair; I wanted to rip it the fuck out.

"Here's the thing…she's going to get hurt, I feel it. I know it in my heart that she's going to get destroyed and I have not a clue how to prevent it. The Madam is obsessed with her and I don't understand why. It's like Ysabelle is everything to her."

She cocked her head to the side. "The only thing I could tell you is to wait. She needs to figure it out on her own. I know that sucks…trust me. I've been there, but she won't realize it if she doesn't figure it out on her own."

"How do you know that?"

She smiled. "I've seen the way she looks at you. She loves you, Sebastian. Women don't walk away from that kind of love. Just give her space…give her time. She'll figure it out."

"What if you're wrong?"

"What if I'm right?" she countered.

All I could do was pray that she was right.

Y

It had been three weeks since I arrived at The Cathouse. Madam was living in a residential medical facility. She was adamant that she wanted to come home, but the doctors ordered that she stay where she would be monitored and they could nurse her back to health. Every time I saw her, she appeared to look better. The bruises had faded and she was walking on her own for the most part. They didn't think she would suffer any long-term impairment.

I hadn't spoken or seen Sebastian since our last encounter and it made my heart bleed more with each passing day.

We had a private party that evening and our presence was required, according to Madam. I hated looking in the mirror, I found myself avoiding it at all costs, and the fact that Sebastian associated my appearance as a whore left a bitter taste in my mouth. I would remember his last words to me and it would make me physically ache. I hated that we hadn't spoken. I knew I told him I needed space, but the longer the days went by, the harder it was to stay away.

My heart called for him.

He was everywhere.

It was on instant replay in my head, over and over again.

I couldn't stop it, and furthermore…I didn't want to.

What the fuck is wrong with me?

I hadn't been to a VIP event since The Gala, and this wasn't even a VIP extravaganza, a client was throwing this shindig. I dressed in a black gown; diamonds were on my ears and neck, along with picture-perfect makeup and a flawless up-do; my matching black heels were sky high.

"Oh, Bella, that bracelet doesn't match that gown. Here let—"

"No." I swiftly moved my hand away. "I'm not taking this off."

She nodded, understanding my silent objection. "Are you ready?"

"As ready as I'll ever be."

There was a stretch white limo in the driveway. We arrived at a mansion the size of The Cathouse in less than thirty minutes. The doors were opened and we were greeted with glasses of champagne. We entered into a palace of hedonism. I could smell the sex in the air. It flowed like a decadence of your favorite dessert. Waitresses were everywhere, dressed in nothing but panties and heels. There were dancers on block stages that wore boudoir lingerie. Cocaine was spread on tables with lines already split and rolled up bills beside it.

Lights…

"Ysabelle, so nice to see you again."

Camera…

"You look amazing, as always."

Action…

I was on.

I batted my eyelashes and smiled like I had just won the goddamn lottery. "Good evening, Charles, always a pleasure."

"So the rumors are true. You've taken over?"

"Not at all. Brooke and I are just babysitting while Madam gets well."

"It's great to see you again. Will you be on the menu tonight?" He winked and I wanted to punch him in the fucking face for even asking me that.

I grinned. "No, Charles, I will not. Like I said, I'm a mere spectator, I don't get to play."

"Such a shame…I would pay anything to get another…taste."

And I would like nothing more than to shove your balls down your pervy little throat. Fucker.

I giggled. "Now, now, you know the rules. All the girls are here. I'd love to set you up with one of them."

"I'm sure I can be persuaded."

I spent the next few hours schmoozing and getting reacquainted. I went to the bathroom and made a wrong turn somewhere. I recognized the sounds instantly, and like a moth to a flame, I followed them. I rounded the corner and I was face-to-face with my past.

VIPs were everywhere; some were straddling men, others were going at it with women, and some were even in groups, taking it in every fucking hole. I watched as they sucked cock and ate pussy or fucked and received pleasure. That used to be me.

Nothing was ever enough.

Always down for a good time.

Never one to say no.

I was a VIP.

It was a slow moving train wreck, except I was tied to the tracks, waiting to be run over by the oncoming force of a mechanical machine. For the first time…I didn't see the glamour or the beauty behind it. There was no, "You're a one of a kind. You're made for this. You're the elite." That's not what it was. I was a whore who used my body to get money. To hurt people. My pussy wasn't made of stone, my heart was.

To have experienced the kind of love that I shared with Sebastian wouldn't even come close to the mockery of the illusion of want and need before me. There was no lust, passion, or even desire. It was primal and seedy. It was heartless and nasty, tainted with drugs and promises of nothing. I was disgusted that this was my life, that I was one of these VIPs and proud to be.

Very Important Pussy was a fuck show.

And I was a puppet.

"Gorgeous." I heard him whisper from behind. "Oh, how I've missed you."

I didn't have to turn to know whose voice murmured in my ear…

Gabriel.

CHAPTER 35

Y

"What are you doing here?" I asked, turning to face him. He looked just as handsome as ever.

"I could ask you the same thing. Are you enjoying the show? Do you miss being the centerpiece of it all?"

I walked around him, knowing he was going to follow. I needed to get air; I felt like I was suffocating. I found a balcony and didn't stop until I was standing beside the railing. I took a deep breath, trying to calm my beating heart that felt like it wanted out of my chest.

"You look stunning in this lighting. You're still the most beautiful woman I have ever seen, Ysabelle."

His fingers crept on my back and he brushed them up and down my spine, my backless gown, giving him the liberty to do so.

"When you left, you took my heart with you…did you know that? Hmmm…did you know that I was in love with you?"

I swallowed the saliva that accumulated in my mouth.

"Of course you did. You loved it, didn't you? Knowing that I wanted you, only you. It was a game to you." He roughly grabbed the nook of my hair, letting my up-do go free; crazy curly hair surrounded my face. I felt nauseous. My present and my past colliding, even though Sebastian wasn't physically there, he made his presence known.

He jerked my head back and I gasped, making me look at him.

"Answer the fucking question, gorgeous. Did you know I was in love with you?"

"Yes…" I breathed out.

"Was I a game to you?"

"Yes…"

"Did you want me to fall in love with you?"

"Yes…"

"Why? Hmm…answer me!"

"Because I could," I simply stated.

He let go and shoved me against the railing. I felt his heat against my back even though he wasn't touching me.

"I could fuck you right now and you would fight me the entire time. My how times have changed. What are you doing here? I can see it written all over your face, you don't belong here anymore."

I took in his words.

"There's no light at the end of the tunnel…is there, gorgeous? Sometimes broken toys can't be fixed. And all that's left is to throw them away," he mocked, making me turn immediately.

"Go to hell."

"Beside you? It'd be a fucking pleasure."

He walked around me, eyeing me up and down. "From the looks of it, you're in purgatory. VIP doesn't have the lure that it used to, does it? You want to know why that is?"

My eyes followed his every movement.

"I was your first…do you remember?"

I nodded.

"Say it."

"Yes…"

"I've fucked you three ways from Sunday. I've tasted you on my mouth for days after devouring you. Do you remember?"

"Yes..."

"I always knew what you were. I've seen inside your soul because I've loved you and you've laughed in my face because of it."

"I'm sorry, Gabriel. I never meant to hurt you. I'm not that person anymore, but I can't go back and change things. I can only go forward."

He laughed. "See…that's where you're wrong. You aren't going anywhere. You're at a standstill. You're like a mouse on a spinning wheel, running round and round with nowhere to go. Aren't you exhausted?"

"What do you want? Did you come here to patronize me?"

"Can't an old friend say hello?"

"You were never my friend."

"Lover then?"

I laughed. "Not even close."

"Ouch…that's not nice, Ysabelle."

"If you'll excuse me, I need to get back," I declared, walking around him.

"Back to what exactly?"

I turned to look at him. "You want to know the difference between you and a lover or even a goddamn friend?"

"Enlighten me."

"You used me, just as much as I used you. You want to pretend like you loved me and justify it…then go right ahead. You never loved me because, one, you don't know the meaning of the word and, two, you don't know who I am."

"That's where you're wrong, gorgeous, I knew then what I know now. You aren't a VIP, you never were. Your Madam knows it, too. It's why she wants you so desperately. You're the first person that's ever told her no, now that's hard to forget."

I backed away from him. "I hope you find happiness one day and it's not at the hand of a whore."

"Like you?" he snarled.

"Always a pleasure."

I left the party without saying goodbye to anyone.

S

"Dad!"

"What's up, bud?"

"Have I told you I love that you've been home these last five weeks?"

"Almost every day."

We had been fishing off the pier for the last few hours. I tried to bury my thoughts with spending as much time as I could with Christian.

"Are you sad?"

"What makes you ask that?" I asked, bumping his shoulder.

"Because you look sad. Do you miss Ysabelle?"

"I do. I miss her very much."

"Mom says that when two people love each other, that they find their way back together. I thought that would happen with you and Mom. I prayed for it every night."

"Christian…"

"I know, Dad. Anthony told me he was going to ask Mom to marry him."

"How do you feel about that?"

He shrugged. "I like Anthony, he's nice. Can I tell you something?"

"You can tell me anything."

"I kinda miss Ysabelle, too."

I laughed. "What? Really?"

"Yeah. She always smelled nice and she was pretty. She had a nice laugh, too. I remember one night when we came to visit you. I pretended like I was sleeping and she came into my room. She pulled the blanket up and made sure I was covered." He looked at me. "She kissed my head and then left. Did you know that?"

I shook my head in complete shock. "No, bud, I had no idea."

"She would make a good stepmom, so if you want to ask her to marry you again, it would be okay with me."

I smiled. "That makes me happy, Christian,"

"Can I ask you something else?"

"Of course."

"If you guys get married, are you going to have more kids?"

I put my arm around him, pulling him to me. "If it were up to me, yes."

"Okay…do you think that you could make it a girl? Because I don't really want a brother, I'd like a baby sister I can take care of."

"You've given this a lot of thought, I see."

"I told Mom the same thing. I want all sisters."

"I'll try to make sure you get sisters."

We fished for another few hours. The tide was coming up and we watched it in comfortable silence. Ysabelle loved high tide, she said something about the moon and the gravitational pull being able to control the water was soothing to her. I thought about her every minute of every day. I was giving her space that she requested. I worried about her decisions and impulses. I prayed that she was taking care of herself. To sit back and wait for the other shoe to drop was pure and utter torture. It was probably one of the hardest things I've ever had to do. A huge part of me wanted her to come to me, to seek me out.

But nothing could have prepared me for what was to come…

Nothing.

Y

By the seventh week, I was restless. Madam was back at The Cathouse, however, she still needed help and for us to be in charge. I took care of everything behind the scenes; I didn't ever go to another party or gathering. Brooke handled all that. She never questioned me about it. She played her part and I played mine. Madam had her chauffeur drive her to her therapy that afternoon. I was handling all the upkeep in making sure all the clients were tested; they routinely needed to provide current medical tests for diseases and good health.

I was searching the files when I came across the name Mika. I opened his folder and there was a picture of him; he looked really young, much younger than the man I had met at the hospital. All his documentation was present, including records of the VIPs he had been with. There were very few, but it said he had been a member since the 70s.

It made no sense.

"It's not nice to spy on someone without their permission, Ysa."

I immediately looked up and our eyes locked.

"I don't think we've been properly introduced," he added, strolling over to me with a powerful presence that I felt with each step he took. He sat in one of the leather chairs in front of the desk. "My name's Mika."

CHAPTER 36

Y

"You don't need to introduce yourself; I know exactly who you are," he remarked with a certain tone.

"Why do you call me Ysa?" I hastily responded.

He grinned and placed his ankle on his knee, sitting back with his arms around the back of the chair. It was the first time I had ever been around a man who screamed sex. It exuded off of him; he had this cocky demeanor without even having to try.

"Isn't that your name?"

"My name is Ysabelle, no one calls me Ysa."

He arched an eyebrow. "What about Sebastian? Does he not count?"

I shook my head and leaned forward. "Who are you?"

"Oh…we're going to start with my introduction. Not exactly how I imagined this going down, but I'm all for spontaneity; life's too short to sweat the small stuff." He nodded toward the folder. "Didn't find out enough information from my file? I'm surprised Angel even has one for me. I've never been much of a client…I hate following the herd, you know? I like to think of myself as an exclusive member to Lilith, more than anything."

"Madam?"

"Oh, yes," he whispered with wide eyes. "Madam."

"Who are you to her?"

He cocked his head. "I don't like labeling our relationship, makes things complicated. Angel isn't too fond of commitment and up until a few months ago, I wasn't either."

"Your file says you're married."

He smiled. "I was. Divorced now. How sad, she hasn't updated my file." He placed his hand on his heart. "I'm hurt. Love is a brutal cunt, isn't she?"

I shook my head and sat up, placing his file back in the cabinet. I rounded the desk and walked to the door with his eyes on me the entire time.

"I'll tell Madam you stopped by," I announced, holding the door open.

"I don't remember saying I was leaving."

"Well, I have somewhere I have to be. I can't babysit you."

He narrowed his eyes. "You lie like her. Your eyes actually glaze over, exactly how hers do. It's poetic. I don't think I have to tell you that you're fucking beautiful. You could make my cock hard without even trying."

I watched as he slowly engulfed every inch of my body, making me feel naked and exposed. He bit his bottom lip when he sensed what I was feeling.

"You know, Ysa, I've known you since you were a baby VIP. I was actually at your first bidding party. I saw you walk in on *Madam's* arm, and I wanted you instantly. You were sinful and you didn't even know it. A man can appreciate a pretty pussy when he sees one. I found her and told her that I would offer double, even triple the amount of money your suitors had bid."

I hadn't moved from the place I was standing, I couldn't. I was glued to the floor.

"She turned me down. Now…when has *Madam* ever turned down money?" he questioned, reading my mind. "I should have known then."

I lowered my eyebrows. "Known what?"

"Who you are."

"What the fuck are you talking about? Stop speaking in code."

"Is that what I'm doing? Thanks for clarifying. Stop being a little bitch and I might tell you."

"Tell me what?"

He stood and walked over to the dresser, grabbing the picture of Madam and me. She had her arms around me and my head was on her shoulder. He peeked up at me with a devilish stare.

"Haven't you ever wondered how she found you? Hmmm…it's all a big coincidence, at least from an outsider looking in."

"Would that make you the outsider?"

His eyes rolled in my direction, but he didn't move his head. "I'd like to think that would be you."

"Me?"

He walked over to the couch and sat down, facing me with the picture still in his hands. He pointed to the couch in front of him for me to sit down; before I could overthink it, I sat. He leaned forward, placing his elbows on his knees. I crossed my legs and placed my hands in my lap. Something about the way he was looking at me made me uncomfortable; I had never been that way around any man. Mika was different, I just didn't know in what sense.

"You're nervous?" he stated as a question. "I can smell it on you, amongst other things." He grinned.

"Do you always use sexual innuendos to get your way?"

"Is that what I'm doing?" he taunted.

"What do you want?"

He sighed. "I want a lot of things. Most of all…I want Angel."

"What does that have to do with me?"

"Everything."

"Care to elaborate?"

He squinted his eyes, taking me in or maybe considering what to say next.

"Want to play a game?" he questioned, catching me off guard.

"Is that what this is to you? A game?" I retorted.

"Oh…Ysa, you have no idea what kind of game you're playing."

"You're right; I don't play games. And if I did…I'd play to win."

He smiled, showing off his bright white teeth. Even though he was an asshole, he was a sexy asshole and the fucker knew it.

"How old are you?" I asked.

"Interested?"

"Not as much as you are."

He clapped his hands and laughed. "I fucking love you! No wonder you're her favorite. I've talked and been around all the VIPs and not once have they challenged me, why you ask? Because they see me with *Madam*. Enough said. You"—he pointed at me—"don't give a fuck, and damn how that makes my cock hard."

"For someone who claims to want *Angel,* you sure have a shitty way of showing it."

"See…that's the difference between you and her. She knows I fuck. That's it. It's who I am. I've loved pussy since before I knew what it was. My mom used to say that it took her years to get me off her tit."

"You're vile."

He chuckled. "Coming from the woman who used to share her pussy with the world and suck cock for a living…doesn't mean much."

I wanted to react to his vicious words, but I knew better. This was foreplay for him.

"I never sucked yours, now why is that? Come to think about it, not many of us have. You've been a member since the late 70s, which would make you somewhere in your late fifties? You're old enough to be my father," I vindictively countered.

He arched an eyebrow. "Except, I wouldn't touch your crack whore of a mother with a ten-foot pole."

"What?" I rashly replied, standing up. "How do you know that? Who the fuck are you?"

He leaned back and looked up at me. "A kitten one second and a lion the next. Must be in your blood." He paused. "Haven't you ever wondered about your life? Huh? You can't tell me you haven't. A rags to riches story; it's like a fucking Lifetime movie. Except, you are not the lead role. *Madam* is."

He stood, walking over to me and standing behind me, placing his face near my neck. "You smell good…" He slowly smelled from my shoulder to the side of my neck, beneath my ear, never touching me but humming the entire time. I didn't back down; he was trying to intimidate me.

I wouldn't let him.

"I bet you taste as sweet as you smell," he murmured, breathing on my neck. "Hmmm…" he groaned. "If I reached into your panties, would you be wet?" His fingers skimmed the side of my arm, moving toward my core. "I'll tell you one thing…" His fingers reached my hip and he stopped. "Your Madam would be drenched, and I'd take those soaking wet panties and shove them in her mouth. All the while…thinking about you." He cupped my sex and I gasped. I turned around and pushed him as hard as I could. He stumbled on his footing, laughing the entire time.

"You son of a bitch," I yelled.

He put his hands in the air, surrendering. “I just wanted to see what all the fuss is about,” he mocked.

I shook my head, backing away. “I’m out of here.” I reached the doorway.

“Don’t you want to know the truth? I know I would if I were you.”

I stopped dead in my tracks and turned around. He was leaning against the desk with one leg over the other and his arms were crossed on his chest. The picture frame was sitting beside him.

“You’re just playing with me. You don’t know a damn thing,” I argued.

“Then why did you stop? If you truly believed that, then you would have kept going.”

“Fuck you!”

“I already tried that. You didn’t like it very much.” He shrugged.

“Tell me! Stop fucking around and just tell me…please…” I begged, not caring anymore.

In an instant, his eyes changed and they were warm and welcoming. He was sad, for whom, I didn’t know. He grabbed the picture and threw it at me. I caught it in the air, holding it and shaking my head in confusion. He nodded toward it for me to look at it and I did.

“Take the picture out.”

I looked up at him. “What?”

“Take. The. Picture. Out.”

I sighed and did as I was told. I popped open the back and there was another picture behind it. I flipped it over, still not understanding. It was a picture of Madam, a young Madam with a woman who appeared to be her mother. They were in a similar embrace as we were in our picture.

“Look at her eyes. Not Madam’s eyes…”

“Oh my God.” Bright, shining green stared back at me.

“You’re right, Ysabelle, it was always a game, except you were never a player. You were a pawn.”

“No…you’re lying!” I threw the frame at his head and he ducked, the glass shattering behind him.

He stood up, straighter. “Your mother was a piece of shit, she still is. It didn’t take much for her to sell you. Who do you think was the bidder?” he sadistically asked.

My eyes widened and I felt nauseous, my hand immediately went to my mouth, and I tried to breath through it.

"How do you think you ended up in Miami? Quite a coincidence, don't you think?"

My face paled and all the blood from my body felt like it was draining. I could barely stand, I was shaking so badly. I looked all around me, trying to keep up with what he was saying and then our eyes locked.

"She was never your Madam," he affirmed, moving his concentrated stare behind me and smiling.

"She is your grandmother."

CHAPTER 37

M

I heard his voice as soon as my heel touched the last step at the top of the stairs.

"How do you think you ended up in Miami? Quite a coincidence, don't you think?"

I ran as fast as I could…

"She was never your Madam."

I stood behind her ready to yell and do whatever I had to do to stop him, but when he looked at me…for the first time after all these decades…I had no idea who he was, and that knocked me on my ass. I was at a loss for words or even movement. His vacant eyes were like looking into a stranger, and he sensed it because he smiled.

"She is your grandmother."

I thought this day would never come, and if it ever did, I imagined it playing out so differently, and never from the mouth of the man that owned my body, heart, and soul. In that moment, I knew what every woman talked about with having their heart shattered. I actually heard it and felt it erupt. It was like a bomb that went off in my body, leaving me cold and broken.

She turned and looked right at me and I swear I was ready to get down on my hands and knees and beg for forgiveness.

"I never knew you at all, did I?" she choked.

"My beautiful—"

"DON'T FUCKING CALL ME THAT!" she screamed, loud enough to break glass.

"Let me explain—"

"Explain what? How you had me raped? Let's start there!"

I put my hands out in front of me, trying to bring her toward me, but she simultaneously backed away. My heart was bleeding, pouring all over my designer suit. I would be nothing after this.

I vigorously shook my head. "No…that's not what happened. He was supposed to scare you—"

"And that makes it okay? You're fucking crazy!"

"No…no…no…Bella Rosa…I made him pay! I swear, I made him pay," I sobbed.

Was I crying?

"You said you loved me! You said you would never hurt me! You promised me that you would be like a mother to me and I believed you! I believed every fucking lie that came out of your mouth!"

"I did everything for you. It was all for you. You have to understand—"

"NO! YOU DID EVERYTHING FOR YOU! I NEVER HAD A CHOICE!"

"Yes…you did. You chose me. You chose this."

"You manipulated me. Everything was a game. Oh my God." She shook, putting her hand up to her mouth and leaning over. "I'm going to be sick."

"Bella Rosa," I whimpered, putting my arms on her shoulders.

She immediately jerked back. "Don't fucking touch me! You have no idea what you did to me! I don't know who I am because of you! It's all been a lie. All of it! MY WHOLE FUCKING LIFE HAS BEEN A FUCKING LIE!" she yelled at the top of her lungs.

"Please…please…" I got down on my knees, putting my hands in a prayer motion. "Forgive me… I can fix this…"

"You're evil. I really did sell my soul to the devil. I fucking hate you. I hate you so much!" she bawled.

"You don't mean that. I'm in your blood, I'm your family you don't mean that."

"Oh my God! I have to get out of here."

I instantly wrapped my arms around her legs, holding her as hard as I could. "Please…don't go…please…I love you so much. You have no idea how much I love you," I wept.

"You don't know anything about love. You have no idea what kind of monster you are. How could you do this to me? How could you make me believe all those lies? I'm so fucked up because of you. You ruined me!" she yelled, hitting me repeatedly in the back to try to break free.

I wouldn't let her go.

Mine.

"Please…please…Mika…help me! PLEASE!" she shouted.

I felt his strong grip around me, prying me loose and away from her like I was nothing more than a ragdoll.

"NO! NO! NO! NO!" I bellowed, watching her reach the doorway. "I LOVE YOU! YOU CAN'T DO THIS!" I fought as hard as I could for him to let me go.

And like that, she was gone.

"Angel…stop…calm down…" I heard him say.

I reacted and turned my hate on the person who deserved it, kicking, scratching, punching, anything I could to make him fucking bleed like I was.

"I FUCKING HATE YOU! YOU STUPID PIECE OF SHIT! WHO THE FUCK DO YOU THINK YOU ARE! I'M GOING TO FUCKING KILL YOU!" I stopped and spit right in his face and he retaliated by shoving me to the ground, holding me down.

"I've told you since day fucking one, Angel, I give you what you need, not what you want!" he roared.

I rolled over and closed my eyes.

Wanting nothing more than to die.

S

They say that twins can feel what the other is feeling, even if they are hundreds, thousands of miles away from each other. It's something about them sharing a womb during conception. I think it's the same for soul mates. I felt her pain in my heart. It ate at me and I found it hard to breathe.

I didn't think twice about it and got on the next flight out.

Y

The world stopped moving and everything that happened next was in slow motion. I was the *outsider* looking in. I left The Cathouse in a blur and ended up on Devon's doorstep. I vaguely remember shaking and him holding me. I wanted to drown out the noises, screams, and memories in my mind. They were on instant reply.

His hands all over me.

His smell.

His movements.

The pain…

So much blood…

Letting the boys touch me. Provoking it. Succumbing.

Miami.

Devon…Devon…Devon…

Madam. The Cathouse. Brooke. Selling myself. All those men. All those women. The orgies. The drugs. The alcohol. Partying. Fucking…over and over again.

Married men. Married women. Couples.

Never say no. Always down for a good time. I'm made like that. You're a treasured jewel. Elite.

Sebastian…my heart…love…hurt…pain…sadness…married.

Whore.

VIP.

Turks and Caicos. Chances. Sebastian. Happy. Confused. Scared. Overwhelmed.

Marriage. Kids. Babies.

Running…

Mika. The truth. Lies. More hurt. More pain. More confusion.

LOST.

I have no idea who the fuck I am.

I never did.

I thought back to the only person that has never lied to me or hurt me, the only person who has always been there for me no matter what.

My savior, my best friend, my protector.

Devon.

I kissed him; I started it.

Please…please…please…make it go away…make it all go away…please…

Did I say that out loud?

He did, with each caress, push and pull, kiss, movement, breath, sigh, groan and moan. Every last bit of it was replaced with tender love and care.

Except, when I opened my eyes, I pretended to see Sebastian. And when I finally came with my release. It all left.

Safe.

Loved.

Wanted.

GONE.

And I felt exactly what I wanted to forget.

Whore.

VIP.

Me.

I couldn't take it anymore.

And I broke down crying.

CHAPTER 38

Y

"Shhh…shhh….shhh….it's okay," he whispered as I was cradled in his arms. "That's it…take deep breaths…in and out…yes. Just like that. Breathe in and breathe out. Shhh…you're okay. I'm here…everything is going to be okay, Kid."

I moved away from him, taking the sheet with me to cover myself. "Oh my God, what the fuck did I just do?"

"It's okay."

"It is NOT okay, Devon; it is so far from okay it's like on the other side of the planet," I irrationally laughed.

"Kid, I think you're having a panic attack or maybe a nervous breakdown. You just need to relax," he coaxed.

"So I decide fucking you was the answer. Jesus Christ…I'm such a whore."

"Stop. Stop talking about yourself like that. I read it wrong, I thought…I don't know what I thought," he explained, shaking his head. "But it's my fault, too. I shouldn't have taken advantage of you. It takes two to tango."

"It doesn't matter! We just had sex. I'm so fucked. Sebastian is never going to forgive me."

"Kid, you and him aren't together. You didn't cheat on him," he reasoned.

"It doesn't fucking matter. It's you. And me. Why would I do this? Why would I fuck up the only good thing in my life? I'm not a good person. I don't know who I am, Devon."

"You need to calm down, you're talking in circles. I can't understand you."

"I need to go."

I jumped off the bed to find my clothes and swiftly put everything on, running for the door. Devon flew out in front of me, blocking my exit with his jeans barely on.

"You're not going anywhere, you can barely talk, let alone drive," he rationalized.

"Stop trying to save me!"

"Ysabelle, this isn't about saving you. I'm not prince charming; I just fucked my best friend and didn't even realize that she wasn't in the mental capacity to do so. Do you have any idea how awful I feel? I'm sorry."

"This isn't your fault. It's mine. I came on to you."

"And I accepted it." He paused. "Just relax, we both fucked up. Equally. It's not a big deal. Now calm down and take a seat and tell me what the hell is going on. Please," he added.

I nodded.

He pointed toward his living room and I went and sat on the couch, he came in a few minutes later with tea and water.

"It's chamomile," he said.

I drank the whole thing in one gulp like it was a shot of whiskey.

"What happened?"

I sighed. "I don't even know where to start."

"The beginning usually works well."

"I was filing clients at The Cathouse and getting everything in order, making sure it was all up to date. I came across Mika's file—"

"Mika from the hospital?" he interrupted.

I looked at him. "How do you know that?"

"We will talk about that later. Just finish."

"Yeah…that guy," I stated confused. "Anyway, he showed up and at first, I thought he was trying to fuck *with* me, and then I actually thought he was trying to fuck me. Make a really long story short, Madam is my grandmother."

His eyes widened. "No…"

"Yeah."

"No way…"

"Yes."

"What?"

"Exactly!" I shouted.

"Jesus…this is like out of a book."

I nodded, half-laughing. “She showed up and it got nasty quick. She’s behind everything, Devon, the rape, me coming to Miami, the night I met her at the bar. She knew who I was because she put me here; she just had to wait until I was an adult before she could make her move.”

He lowered his eyebrows. “I don’t understand. Your mom is her daughter? Then why were you raised like that? Why wasn’t your mom a VIP?”

I shrugged. “I don’t know. My mom never talked about any family. I have not a clue. I know I need answers, and the only way I’m going to get them is through her. Just the thought of having to face her again makes me ill.”

“So, Mika told you?”

“Every last detail.”

“Who is he?”

I shook my head. “I have no idea. I’m assuming from the way he spoke about her, some sort of lover.”

“Why did he tell you?”

I stood up, frustrated. “Devon, you’re asking all these questions and I don’t know the answers. I’m so lost. I have no idea who I am. I never did. I was a puppet and she pulled the strings. She has controlled my entire life and made me think that she was a mother to me. She still thinks she is. You should have seen her! I’ve never seen the woman shed a goddamn tear, let alone frown, and she was on her hands and knees, bawling for me to forgive her.”

“Wow.”

“Queen of Miami, leader of VIP, the most exclusive and elite whorehouse in all the world, is my grandmother. That’s why she wants to give me VIP. Brooke once told me that it’s been in her family for generations; she was born into this life. I’m the key to keeping it going. Hence, why I’m back here. At this point, I wouldn’t be surprised if she faked getting beaten.”

“She was on her deathbed. There’s no way.”

“She’s fucking insane.”

I sat down next to him, both of us in shock from everything I disclosed.

“What are you going to do now?” he sincerely questioned.

“Obviously, I fuck my best friend. I mean why not…let’s just add icing on the cake.” I placed my head in my lap. “I’m so fucked up.”

He rubbed my back. "Kid…"

"Hmmm…"

"I love you."

I smiled. "I love you too, Devon."

"No…I love you."

My eyes immediately opened. "Please tell me you're joking," I replied, not moving.

"Hear me out. I've known you for over ten years now. When you first walked into my bar, I thought you were the most beautiful girl I had ever seen. That night when you came home with me, I had this instinctual desire to want to protect you. I still do. When I found your license and realized that you were sixteen, I knew you were running from something. It had to be bad; you were taking a risk and I decided in that second to take one with you. When you left the bar, I felt it. You wanted more out of life and I let you go."

I sat up and turned to look at him.

"Over the years, our friendship got stronger and the feelings of love grew. I thought I was in love with you. That's why Christine hated you so much; she knew it. You never looked at me the way you look at Sebastian, not one time. When you walked through my door just now…I thought…I thought you wanted me. And I jumped at the chance to be with you. I'm an asshole."

"Dev—"

"No…I am. In a weird, fucked up sort of way. I'm glad it happened. I love you, Kid. I always will. I think somewhere along the way, I confused that love into something that it's not. It got twisted."

I frowned.

"I slept with Brooke. Let me rephrase that…I've been sleeping with Brooke since that night at the club."

My mouth dropped open. "Oh my God! She hasn't said a word." I was stunned.

"Well…at least that answers that."

"Brooke is—"

"I know what Brooke is. I think I'm falling in love with her, though, and sleeping with you just made me realize that."

I was at a loss for words. This night was a shit show.

"I've never met anyone like her. There's something beautifully broken about her. I can't stay away."

"I don't know what to tell you. How often do you see her?"

"Often enough."

"Are you going to tell her?"

"I don't know. Are you?"

"Devon, please…I don't want you to get hurt."

"I can take care of myself, Kid."

I nodded.

"Think of it this way, I got to fuck two VIPs and I didn't have to pay," he chuckled.

My head jerked back, wide-eyed. "Oh my God! You're not paying for Brooke?"

"That's your response?" He grinned. "Of course not."

"Ever?"

"No, not once."

"And she knows that?"

"Yeah. She wanted it that way."

"Brooke? She wanted you to not pay?"

He nodded and I laughed. He had no idea the hell of a ride that he was in for and for some reason, I knew that Brooke didn't know, either.

"What time is it?" I asked, changing the subject.

He looked at his phone. "It's almost midnight."

"I left Chance at Brooke's house; I need to go let him out. She's probably wondering where the hell I am."

I walked toward the door and he followed.

"It's not going to be weird now, right? You know…now that we've…you know…" I mumbled, facing him.

"Seen each other naked?" he casually replied.

"That and..."

"Fucked?"

"Yeah," I answered, looking away.

"I don't think I've ever seen you shy and nervous? Is it because my cock is so huge?"

I smiled. "No, that was a nice surprise."

"You did come…twice." He stretched his arms. "Just saying."

I slapped him in the chest and he fell forward with an oomph.

"Let's pretend like it didn't happen. Think we could do that?"

He bit his bottom lip. "Damn…I don't know, Kid, that booty and that pussy…"

I gasped; I had never heard him talk like that. Something told me that I didn't experience the same treatment that Brooke was receiving. I started to think that maybe she knew a whole different side to him.

"I'm kidding. To be honest, it was like having sex with my sister."

"Eww…now you're being disgusting."

He rolled his eyes. "Come here." He pulled me into a tight embrace. "I love you. Nothing and no one is going to change that. You and me, we're together till the end. Got it?" he whispered into the side of my neck.

I took a deep breath, knowing he meant every word.

S

Ysabelle wasn't answering her phone. I called the only other number I knew.

"Hello," Brooke answered.

"Hey, it's Sebastian."

"Hi, how are you?"

"I wish I were better, I've been looking for Ysa and she's not answering her phone. You don't happen to know where she might be, do you?"

"Oh…she actually just grabbed Chance about ten minutes ago. She said she was taking him to the dog park up the road. Do you know the one?"

"Yeah…" Sadly I did.

"Sebastian?"

"Yes."

"Ummm…she doesn't look so good. I don't know what happened, but I have a feeling that it's something bad. I'm glad you're here."

"Thanks, Brooke. I appreciate that."

"And Sebastian?"

"Hmmm…"

"Be nice to her, okay?"

"I'll try," I said and hung up.

As soon as I walked into the park, Chance came running over to me. I greeted him and frantically looked around for her. She was sitting on a bench in the back corner, leaning forward with her head in her hands. Chance followed me as I made my way over.

"How did you find me?" she whispered, just loud enough for me to hear.

"Brooke."

"What are you doing here?"

"Why do you think I'm here? I told you I would follow you anywhere."

"We've made it full circle, Sebastian. We're in the exact place that I saw you with your family." She finally looked up at me, tears streaming down her face. Her eyes looked desolate. "And now you're seeing me with mine."

I cocked my head to the side in confusion and her body fell over, sobbing; it took everything in me not to go to her.

"I'm so sorry. I'm so fucking sorry."

That did it. I immediately fell to my knees in front of her, placing my hands on the sides of her face, making her look at me. She did.

"My girl…I've missed you so much. Please don't cry. I'm here now."

"Sebastian, I'm so sorry. You have to forgive me."

"Ysa, it's okay; everything is going to be okay."

She frankly shook her head in my hands, weeping and slightly hyperventilating.

"You have to calm down. Shhh…"

"No. I'm sorry. I'm sorry. I'm sorry," she repeated in a trance.

"Ysa, I know. I know, baby; it's okay."

"It's not okay," she reiterated, still shaking head.

"We're together it's fine. Calm down."

I'll remember the next words that came out of her mouth until the day I die.

"Sebastian, I had sex with Devon and I'm pregnant."

CHAPTER 39

S

I ran. I ran as fast as my legs would let me. I vaguely heard her yelling my name from behind me. Chance was barking as I hit the keyless entry to my car. I jumped in and had the car in reverse before I even had the door closed. The tires skid out as she was running out the gate, still screaming my name.

"I need the address of Devon Hill," I said to my phone.

"There are two Devon Hills in the area," the automated voice replied.

"Give me the closest."

"Devon Hill. 345 Bayshore Boulevard, Miami Florida, 33011."

"Directions," I added.

I pulled up to his house and he was walking out as I was parking. I got out of the car, leaving the engine on and the door open.

"Listen, man, it's not what you—"

My fist collided with his face before he got the last word out. His head whooshed back, taking half of his body with him. He stumbled, shaking it off.

"This is how it's going to be?" he asked, spitting blood onto the ground.

"Hell yeah; it's go time, motherfucker. I've been waiting for it."

I charged him, ramming my body into his torso, taking him to the ground. He was prepared for it and he instantly fought back. We wrestled around in the grass for a few minutes, each of us trying to get the upper hand on the other. He was able to get on top of me and got in a few hits to my face.

"I don't want to fucking fight you! You fuck! Calm down and let me explain!"

I hit him in the gut and he fell forward. I flipped us over, locking him in with my weight. Car tires screeched on the road and I knew it was Ysabelle barreling out.

"Shit!" she yelled, running over to us.

"You fucking son of a bitch!" I hit him. "You fucked her!" I hit him again. "And then you knock her up!" I hit him twice.

"What the fuck are you talking about?" he yelled, blocking another blow.

"Sebastian, stop!" she shouted, trying to pull me away. "I just had sex with him. Tonight! The baby's yours. I'm pregnant with your child."

I instantly stopped, both of us breathing heavily, sweating profusely all over the place. I removed myself from him, never taking our intense, crazed stares away from each other. I stood up, needing to take a few steps back to collect myself. She immediately got on her knees and went to him.

"Are you fucking kidding me? You go to him?" I seethed.

She aggressively looked up at me. There was no love in her eyes. Nothing.

"Jesus Christ, Sebastian; he's on the ground, you're standing."

"When?" I retorted, not having any patience left in my body.

"You want to talk about this now? Are you serious?"

"When?" I snarled through gritted teeth.

She looked down at him and then back at me. "March 3rd."

"The day we bought the house?"

She nodded. "Yeah, Sebastian, you got one past the goalie on the stairs. Con-grat-u-fucking-lations," she angrily spewed.

"You've known this whole time that you were carrying my child?"

Devon grabbed her hand and she helped him up, she put his arm around her neck and he leaned on her.

"I found out the morning of our anniversary. The doctor told me then."

I almost fell to the ground, stunned. I watched as she helped him sit on the chair on his patio and then she walked right past me. I grabbed her by the arm.

She roughly pulled it away. “I’m getting him some ice.” She tended to him for the next several minutes and I let her. I was at a loss. I needed to gather my thoughts and regain my sanity. I felt like I was going crazy in some fucked up version of *The Twilight Zone.*

“I think he might have a concussion and a broken rib, he needs to go to the hospital,” she stated, standing before me.

“Fuck him. Oh, right…you already did that.”

Her eyes widened.

“You fucked another man with my child inside you.” I shook my head, disgusted by the turn of events. “You thought all along that you didn’t know who you are, but the truth is, I didn’t know. The woman I know wouldn’t have kept this secret from me.” I banged at my chest. “The woman I know wouldn’t have run, knowing she was pregnant with my child. A child that I’ve wanted since the moment I laid eyes on her. The woman I know wouldn’t have fucked another man.”

Tears fell down her face.

“You’re a whore. Congratulations, Ysa; you’re a VIP. That’s who you are.”

She wrapped her arms around her tiny frame in a comforting gesture. She looked so small and frail and I quickly thought about my child growing inside her.

“Have you even been taking care of yourself?”

“Of course,” she wept.

“How far along are you?”

“Thirteen weeks.”

“How?”

She lowered her eyebrows and her face wrinkled. “What?” The mascara dripping down her face made her look more beautiful. The pregnancy glow was all around her and I wanted to desperately hold her and kiss her belly.

Our baby.

“How did this happen?” I questioned, trying to get rid of the image that I’ve wanted for so long.

“Sebastian, you were—”

“Not that,” I interrupted. “You were on birth control.”

She bowed her head. Almost like she was ashamed. “I opened a new pack of pills and the date on them was wrong. I was behind. I’m always so careful and I must have missed some days with everything that…I’m sorry. I was tired and not feeling well and I went to the doctor that morning. I took a test out of precaution because she didn't want to write me a script for medicine."

I nodded. "Look at me," I ordered.

She shut her eyes in pain and then looked up.

"That's why you ran?"

"Yes. I wasn't going to, but then I found the picture of Olivia and I just needed to get away. It was all too much."

"I see. So you find a picture of my *dead* friend and you decide that leaving, pregnant with my child, was the right choice? Oh yeah…I completely understand."

She cocked her head to the side in disbelief. "Come on…you know it was much more than that. Give me some credit."

"Like you gave me? Huh? When you decided to take away my baby without even fucking telling me? I'm supposed to give you sympathy? I'm supposed to feel bad for you? That's what you want, right?" I moved closer and grabbed her chin. "Am I supposed to feel bad for you because you fucked Devon? Hmmm…how far is my sympathy supposed to go? Please tell me?" I cruelly mocked, holding back the last bit of restraint that I had.

"I'm sorry…" she murmured.

"That makes it better? Does that make everything okay? You've been working for Satan for the last seven weeks, putting my child in harm's way—"

She tried to pull away, but I held her firmer. "It was never in harm's way," she objected.

"Right…" I stated, running my thumb on her lips. "Did he kiss you?" I impulsively asked, not able to control my turmoil anymore.

Her eyes widened in surprise.

I continued to rub at her pouty mouth. "Hmmm…tell me…did he touch you the way you love?" I paused. "Come on, baby, tell me how much you rode his cock? Did you scream out his name like you do mine? Did you even think of me when he was fucking you? Or did you just spread your legs like a VIP?" I urgently pushed my thumb into her mouth. "Did he make you come? How many times did you come like a good little girl?" I viscously ridiculed, pulling down her jaw. "Did he come inside you, huh? With my child in there? If you're going to act like a *VIP,* I'm going to treat you like one."

"That's fucking enough," he announced from behind me.

She freed herself from my grasp. "Devon, stay out of it," she hissed, only looking at me.

I cunningly smiled. "Yeah, Devon, stay out of it and maybe she will fu—"

She cold clocked me, making my head sway from the unexpected blow to the face. I grabbed my jaw, moving it around as she shook out her hand from the throbbing, I was sure.

"You have no idea what I've been through tonight." She sniffed. "I deserve your anger, but you do not get to treat me like that."

"I can't even look at you right now. Do you have any idea how much it pains me not to be able to look at you? You're my favorite fucking thing to look at," I choked, holding back my emotions. "I would have followed you to hell, and from the looks of it, I have. I fucked up the first time around and I did nothing but grovel at your feet for forgiveness. I have been patient, and I would have taken you any way I could have had you. Any. Way."

She sucked in air from the tears that were flowing.

"You want this life? Have it. Take it all. You want to run VIP? Go for it. We're done. Do you hear me? DONE!"

She shook her head. "You don't mean that. You're upset and you don't mean that. You know I love you. I'm sorry, Sebastian. I was upset and hurt and I just wanted to forget. For one second, I wanted to forget about everything. I went to Devon because he's the only person that has never disappointed me. I didn't do it out of spite. I feel awful. I would never want to hurt you. Never. You don't have to tell me that I'm a whore because I already feel like one. Do you understand? I'm fucked up. I know that. I've told you that," she openly sobbed. "But…I'm so fucking sorry…please…just please…stop…stop saying things you don't mean…"

I looked back at Devon. "Make sure she gets home okay."

"No!" she yelled, grabbing my arm. "Look at me! Please! Look at me…I'm Ysa; I'm your girl…just look at me, please! Look into my eyes…I'm yours…"

I stared right at her, right where she wanted me to, and the depths of her soul were staring right back at me.

Love.

Soul mate.

Ysa.

My girl.

Mine.

Now all I can think about and see is…

Broken.

Hurt.

Destroyed.

Betrayed.

I forcefully grabbed the back of her neck and kissed her. I kissed her with everything I could muster. I kissed her until the earth stopped moving and time stood still. I leaned my forehead on hers and looked into her bright, beautiful green eyes that always showed me the world.

"I can smell him on you," I whispered.

She bawled.

I backed away from her and she fell to the ground, crying. I'd never seen her cry so hard, and for the first time, I didn't want to hold her. I didn't want to comfort her. I wanted her to hurt. I wanted her to feel an ounce of what I was feeling.

"That child inside of you is *mine.*"

She wiped at her face and looked up at me, barely breathing, sucking in the air, trying to hold it all together, but shattering right before my eyes.

Now both of our hearts are broken.

"This is what you want. I don't care anymore, but that child is *mine* and I will fight you tooth and nail in court for custody. It will never grow up in this environment. Do you understand me?" I roared, making her jump. "I will die before I ever see my child in The Cathouse. So you better lawyer the fuck up, I don't care if I have to play dirty. I won't stop until I have custody."

She hyperventilated and I looked over at Devon.

"You win. She's all yours."

I took one last look at her…

Turned and walked out on her for the last time.

CHAPTER 40

Y

Devon picked me up off the ground. We lay in his bed for what felt like years. I cried the entire night and he stayed right by my side, not saying a word. He just played with my hair and let me openly bawl my eyes out. I cried so hard it hurt my entire body and I was sore the next morning. I didn't know when I fell asleep, but he woke me up with a glass of milk and breakfast.

"No…I'm not hungry."

"Kid, it's not for you."

My heart hurt. I nodded, understanding his innuendo. I ate every last bite, drank the entire glass of milk, and it made me feel better. He took away the tray of food and placed it on the ground.

He genuinely smiled. "You're going to be a mom."

I breathed out, laughing, "Yeah."

"You're going to be such an amazing mom."

"I hope."

"I know. That baby is so lucky. He's going to have an amazing Uncle Devon and cousin Ethan."

I nodded. "Yeah."

"You're going to be okay. Have faith that everything will fall into place."

"You promise?"

"Promise."

A week later, I was walking up the steps and into an office I never thought I'd step in again.

"Bella Rosa." Madam embraced me and I let her. "You have no idea how much it means to me that you're here."

I smiled. "We need to talk."

"I know. I've wanted to call a million times, but I knew, I knew in my heart that you would come back. You're my granddaughter. Do you have any idea how happy I am to be able to say that to you?"

"I'm happy to see you, too."

"Come…come have a seat. I had the chef prepare all of your favorite foods. Let's have lunch and talk."

"Okay."

We ate and she told me about everything. I didn't even have to ask.

Her pregnancy.

Her mother.

My mother.

How she took over VIP.

How she found me.

The accidental rape.

Getting me to Miami.

And everything else is history.

Although she didn't say that her accident was planned, I knew it was. That's just the kind of woman she was. I also didn't have to question her about Mika. I honestly…didn't want to know. I imagined he had some story to tell, but I didn't care to have her share it with me.

"Bella Rosa, can you ever forgive me for everything?" she asked with sincerity in her voice.

"Of course. I wouldn't be here if I hadn't. I'm ready. I want to make you proud, Grandmother."

Her eyes shined bright. "Well…no time like the present. Let's get everything in order."

"Perfect."

I spent the next week signing away my life.

VIP was mine.

I was The Madam.

Another month went by and I was nineteen weeks pregnant. The doorbell rang to The Cathouse and Chance was barking incessantly.

"Stop! Shhh…go, Chance, go!" I shouted, making him run along. I opened the door and I was slammed with papers in my face.

"Ysabelle Telle?" she asked.

I nodded.

"You've been served," a woman stated, giving me the envelope.

"Served?" I called out. She didn't stop and drove away.

I walked into the kitchen and grabbed a bottled water from the fridge. Pregnancy was turning out to be fairly easy. I drank half the water not realizing how thirsty I really was. I sat down at the island and opened the yellow envelope. There was a letter among a stack of papers.

ABF Defendant to Miss Telle,

Sebastian Vanwell has hired the legal representation of Jacobson and Myor Associates. Attached are two documents; Child Custody Legal Rights in regard to full custody of said child, and Dissolution of Community Property of estate 96 Sunrise Drive in Turks and Caicos.

Mr. Vanwell has agreed to divide said estate mutually and earnings will be split 50/50.

Mr. Vanwell has agreed for visitation rights ONLY in his presence. OR away from defendants property titled, "The Cathouse."

Mr. Vanwell has agreed for the defendant to be involved in any of the child's upbringing as long as it's away from defendant's business or The Cathouse residence.

Mr. Vanwell wants to be informed of every doctor's appointment and be updated on the health and progress of said child.

Mr. Vanwell wants to be in the delivery room when said child is born.

Mr. Vanwell will be on the estate property of 96 Sunrise Drive from September 19 – September 29, collecting his personal items. He has requested that you not be present during that time.

Defendant has thirty days to respond to the affidavit.

Sincerely,

Jacobson and Myor

I think I read the letter ten times before it processed. There it was, in black and white, everything I lost. I rubbed my belly, wanting to feel comfort and it helped.

I looked over at my phone. "Shit!" I said to myself.

I drove in a blur for the next twenty minutes and pulled into a parking lot, parking my car beside the last person I expected to be meeting. I got out of the car and she walked over to me.

"I'm sorry I'm running behind, Julia."

She smiled. "It's okay. I'm surprised and happy that you called me."

"I'm thrilled you accepted."

"Can I?" she asked, pointing to my belly.

I nodded. "Of course."

She placed her hand on my stomach. "Can I say I hate you a little bit?" she laughed, making me nervous. "You're five months tomorrow and you're barely showing. You don't even look pregnant, how unfair is that?"

I immediately felt at ease. We walked into the restaurant and they seated us in a booth. I ordered milk and she had a glass of wine.

"I craved milk when I was pregnant with Christian, too," she announced.

"It's weird, I hated the stuff before. Sebastian drank it by the gallon." I shrugged. "So…"

She sadly smiled. "Have you talked to him?"

I shook my head. "No. Not since…no. I did get served with papers today, though."

She sighed. "Yeah…he told me they were on their way."

"I don't blame him. I would do the same thing if I were in his position."

"Are you going to fight him on it?"

"I don't know. He's selling our house…I just can't believe this is even happening."

"I understand."

"I love him, Julia. I'm pregnant with his baby and it's the only thing that has kept me going. I'm so fucking stupid."

"Ysabelle, you made a mistake, people make mistakes."

"I know, but he can't forgive me. He hasn't even tried to contact me."

She grabbed my hands on the table. "I don't want to get involved, but I promise you that he is hurting, too. He's a mess."

I bit my lip.

"Anyway, I didn't call you here for this. I don't want to put you in the middle."

She nodded.

"I wanted to say that I'm sorry. I'm sorry for everything that I did. There hasn't been a day that has gone by that I haven't thought about what I did to you. I wish I could tell you that I regretted it, but I can't. The only thing that I do regret is that it hurt you. I knew he was happily married and I didn't care. I never once thought about you or how any of it would affect you. I'll never forgive myself for breaking up your marriage," I sincerely stated.

I felt like I had been liberated. It didn't matter if she threw her glass of wine in my face, being able to tell her how I felt and apologize to her was enough for me.

"You're an amazing mother and if I can be half the mother you are, I'll be lucky and grateful."

Her eyes widened and she frowned. "I lost Christian at Niemen Marcus when he was four years old," she blurted, her eyes started to water like she was reliving it. "I let go of his hand and turned my back to look at the new fall wardrobe, I forgot about him. I forgot about my child for a designer. I looked down, remembering that he was with me and he was nowhere to be found. I ran around the aisles for ten minutes and then I told the saleswoman that I lost my kid." She paused.

"Ten minutes. Do you have any idea how much could happen in ten minutes? I should have told them the second I didn't see him. I should have never let go of his hand."

I couldn't believe what she was disclosing and I took in every word.

"It took security another twenty minutes to find him. I called Sebastian franticly and he immediately told me to look under the dresses on the hanging racks. He said Christian loved to play hide-and-go-seek in them. I told security and they found him a minute later. He's my child and I didn't know any of that. He used to cry all the time when he was a newborn and I would panic every time. Sebastian always calmed him, always, no matter what. For the first six months, I thought he hated me."

I listened to her like she was telling me a bedtime story.

"The first time we took him to the emergency room was because he burned himself with my curling iron. The one I left on, knowing my toddler was beside me. Thank God it had barely warmed and didn't hurt him. I could go on and on about the mistakes I've made." She hesitated, thinking about what she was about to share.

"My worst mistake was marrying a man I knew wasn't in love with me. I manipulated both Olivia and Sebastian so they couldn't be together. I precisely stepped in the way of my sister's happiness because I was jealous and wanted him for myself. Karma is an evil and brutal bitch. I'm not perfect, I'm so far from it it's not even funny."

I squeezed her hand.

"The second I saw Sebastian look at you at The Gala, it was a rude awakening. I always thought that the way he looked at Olivia was true love. I was wrong. The way he looks at you, words can't even describe it. Love has a way of finding you when you least expect it. I'm engaged to Anthony and I've never been happier. If it weren't for you, Sebastian and I would probably still be playing house." She shrugged. "Sometimes people have to walk away to realize what they have."

I nodded. "Thank you."

"No, Ysabelle, thank you."

CHAPTER 41

M

It had been six weeks since Ysabelle became The Madam. It took a week to get all the documentation in order and for her to take ownership. I spent the next few weeks traveling and letting clients know that I had stepped down and my granddaughter had taken over.

Mika was dead to me.

He had a story to tell, but I didn't give a fuck about it.

Once I landed, I immediately went to The Cathouse. I told Hector to let Ysabelle know that I would be there in the afternoon. I could barely contain my excitement as the limo drove. I had waited for this moment for the last fifteen years. She was finally following in my footsteps.

My legacy would live on.

VIP would remain in my family.

Forever.

Everything was as it should be.

Mine.

I walked up the stairs, opening the double doors to *her* office. I saw the back of the leather office chair.

"Bella Rosa, you have no idea how long I've waited for this moment. I've dreamt about it since I looked into your bright, vibrant green eyes. You're finally where you belong…home," I praised.

As the chair gradually turned around, the air from my body began to bleed from my lungs. She was sitting with her legs crossed and her arms folded over her chest, fully facing me.

"Hello, *Lilith*." She smiled with devious eyes and cocked her head to the side. "Like what you see?"

I narrowed my eyes. "Brooke, where's Ysabelle?"

She waved her manicured finger in the air. "Now, that's Madam to you, *darling*."

"What the fuck are you talking about?" I argued.

"Angry is really not a good look for you. You're getting old, Lilith, wrinkles…you know…they don't forgive," she mocked in a condescending tone. "Ysabelle is where she is supposed to be, as am I. Although, I don't really like the term *Madam*, it's so…old, kind of like you. I may retire it. I happen to like my name Brooke; besides, I don't need to feel like queen, I'm already one. That's the difference between you and me. I don't need people kissing my ass and fearing me. Oh my…VIP is in for a change, darling."

"If you so think—"

"I don't think." She shook her head and looked at her watch, glancing back up at me. "I don't have time for this and I honestly don't care to explain myself to you. You fucked with the wrong VIP, and if you want some answers, there's a letter on *my* desk for you. It's more of a consideration than I would have given you, but Ysa is a good soul. She may have your blood but not your heart."

She rounded the desk and stopped right behind me. "You have twenty minutes to get the fuck off my property or you'll be escorted out. Have a nice life." She kissed the air twice and left.

My feet moved on their own accord and I had the letter in my hands.

Lilith,

If you're reading this letter then I don't have to explain to you that Brooke has taken over. When you signed VIP away to me, I signed it right back to Brooke. She wants it, she always wanted it and she will do a hell of a lot better job than you ever did. You have no say in this. I know your mind is already spinning on how to take it out from under her. The contracts are iron clad, not only that…I have more than enough documented proof of the shit you have done with VIP. Something happens to her, it's going right to the district attorney and the Chief of Police, who you know are great friends of ours. They would love nothing more than to see

your ass rot in prison. Aside from that, I no longer have any reason to hear from you, speak to you, or see you.

We're DONE. It was NEVER about me, not once. It was ALWAYS about you. This was your legacy, not mine. You have ten more minutes to get the fuck off the property, I know Brooke seems dainty but I wouldn't fuck with her if I were you.

In the words of the late great Madam, "Go Fuck Yourself."

Ysa

I fell to the ground, wallowing in my own misery, the misery that I created. I never imagined that I would end up alone.

Tick tock…it was NEVER for her…

It was for me.

"Angel."

I glanced up and there he was…

EPILOGUE

Y

I was six and a half months pregnant and finally started showing. I was beginning to wonder if there was even a baby in there, and then one day, I woke up and there it was. I blossomed overnight. After I had given VIP to Brooke, I went on a sabbatical, so to speak. I spent time alone, just the baby and me. I went back to my hometown and showed the baby where I came from. It was silly since the baby was still in my stomach, but it helped nonetheless. It was like closing a chapter of my life that would never be reopened. I wouldn't be like any of them. I knew that now.

I had come so far from the broken home I grew up in. To look at it with my baby inside of me was therapeutic. I would never let anyone hurt him or her. This baby was mine. I created something amazing out of pure love, and to know that it was living inside of me, nothing compared to that or even came close. The bond that I had formed with my little person was endless.

Just like my love for Sebastian.

I knew what I did was wrong. I never claimed to be a perfect person. I'm far from it. I had accepted my mistakes and all I could do was pray that he would forgive me. I needed to love myself and know who that person truly was. It took me leaving…running…to find that there was no place like home. It was with him all along. I always knew who I was when I was with him; I just didn't realize it until it was too late. Words could not describe how messed up I was. I never came up for air. Not one time after I left VIP. I thought leaving the first time I would be miraculously healed. I couldn't have been more wrong.

It was just the beginning.

I had no ties to VIP anymore, and I think a part of me always knew that something was holding me back; I just didn't know what it was until it all came to light. It may have been one of the worst memories of my life, but it was also one of the happiest. I didn't have to wonder who I was anymore.

I wasn't a VIP.

I wasn't Lilith's granddaughter.

I wasn't my mom's child.

I was Ysa. I was going to be a mom. I was going to have a baby and I couldn't have been more excited. I had a best friend who would do anything for me. And I had a sister that, no matter what, was my ride or die girl.

All that was missing was…

Sebastian.

I was just a woman in love with a man who was my everything. The baby growing inside of me was a miracle and I knew that God put him or her in my life for a reason. Everything in life happens for a reason.

And he was my reason.

Always and forever.

"All right, little person, if you would like to be absolutely adorable right now, it might help. Feel free to kick and move around inside me, especially if you hear your daddy's voice. Maybe if he tries to touch my belly, you could kick or something," I said, rubbing my stomach as I drove my car.

"I know that I have messed up so much of your life already and you're not even born yet. I'm sorry about that. Your daddy should have been able to watch you grow while you've been inside me, but I promise to make up for it for the rest of your life. I promise to be the best mom I can be. I know it sounds ridiculous, but I have no idea what I am doing. From what I have been told, though…most moms don't. We're supposed to learn as we go or something. I think that might be a load of…shiii…poo…I think moms just tell other moms that so that we're not freaking out from something coming out of our vaginas, and we don't know what to do with them once they're real people." I rubbed my belly some more.

"I never thought I would enjoy being pregnant. That's been a nice surprise. You have made it pretty easy and soothing. You must get that from your daddy. He was always able to comfort me when I didn't know I needed it. He's the best man I know and he is going to be an amazing father to you. I wish I could tell you that we're going to get a happily ever after, but I can promise you that I will always be here for you. No matter what. You have a lot of people who are waiting for your arrival; you're going to have so much love around you. I promise. I love you so much. I hope you know that."

I pulled up to the estate and there were moving trucks parked right in front. I wanted to break down and cry, but the baby kicked me. I smiled and laughed, taking it as a sign to keep going. Chance, of course, went barreling out of the car and into the house.

I swear I need to teach that dog some manners.

I followed him inside, hoping to start a new chapter in my life. I found Sebastian in his office. He was on his knees, petting Chance, and stood up when he saw me leaning on the doorframe.

"I specifically told my attorneys to advise you when I would be here so that I didn't have to see you."

"Right…you're supposed to meet with the new owner."

"Yeah." He nodded, staring at my belly.

"I'm the new owner," I acknowledged.

He looked back up at me. "That's why the buyer wanted to keep all their information private."

"Mmm hmm…"

We stood there for a few minutes, neither one of us saying anything. When he started walking over to me, I thought I was going to pass out from the anticipation of what he was going to say or do. He stopped when we were a few inches apart.

"Can I?" he asked, pointing to my stomach.

"Of course."

As soon as he placed his hand on my belly, the baby kicked, and we both looked at each other wide-eyed.

"Oh my God, it recognizes you and listens to me," I excitingly stated.

"It?" he questioned, never moving his hand from the kicking little person inside me.

"I don't know the sex yet. I didn't want to find out alone."

He sadly smiled and kneeled down, placing both his hands on the side of my growing belly.

"Hey…I'm your daddy. I can't wait to meet you. I love you so much," he whispered just loud enough for me to hear.

My emotions and hormones were all over the place. I cried all the time about random things, and I was never a crier. Tears fell down my face; I couldn't stop them.

And just when I thought I had a chance…we had a chance.

"Sebastian, what do you want me to do with this?" an attractive woman asked, coming out of our old bedroom.

Then it was gone…

This was the worst memory of my life.

I've told you since the beginning that this wasn't a love story but a story about love. I've been asked several times if it was all worth it. I used to answer that question the same way—if it's all you've ever known, then you don't know what to expect.

Not anymore.

I didn't regret one thing.

It all led me back right where I belonged.

S

"Ysabelle this is my assistant, Amy," I quickly stated, taking in her face of pure panic and standing up.

"Oh," she breathed out, relaxing immediately.

"I'm sorry I didn't know anyone else was here. I'm Amy," she greeted, sticking out her right hand.

"Ysa," she replied, shaking hands.

Hearing her say Ysa made my heart ache and she knew it.

"I'll leave you two alone," Amy announced, leaving.

Ysabelle placed her hand on her heart. "I think I just had a heart attack," she laughed to herself.

I tried like hell to ignore her inner turmoil. "I don't have much more to do and I'll be on my way," I informed, moving back to my desk.

"Okay," she choked, holding in her emotions and backing away.

"Why did you buy this house?" I impulsively asked, stopping her dead in her tracks.

She turned around to look at me. "It's my home."

"No. It was our house. Why do you want it?"

"I want to raise our baby here. I didn't want anyone else to have it. It's ours."

"You're moving back?" I questioned confused.

"I never moved away. I'm done with VIP."

"In the papers—"

"It was never mine, Sebastian. I needed Lilith to believe that it was."

I nodded. I had read in the papers the story of Ysabelle's life. It was there in black and white, everything she wanted to know.

"It's Brooke's. I signed it over to her. My life is here."

"What do you want to do about the baby?" I immediately interjected.

"What do you mean?"

"Ysabelle—"

"Will you stop calling me that?" She frowned. "Please," she added.

I took in her request; I didn't want to cause her or my child any stress. "I know you're going to be an amazing mother, I always did. I wanted sole custody when I thought you were going to take over VIP. Since that's changed, I will agree to joint custody."

Her face got gloomier like she was expecting me to say something else.

What did she want from me?

"Are you staying on the island?"

"Of course. It's my home, too. Unlike you, I never left," I spitefully reminded without thinking. "I shouldn't have said that."

"It's fine," she sulked. "I left all the paperwork at Chances; I've been staying there for the last few days. It's all signed."

I nodded. "I'll come by and get it this afternoon."

"Okay. I'll see you then."

I was done by early evening and made my way over to her bar. I thought about her the entire fucking day. The way she looked, her smell, her pouty lips, her growing belly, my child, our family, and her bright green eyes that had the power to bring me to my knees. I loved her. I never stopped loving her. And will always love her. I didn't know what the future would hold, I was still pissed at her, but two wrongs didn't make a right. We've both made mistakes that have cost us the other person at one time or another. I wasn't trying to say that we were even…

However, it appeared to be so.

She was lying in the very same hammock that she was in when I first found her. Chance came and greeted me the exact same way and she followed.

She was wearing a bathing suit top and shorts, her belly was sticking out and her curly hair was flowing. She looked fucking gorgeous. It pained me to watch.

She reassuringly smiled. "We're standing in the exact same place that you found me. Do you remember?"

"I was thinking the same thing."

She smiled higher. "Good." She paused, taking a deep breath. "I have fucked up so bad." She looked down at her stomach and rubbed. "Sorry, baby," she apologized, looking back up at me with her green eyes that showed more love for me than I have ever seen before.

"There is more to me than meets the eye, if that makes any sense. I have made mistake, after mistake, after mistake. I don't expect you to forget what I've done, but maybe you could forgive…I don't assume that you would understand; however, maybe you could listen?"

I didn't answer or move.

"I'll take that as a yes." She paused. "To come from where I've been is like dying and being reborn again. Everything I thought to be true wasn't. How could I move forward if I was still stuck in the past? I wanted so desperately to be with you. I still do. My mind just couldn't catch up to my heart. I tried. I swear to you on our baby's life, I tried. It was like a boulder was chained to my leg and I was struggling to stay above the surface, to breathe. Though, I couldn't. I drowned. It wasn't until I found out the truth that I was really free. I don't know any other way to explain it to you. I never meant to hurt you. I would die before I would ever want to hurt you. You're the best thing that's ever happened to me, Sebastian." She placed her hands on her stomach.

"This is the best thing that's ever happened to me. We made something together out of our love. A love that I never thought was possible for me. I was lost until I found you. Until we found each other. I love you. You taught me the meaning of the word."

My heart was racing and I could hear my pulse through my ears.

"Ysab…Ysa—"

She got down on her knees and I stopped breathing. She held onto my legs and looked up at me with more love than I have ever seen before.

"I want to spend the rest of my life with you. I want to have more babies with you. I want my home with you. You're the air I breathe, the nourishment that I need to keep going, without you I'm not living. You're my beginning, my middle, my ending. I'm your girl," she choked, soaking her face with tears. She pulled a ring out from her pocket. "Marry me."

It wasn't a question; it was the very same words I had said to her.

I didn't care about the past. We've both made mistakes and paid for them. People aren't perfect and neither is love.

All I cared about was the future.

We had truly come full circle. It wasn't that night at the park. Now…this…moment…it led us back to each other and that's all that mattered. She was the other half of my heart, without it I'm incomplete.

Mine.

I got down on my knees to her level. Her eyes widened as I pulled out a diamond ring.

"I bought this the day before I found you. I actually had it in my pocket in this very spot that we're both kneeling in now."

She laughed, crying.

"What kind of a man would I be if I let you propose to me and not do it back? Marry me, Ysa."

She tackled me to the ground and kissed me. We kissed like we were both starving for it. The baby sensed it, too, because he or she started kicking, making us both laugh.

I placed my ring on her finger, right where it belonged.

Y

Love isn't always perfect. It will make you cry, it will make you hurt, it could even make you bleed, bringing you down to the ground in agony. I had personally witnessed it time and time again. It's messy, it's chaotic, it can be ugly, or it can be fucking beautiful. Taking away your breath with each moment and memory. Our love didn't come packaged in a bright red bow, but that didn't make it any less real.

You have to find yourself before you can fully give yourself to another person. And we both did that for each other, except it didn't happen at the same times. It didn't matter…

It led us right back to where it all began.

Life is funny like that.

Our love story is far from perfect…

But it's ours.

And I wouldn't trade it for the world.

…

Eight months later…

"Lilah, you're going to have a very special day today. People have flown from all over the world just for you, little lady. Your brother Christian, your Aunt Julia and Uncle Anthony."

I grinned as I heard Sebastian's voice through the baby monitor.

"And then maybe you will cut your daddy some slack and let him play with your mommy. Oh yes!" His voice got higher. "Yes! You little pee pee blocker. How am I suppose to give you a brother or sister if you won't let me get back inside Mommy?"

"Sebastian!" I scolded, standing in the doorway of her nursery.

He smiled, holding her up and blowing kisses on her neck. "She doesn't understand a word I'm saying. Do you?"

She giggled.

I loved her sweet face.

"Then why did you say pee pee?" I asked, chuckling because their laughter was contagious.

He ignored me. "You are the prettiest baby ever. Just like your mommy; look at those bright green eyes." He kissed all over her face.

"Sebastian, you're wrinkling her dress. Brooke will shit if she sees what you've done to that designer dress that she had custom made for her goddaughter."

It was Lilah's baptism. Brooke was the godmother, and after arguing with Sebastian for weeks, he finally agreed to have Devon be the godfather. They went on some fishing trip hating each other, and came back the best of friends.

"She hates the dress; it's stupid. She wants to be naked, not dressed like a doll."

I rolled my eyes. "Oh my God, give me my baby."

He pulled her back. "Our baby," he stated, pulling me into both of them. I smiled and he kissed me like we weren't in front of Lilah.

My family.

My husband.

My daughter.

My love.

My life.

The End.

Connect with M. Robinson

Website:
www.authormrobinson.com

Friend request me:
https://www.facebook.com/monica.robinson.5895

Like my FB page:
https://www.facebook.com/pages/Author-MRobinson/210420085749056?ref=hl

Follow me on Instagram:
http://instagram.com/authormrobinson

Follow me on Twitter:
https://twitter.com/AuthorMRobinson

Amazon author page:
http://www.amazon.com/M.-Robinson/e/B00H4HJYDQ/ref=sr_ntt_srch_lnk_1?qid=1417487652&sr=8-1

Email:
m.robinson.author@gmail.com

65900332R00146

Made in the USA
San Bernardino, CA
06 January 2018